COUNT JULIAN

COUNT JULIAN

JUAN GOYTISOLO

Translated by Helen Lane

SERPENT'S
TAIL

The publishers thank Kathy Acker, Mark Ainley, Martin Chalmers, John Kraniauskas, Bob Lumley, Enrico Palandri, Kate Pullinger, Antonio Sanchez for their advice and assistance.

British Library Cataloguing in Publication Data
Goytisolo, Juan, *1931-*
    Count Julian. - (Masks)
    I. Title
    863'.64 [F]
    ISBN 1-85242-158-4

First published 1970 as *Reivindicacion del Conde Don Julian* by Editorial Joaquin Mortiz, S.A. Copyright © 1970 by Juan Goytisolo
First published in English by The Viking Press, New York
Translation copyright © 1974 by The Viking Press

This edition first published 1989 by
Serpent's Tail, 4 Blackstock Mews, London N4
Second printing 1990

Printed in Great Britain by
WBC Print (Bristol) Ltd.

In their struggle against the Byzantines and the Berbers, the Arab chieftains had greatly extended their African dominions, and as early as the year 682 Uqba had reached the shores of the Atlantic, but he was unable to occupy Tangier, for he was forced to turn back toward the Atlas Mountains by a mysterious person whom Moslem historians almost always refer to as Ulyan, though his real name was probably Julian, or perhaps Urban or Ulbán or Bulian. Soon thereafter he became a legendary figure, known as "Count Julian." We are not certain whether he was a Berber, a Visigoth, or a Byzantine; as a "count" he may have been the ruler of the fortress of Septem, once part of the Visigoth kingdom; or he may have been an exarch or a governor ruling in the name of the Byzantine Empire: or, as appears more likely, he may have been a Berber who was the lord and master of the Catholic tribe of Gomera . . .

—L. G. DE V., *Historia de España*

Accursed be the fury of the traitor Julian, of which we were long the victims; accursed be his wrath, for it was cruel and evil; his rage was boundless and his hatred intractable, his madness precocious; he was incapable of loyalty, respected no law of the land, and scorned God; a pitiless man, the murderer of his suzerain, the enemy of his own house, the destroyer of his own land, perfidious and treacherous and guilty of many grave misdeeds against his own people; there is a bitter ring to his name in the mouths of those who utter it; the very memory of him brings pain and sorrow to the heart of anyone who speaks of him, and his name will be forever accursed by all who mention it.

—ALFONSO X EL SABIO, *Crónica General*

I should like to discover a crime the effect of which would be actively felt forever, long after my own active efforts had ceased, so that every single instant of my life, even when sleeping, would become the cause of some sort of disorder, which would then spread so widely as to bring on such general corruption or such absolute disruption that the effect of it would be prolonged far beyond my own lifetime.

—D. A. F. DE SADE

part one

I dreamed of Tangier, whose proximity fascinated me, and the prestige of this city that is more or less a favorite haunt of traitors.

—JEAN GENET, *The Thief's Journal*

harsh homeland, the falsest, most miserable imaginable, I shall never return to you: with eyes still closed, it is there before you, enveloped in the blurry ubiquity of sleep and thus invisible, but nonetheless cleverly and subtly suggested, foreshortened and far in the distance: with even the tiniest details recognizable, outlined, as you yourself admit, with such scrupulous accuracy as to border on the maniacal: one day, another, and yet another: ever the same: a predictable sharpness of contour, a mere cardboard model, in reduced scale, of a familiar landscape: burning beneath a fiery sun perhaps? or enveloped in lowering clouds?: impossible to say: an unpredictable climate, this, subject to constantly changing, contradictory influences: currents, low-pressure areas, storms, sudden periods of calm that no meteorologist would venture to predict for fear of being laughed at or called a liar: an insolent light, a sarcastic sun, where there ought, rather, to be a low, flat horizon, a hermetic sky, huge thunderheads under full sail, an incredible flotilla, like great, dark, tentacular sponges: infallible doctrine supplanted by a pragmatism just a shade decadent and skeptical: the famous anticyclone of the Azores, suddenly changing direction and following a north-south axis, driving down toward the Straits of Gibraltar masses of air that ordinarily blow in over the continent farther north, so that the southern edge of these cold fronts affects the entire region: the effect of these anticyclones is extremely severe, but often they cause a general low barometric pressure in the entire area, with possible storms or squalls and even heavy, unexpected downpours: and the sage who had predicted clear skies and smooth seas thanks to the beneficent influence of the sun discovers a few hours later that the celestial he-goat is growing fainter and paler, becoming indolent and abulic and dispirited in the fog that now veils it and shrouds the roiled waters of the sea, thus giving the expert pause to ponder as he sits marinating in his laurel leaves, gazing at his little dials in order to predict temperatures, degrees of humidity, barometric pressures, wind velocity, and the amount of rainfall per square inch with the aplomb and gravity of a Roman haruspex: he's been caught with his pants down, there's no doubt of that, and the only thing left for him to do is shave off his mustache: as the person in question did in fact do once upon a time, giving rise to the most derisive remarks on the part of some people and the sympathetic commiseration of others: eyes still closed, at a distance of barely ten feet from the light: the daily struggle of climbing out of bed, putting on a pair of house slippers, walking across the room toward the bright parallel stripes of light, pulling on the cord of the venetian blinds like a person drawing water from a well: an apathetic sun?: threatening thunderheads?: blinding light rearing in fury?: a dead land, a chimerical sea: mountains along the coast, a monotonous ebb and flow of the tide: range upon range of deserted, arid, bare crests: bleak moors, vast expanses of barren soil: an inorganic realm seared by the fire of the low-water mark, cruelly chiseled by cold northern blasts: lying there motionless, you allow yourself a few brief moments of respite: at times, the cold masses of air moving in from the high-pressure area of the Azores invade the Mediterranean basin and condense between the two shores as though passing through a funnel, blotting out the landscape: a new Atlantis, your homeland has at last foundered and disappeared from sight: a terrible cataclysm, a blessed relief: the few friends you still have were doubtless saved: no need, then, for sorrow or remorse: at other times, the fog seems to shorten distances: the sea, having turned into a lake, links you to the other shore, as the fetus is tied to the mother's blood-engorged womb, the umbilical cord between them coiling like a long, sinuous strip of *serpentin*: you are overcome with anxiety: cold sweats, a racing heartbeat, palpitations: you are trapped, imprisoned, encapsulated, digested, expelled: the classical life cycle by way of the passages and tunnels of the digestive-reproductive system, the ultimate destiny of the cell, of every living organism: you open one eye: a ceiling flaking from the dampness, bare walls, this new day awaiting you behind the curtain, a Pandora's box: handcuffed beneath the blade of the guillotine: one minute more, Mr. Executioner, just a few more seconds: invent, compose, lie, make up stories: repeat Scheherazade's marvelous exploit spanning a thousand and one brief, inexorable nights: once upon a time there was a darling little boy, the most delightful youngster imaginable: Little Red Riding Hood and the big bad wolf, a new psychoanalytic version complete with mutilations, fetishism, blood: wide awake now: eyes open, attentively following the sly games and tricky maneuvers of the light in the cloudless sky: a slight effort: ten feet, getting up out of bed, putting on slippers, pulling the cord to open the venetian blind: and: silence, please, ladies and gentlemen, the curtain is about to go up: the play is beginning: the stage setting is very spare, schematic: rocks, schist, granite, stone: an untamed land that refuses to submit to domestic crops, to work in common by colonies of diligent ants: some years ago, in the limbo of your endless exile, you thought that homesickness was the worst of punishments: a mental compensation, a classic neurosis: a difficult, arduous process of sublimation: and then a feeling of alienation, dis-affection, indifference: separation was not enough for you if you were unable to measure it: nor fuzzy-minded awakenings in an anonymous city not knowing where you were: inside, outside?: anxiously searching for some sort of security: Africa and your first visit to the mirador of the Casbah, with its com-forting view of the other shore and the tranquil sea between the two of you: a daily, necessary confirmation: a last guarantee that you were safe from the wild beast, out of reach of its fangs and claws: its burnished muscles gleaming in the sun, its jaw set, crouching, all prepared to attack you at any moment: right there in front of you: ten feet, get up out of

bed, put on your slippers, pull the cord of the venetian blind:
looking round about you and drawing up a meticulous, frantic
inventory of all your worldly goods and possessions: two chairs,
a standing wardrobe built into the wall, a night table, a gas
stove: a map of Morocco, scale 1:1,000,000, printed by Hall-
wag, Bern, Switzerland: a colored print showing different
varieties of leaves: ensheathed (wheat), cordate (buckwheat),
dentate (nettle), digitate (chestnut), verticillate (madder): on
the back of the chair: a corduroy jacket, a pair of dacron and
wool pants, a plaid shirt, a wrinkled wool sweater; at the foot of
the chair: a pair of shoes, one sock rolled into a ball and
another just lying there, a dirty handkerchief, undershirt and
shorts: on the night table: a lamp, an ashtray full of cigarette
butts, a schoolchild's red composition book with the multiplication table printed on the back cover, a little folder of cigarette
paper, the kind that Tariq uses to roll joints: nothing more?:
oh yes, the light fixture on the ceiling, with four arms and glass
teardrops: two of the bulbs have burned out, as a matter of
fact, must remember to hunt up new ones, 90 watts each:
there's no way out of it, out of bed and on your feet, you, at
the mercy of another day and its nasty surprises: infested with
germs, rotten to the bone: one last effort, damn, ten feet, etc.,
etc.: hurriedly finishing up the minutely detailed inventory:
a limp beat-up leather wallet, an unused Paris Metro ticket,
a check drawn on the Commercial Bank of Morocco, two
hundred-dirhem bills, an old photo of Tariq looking like a tiger
in his striped djellaba, the ends of his handlebar mustache
curving up to a sharp point: not to mention the book of the
Poet, a haughty falcon who scorns the low-lying fog that veils
the truth and soars far above in search of a purer light:
prudently putting your feet in your slippers, enveloped in the
reassuring fetal shadows, groping about in the soothing womb:
a sudden flood of light, like that a man condemned to death is

bathed in, as you pull the cord of the venetian blind, eyelids
blinking frantically as the blinding sun streams in: light that
shimmers in the heat? light wearing a turban of white clouds?:
not at all: the sea, bright blue and dancing merrily, the distant
mountains canonized by foamy little white halos of fog: yes,
that's really your homeland: moody, violent, within arm's reach,
as the saying goes: the anticyclone didn't blow in from the
Azores after all, the sky above the turbulent waters of the Straits
is perfectly clear as far as the eye can see: a sky for a Murillo
Madonna, with little angels gamboling and frolicking on the
soft eiderdown of a cloud: a boat glides swiftly away into the
distance as you lean on the window sill, as you recite, like a
Romantic, like a Lermontov, the dark magic incantation: farewell, foul Stepmother, land of masters and slaves: farewell,
black patent-leather tricornes and you, my people who tolerate
them: may the sea of the Straits deliver me from your
guardians: from their eyes that see everything, from their evil
tongues that know everything: realizing once again, with calm
resignation, that invective does not ease your pain: that the
Stepmother is still there, lying in wait, motionless, ready to
spring: that the invasion which will lay waste to everything has
not yet taken place: flames, suffering, wars, deaths, desolation,
evil deeds: patience, the hour will come: the cruel Arab is
joyously brandishing his lance: warriors with kinky hair, pure-
blooded Bedouins will one day occupy the entire length and
breadth of Spain, that vast, sad land, and be welcomed by a
great chorus of moans and lamentations and supplications:
sleep, sleep in peace: no one suspects you in the least and your
plan is taking shape nicely: to relive the memory of the affronts
and the humiliations you suffered, storing up your hatred, drop
by drop: without Rodrigo, or Frandina, or Cava: another Count
Julian, hatching dark and treacherous plots

once the window is opened, a melody pours into the room: a
single sustained note sometimes, or perhaps a brief arpeggio:
played on the shepherd's flute of one of Pan's disciples, a
companion of Bacchus and a pursuer of nymphs: a spare,
subtle, haunting melody: full of suggestions, temptations,
promises: running away from home, fleeing to the mountains,
roughing it, living like a nomad: all sorts of regrets and
nostalgias condensed in a simple chord that the itinerant tool-
sharpener tirelessly repeats, day after day: a young man
perhaps, recently forced to leave his village to earn a living as
best he can in the unfamiliar streets of some large city, that
urbanized jungle that is so attractive in these parlous times:
with his bicycle, his pulley, his razor strap, his emery wheel:
his mouth hidden from view in a thick growth of beard many
days old, his shirttails hanging out over a much mended pair of
pants: and perhaps a little kid tagging after him, staring
attentively at the ground, searching for an empty cigarette
package or tops off bottles of Islamized Coca-Cola: proclaiming,
in his inimitable accent of a Hispano-Moorish vagabond, of the
last of the Abencerrages, his talents and capabilities, the vast
range of services he has to offer: the sharpening of razors,
knives, letter-openers, scrapers, scissors: glancing up toward
windows that never open, or open only very infrequently, before
raising the flute to his lips again and once more casting his
melodious, subtle spell, apparently meant especially for your
ears: the portent of a better, freer life, far from the dreary
Peninsula and its lethargic fauna: a thread of sound possessed
of a penetrating, enigmatic simplicity: a soothing reveille
announcing the dawn of the new day, a compensation and an
antidote for the brutal awakening you have had: posted in his
usual place around the corner, doubtless within a few yards of
the vacant lot overgrown with weeds across the way: for sale,
address all inquiries c/o Agencia Hércules, Sanlúcar 52,
Tangier: as on other days, the little neighborhood ragamuffins

appear to have congregated there in the vacant lot amid the
debris and the bushes: there are eight or ten of them who come
there almost every day to play cops and robbers, but today they
are acting out a kind of silent, mysterious ritual: carrying long
sticks and rods, they are wordlessly advancing, in some sort of
strict geometrical pattern, toward the newly appointed, for-
bidding-looking high priest of their cult: a young European boy,
with a Texas sombrero on his head and two silver-plated
revolvers stuck in his belt: precocious guerrilla-fighters fanning
out through the bushes, reassembling at a sign from their leader,
commending their spirits to their dubious divinity of the
moment, and then immediately afterward raising their flexible
rods in unison and furiously beating the greenery, launching a
desperate attack on the secret jealously guarded by the straggly
bushes, the goal of their hazardous journey, of their dark,
gnostic initiation: a secret visible now, as a result of the
blows raining down on it, driving it this way and that: the
already rigid dead body of a mangy cat with great bald patches
of skin, whose long and perilous journey, fraught with suffering
and misfortune, has ended here in this unkempt patch of weeds:
the final stopping-off place of a disastrous life of starvation,
want, privations: kicks in the ribs, physical abuse, stonings: an
existence possibly redeemed by furtive moments of love: nights
of burning passion in the course of the African winter, affording
every sort of ecstasy, every variety of oblivion: incredibly erotic,
raucous meowing that has often kept you awake in the middle
of the night: replaced now by the sinuous modulations of the
notes being played on the flute: a tenuous, subtle, almost sly
melodic line: as though the itinerant knife-grinder, abandoning
the beaten path, were venturing farther to try his luck: wandering off in the direction of the vacant lots bordering the Avenida
de Madrid, toward the population centers whose development
was suddenly interrupted by political independence, which
subsequently brought on the massive flight of undeclared and

undeclarable capital to more clement latitudes, milder climes:
the flute melody eventually blending in with the booming
heartbeat of the city as you light a cigarette and proceed, as you
do every morning, to the kitchen to cast a quick glance at the
holocaust of diptera and hymenoptera, the death toll that greets
your eye at the beginning of each day: all sorts of different
winged species, done in by a powerful insecticide as the inhabitants of Herculaneum and Pompeii were annihilated by the
lava pouring down from the roaring volcano: sudden death
extending its voracious tentacles through the Forum and the
Stabian Baths, the Temple of Isis and the House of the Amorini
Dorati: wings with fine veins, balance mechanisms, sucking
tubes perfectly conserved amid peristyles with Doric columns,
marble porticoes, Pompeian friezes: awaiting Bulwer's pen to
immortalize them: clumsy thick-bodied flies, ants with styli d
bodies and the slenderest of appendages; horseflies that have
undergone a complicated metamorphosis, with a lower mandible
that has assumed the shape of a tube: a bee here and there, or
a cockroach, dying in the midst of performing their digestive or
reproductive functions: in the euphoria of a sumptuous banquet
or prolonged, languid copulation: in the butcher's stall or the
brothel: as you untie the pouch and brush the victims into it,
with the aid of an old picture post card: a photo of a young Arab
girl of the sort very popular at the turn of the century, retouched
in the most garish colors: not forgetting, however, to make a
rough estimate of the number of dead: corpse upon corpse piled
up around the trap of flesh and the little white mounds: swiftly
swept up with the post card and placed in the pouch with the
drawstring open: fifty? a hundred?: and then it's the turn of
the others, the ones on the edges, the outskirts, the periphery:
among the cypresses of the Villa of Mysteries or on the esplanade
of the gladiators' barracks: and once every trace of the ambush
has been erased, throwing the window open wide to clear the
air, heavy with the smell of the tempting twofold invitation:

chicken giblets and powdered sugar: delicious honeycomb that
gourmands, past, present, and future, will die of: thereby satisfying the ravenous appetite of the pouch with the tight drawstring: all ready to be slipped into your jacket pocket and taken
with you on your daily walk to the library along the boulevard:
as you wait for new volunteers to appear and fall into the same
trap on your return to your apartment a few hours later: you
cut off any possible retreat on their part by squirting them with
DDT: your mechanism for attracting them with sugar and
chicken giblets is all set up: in less time than it takes to tell,
you are bathed and dressed: the pouch containing your treasure-
trove is on the kitchen table and you carefully slip it into the left
pocket of your jacket: without so much as a glance at the
enemy coast, though you might easily catch a glimpse of it between the articles of clothing hung out to dry on the balcony
and the chimneys of the building next door, you bolt your door,
wait for the elevator, and cautiously step out into the street

the life of an émigré of your stripe is made up of a discontinuous
series of events that are very difficult to assemble into a coherent
whole: though it no longer enjoys its former prestigious international status, the city is still a melting pot for all sorts of
exiles, and its inhabitants appear to be living in an uncertain
present that is very enjoyable and full of material riches for
certain people and a time of hardship and austerity for the rest:
a test tube for complicated chemical experiments involving
elements of the most disparate origins and background:
cautious bourgeois, nobles mournfully remembering the past,
suspect petty tradesmen, dishonest speculators, examples of all
the infinite gradations and subtle shadings within the very
complex, multicolored, prodigious family of sexual flora: ingredients that are juxtaposed but never mingle: like geological
strata formed by centuries of sedimentation, or liquids of

different densities that never mix in the test tube of the scientist or the researcher: lying one atop the other without ever combining: the specific gravitational force exerted upon them by their common center depends, as Figaro observed, on the greater or lesser quantity of molecules of which they are composed: solids, liquids, and gases: at the very bottom, the most solid of solids: the earth's crust, the base of the social edifice, on which we tread, from which we work our way upward: exactly like a stone: in the middle, man-the-liquid, meandering across the stratum beneath: continuously moving about in search of a job or a vacant post: today a little brook, tomorrow a river: and at the very top, the Arctic realm of thought: man-the-gas, man-the-balloon, a creature of amazing splendor and grandeur and glory: rising to sublime, Olympian heights: with irresistible force, like a champagne cork: these are sharply defined strata, recognizable at a glance: the marvelous benefits of the consumer society have not yet reached these parts, and fashion has not yet made the members of these various levels all resemble peas in a pod, and thus the very obvious inequalities, the sharp contrasts, seem even more shocking here: especially to the foreigner, the outsider: the aged blind man, his hand on the shoulder of his young guide, zigzagging from one sidewalk to the other, at every hour of the day, in every quarter of the city: or the little old woman wrapped in a ragged, threadbare length of cloth, squatting motionless against the wall, with her hand outstretched, opening out like a starfish: staring after you with pleading eyes: not saying a word: a mute reproach? a mute question?: as you rummage through your pockets for a coin: looking the other way and crossing over to the opposite side of the street when you don't have one to give her: or depositing it in the central disk of this human asteroid whose fingers close over their prey and swallow it as if it were an oyster: though never without first determining the denomination of the coin: ten, twenty, fifty centimes: and murmuring in

a barely intelligible voice: *el-jamdul-lah*: habitual interferences
these, part of the normal order of things, part of the mechanism
assuring the proper functioning of the whole: bearing no resemblance to encounters with the professional sponger, the
timid fellow down on his luck, whose pleas are completely un-
planned, improvised on the spot as the occasion demands: the
poor man must be listened to and pitied, for he has been over-
whelmed by an incredible succession of every imaginable sort of
disaster, and all the numerous members of his unfortunate
family have suffered the cruelest blows of fate conceivable: an
endless tale of terrible sorrows, sicknesses, accidents, recited in
a monotone followed by hints of the meager physical resources
at his disposal: he is suitably dressed for the occasion, in an
overcoat that is just a bit shabby and missing several buttons,
the collar pulled up around his ears: the pants legs of his
worn-out trousers drooping, his feet shod in pitifully misshapen
tennis shoes: walking toward you with a grave, tortured smile
on his face: his right hand groping for yours with respectful
alacrity: good day, sir: and inquiring as to your state of health,
as solid as an oak: a necessary, indispensable contrast to his
own state of health, so fragile and wretched: feeling just so-so:
that damned liver of mine is acting up again, as usual: all
said in the confidential tone of voice of a person who has spent
half his life in the anterooms and the offices of the now defunct
Spanish administrative apparatus, seeking some vague sort of
job or sinecure or begging for help that most likely was never
forthcoming: contaminated by the aristocratic, military atmosphere, the brusque, condescending paternalism that fauna of
your species live amid: an errand boy, a batman, a factotum for
some satrap with a whole sleeveful of stars or at least hopes for
one or two: for some petty tyrant ruling over the list of Army
promotions, himself the slave of the Military Code and the
decrees of the Official Journal: his shifty eyes stealthily glancing
at you as he sketches the sorry picture of his sad state: all

decked out in breastplate, face mask, fencing gauntlets, ready
to thrust with his saber: the doctor gave me a prescription for
some wonderful medicine: English aspirins, no, not aspirins,
exactly: some little pills for that liver of mine: marvelous,
really marvelous: pause: but frightfully expensive: the damned
things cost ten dirhems apiece, can you imagine?: no, twelve
dirhems, come to think of it: I'm sure they'll cure my liver
trouble right up: but where am I going to find the money to
pay for them, I ask you?: and then passing from the singular
to the plural, from the personal case to the family case, and
unveiling even vaster and more heart-rending perspectives,
he assumes the *en garde* position and points his foil straight at
your heart: Mama, poor thing, is the same as ever, slowly
wasting away: she's over seventy now, her health's failing, and
she's got lots of worries: her head aches constantly: she can
hardly eat a bite, poor dear: a little bit of bread in the morning
and a bowl of *jarira* in the evening, and even that's too much
for her: it's as bad as fasting during Ramadan: and aspirin too,
of course: twice a day, with a few swallows of water: from
the mosque to the house, from the house to the mosque:
meditating and praying all day long: for her children: for her
relatives back in her village: they're good people: not trash
and riffraff from heaven only knows where: good, solid country
folk born right here in Morocco; nice, quiet people: one of
them is a handyman, another one earns a living as best he
can and the third is in the process of getting his passport in
order: they're a bit pressed for money, it's true: decent jobs
are hard to find: but they haven't lost their faith in God: they
keep hoping that things will get better, that some charitable
soul will think of them and give them a helping hand: and then
he flourishes his sword and goes in for the kill: he's not asking
for much this time, practically nothing, really: a mere fifteen
or twenty dirhems, just enough to tide him over for a little
while: you barely have time to escape around the corner before

he spies you and you meet him face to face: walking toward you with a grave, tortured smile, his right hand groping for yours with respectful alacrity: good day, sir: and after inquiring about your state of health, launching into a long involved description of his own: his liver, as usual: or more trouble with those kidneys of his that are always acting up: the worst of it's over now, thank goodness: but something's still wrong with them: yes, a kidney stone apparently: and Mama, poor thing, slowly wasting away: she's over seventy now, her health's failing, and she's got lots of worries: she's so concerned about her children she scarcely eats: just her aspirin with a few swallows of water: good people: not riffraff, good, solid country folk: a little pressed for money of course: but they still haven't lost their faith in God: practically nothing: just enough to buy a few pounds of flour: twenty, thirty dirhems: hanging his head, blushing with shame: the saber thrust in up to the hilt: as you hurry off in the opposite direction as fast as your legs can carry you, hugging the brick wall around the vacant lot down the street: your heart is pounding violently and you feel utterly exhausted, as though you were being pursued by a pack of bloodhounds: staring fixedly at the entrance to the little alleyway that will allow you to escape him: finally reaching it, with a feeling of vast relief, only to run into him again: suitably dressed for the occasion, in an old overcoat buttoned up to the ears, the pants legs of his worn-out trousers drooping, pitifully misshapen tennis shoes: good day, sir: his shifty eyes stealthily glancing at you as he recounts every last detail of his sad story: yes, that's right, my liver: she's over seventy, her health is failing, and she's got lots of worries: very nice, very quiet people: hoping that things will get better: almost nothing this time: a hundred dirhems: stealing down the street to the boulevard: casting a wary glance in the direction of the park benches along the esplanade, the railway embankment, the public baths: the wind is stirring the branches of the palm trees: and some kids are trying to knock down a fat, ripe bunch of dates on one of them by throwing stones up at it: a number of cars drive slowly by, and now and again a taxi cruises past: and the usual sort of people in the streets: tourists in pairs, the same hordes of idle good-for-nothings everybody expects to see loitering about here, a group of peasant women driving their donkeys toward the market: not the least sign of danger, either to the left or to the right: so you feel rather happy and more or less optimistic: you're far beyond their hunting grounds: as you light a cigarette and inhale the smoke you're almost positive that today at least you've escaped them and are safe and sound

the sea is not deaf, and the store of knowledge you've acquired may be deceptive: your premonitions are often wrong too: the road ahead is clear, the day belongs to you: you are the protean master of your fate, and better still, you've dropped out from the march of history, you're playing no part in the rapid process of development which, according to all witnesses, is rejuvenating the face of an ancient country that yesterday was both forbiddingly grim and drowsy, and today is flowering and humming with activity: service stations and motels, daring films and foreign girls in bikinis on the beaches: different, yes: possessed of a typical Spanish flavor, a warm, sunny charm: bullfights, manzanilla, guitars: light, color, flamenco: the subtle spell of nights in the gardens of Spain; *populorum progressio*: thanks to the cleverness and the competence of your brilliant technocrats, the zealous male nurses of a patient who had been ill for decades, who despite a provident bloodletting was under strict orders to remain in bed around the clock and not move a muscle, to take a sleep cure, to stick to a diet of plain water: but who now is on the way to recovery thanks to the ubiquitous power of a certain barrel-shaped gentleman: ready to climb out of bed, speak in a soft voice, take his first steps: little walks in the garden of the clinic: not at all impatient to visit the gymnasium again or turn somersaults: possessed of a sense of prudence and caution that seems more and more attractive to more and more people with each passing day, in these depressing times in which there are nonetheless hopes of better things: a television set, a Seat 600, and all the rest: you're on the station platform, that's where: having just climbed off the train that is laboriously chugging ahead, slowly but surely: without demanding a place at this feast that is not eucharistic by any stretch of the imagination: without staking a claim to any of the crumbs so passionately fought over: in the limbo of a time without boundaries: in merciful oblivion: free to follow your feet wherever they take you: to contemplate the flowerbeds around the station, the buses constantly shuttling back and forth: to flee the spiel of the vendor hawking lottery tickets, the insistent bootblack tugging at your sleeve: as all the others file slowly past you: peasant girls in straw hats, soldiers on leave, veiled women, an old man on a white horse (one of the Dioscuri?), a Riff with a grim, enigmatic expression on his face: and suddenly a brief hurricane: a young girl who could not be anything but Spanish, bouncing along, her step light and agile, as though propelled by the admiration she arouses: the eyes of all the males in the crowd riveted on her: on her innocent jutting breasts, on her zealously guarded treasure: a theological fortress, a sacred grotto: stubbornly defended and impregnable: a subject for literary contests, for learned, abstruse plays on words: fancy figures of speech revealing yet again the talents of a people with a natural gift for elegant compliments, for high-flown verbal gallantry: the apogee of a national style of rhetoric that has been a tradition for generations: raving beauty, blushing rose, gorgeous creature, queen of the pin-ups, living doll: flattering remarks spoken in a soft voice, the saliva drooling, which she pretends not to hear or really does not hear, being totally absorbed by the assault on her sanctum sanctorum: the males closing ranks, weapons at the ready: as she passes within three feet of your table, offering marvelous spheres, solid possibilities for speculative reflection: which wriggle and oscillate in helicoidal arcs as she walks away from you and all her rejected suitors: would-be speleologists dreaming of exploring the crypt, the secret cavities: remains of the civilizing Hispanic presence in these parts, holdovers from another era, more or less falling apart from old age and chronic ailments, resigned to genteel, messianic poverty, with a tooth-pick hanging sententiously from their mouths; she is now braving the bards in the café next door, standing there next to the bus schedule posted on the wall and the silhouette in profile of a man with a silent, eloquent revolver: JAMES BOND, THUNDERBALL, final week: then at last she disappears from view, thereby suddenly destroying the vague dreams, bitterly disappointing yet again the hopes of these coarse Hispano males who like to think of themselves as irresistible Don Juans: suave seduction scenes, soft overtures with no vocal accompaniment, a fertile, generative puff of breath into the instrument: your compatriots have once again buried their noses in the local herald, in the no man's land of the day's news items, in the dialectical pap: an impressive demonstration of your fellow countrymen's accomplishments in this important area: discussing current events with the man at the next table and carefully pointing out the crucial significance of certain developments if need be: in the cavernous voice of the former civil servant or the retired warrant officer: in order to roundly condemn instances of irresponsible behavior, which, alas, are so frequent at this particular time, so fraught with bitter polemic: and then reduce them to their proper proportions: acts of men con-taminated by the violently argumentative tone of editorial-writers: behavior sanctioned by all the force of their rasping, hoarse-voiced authority

I am persuaded, however, that this is typical only of a very small minority

you drain your cup of coffee in one gulp, pay the check, and retrace your steps: in the direction of the bus schedule and the silhouette in profile of the man with the revolver: caressed by the generous warmth of the sun, so charitable toward the underdeveloped countries or those in the process of development: far from the chill North, from nasty fogs: a climate you managed, incredibly enough, to live in for years: thick clouds, dense plumes of smoke expelled by chimneys of factories that always appeared to be teeming with repressed tensions, on the very verge of revolution; whereas here a conscientious sun, calm nights are the rule: a crescent moon, bright battalions of stars: unless an anticyclone unexpectedly blows in: looking around for the poster of the Red Crescent, faded by the rain and torn by the wind, but still readable: DONNEZ VOTRE SANG, SAUVEZ UNE VIE: and rushing to the closest dispensary: in the propitious twilight shadows: wearing dark glasses and a false mustache: rich, thick, beneficial sap: bottled, distributed, injected: swirling through the pleiades of ganglia, a blossoming apotheosis: turning off down the first street then and slipping through the half-open door: a rectangular room, with shelves full of bottles and vials each bearing a label, a necessary stop in the course of your aimless wanderings through the city: consolation and relief for every pain, every ill that the old man unhurriedly offers, meanwhile discussing the Sunday afternoon national championship soccer match with the future local Pelé: a youngster about twenty years old, a nice-looking chap, whose Moorish bonnet topped with a pom-pom barely covers his mass of kinky, matted hair: a center forward, apparently, on a team of local lads who has hopes of making the big time and playing on a peninsular team, and meanwhile plainly spending a great deal of his time in gay bars: during those odd hours of the night when you close your eyes to what other people are doing and live and let live, when moral standards become very flexible and permissive: hours curiously situated, *consensus omnium*, beyond good and evil: an eighteen-carat-gold chronometer-wristwatch, a cashmere sweater, pants of fine Manchester wool: with his card identifying him as a professional player that he uses as a master key and the photo of his fiancée in his wallet: which he displays with pride, doubtless, in the tenderest moments of abandon, at the height of passionate love-making: he's prattling on and on about the knee operation performed on so-and-so and its possible effects on the future of the nation as the old man pulls back the dirty curtain and invites you to come in: I'll be with you in just a minute: with your belt already loosened and your gaze fixed on the shelves loaded with all sorts of objects, on the little table on wheels, on the glass jar: as always after the blood test: waiting with claustrophobic anxiety: with the total apprehension of the insect threatened with destruction: intuitively aware of the lethal presence of the enemy only inches away: the arthropod with crablike pincers and an abdomen tapering to a sharp point; pedipalpi not very highly developed, four pairs of stigmata: a chitinous carapace, spiracles, a poisonous stinger: shut up with the creature in the hermetically sealed cage during the required hours in the Natural Science lab: trying to get out, falling down, trying again, falling again: with the impassive eyes of the Reverend Father and the other students riveted upon you: your still-tender heart skipping beats: fascinated by the rigidity of the ringed segments, by the sudden raising of the pincers: as the old man prepares the sharp-pointed instrument and refills it: trapped in the narrow cage: instinctively turning your eyes away, refusing to watch the harmless, horrible operation: the faces of the youngsters trapped in the cage and

the angelic smile of the Reverend Father: the dull echo of your
past anguish thudding in your ears and your forehead bathed
with sweat: there, he's done it: and now he's slowly injecting
the poison that will spread through the veins, paralyze
the nervous and motor centers, and inevitably invade the
brain: all set now for the copious funeral repast, for the usual
depressing finale: in a kindly voice: I'm not hurting you, am
I?: and your stoic answer: no, not in the least: but breathing
a sigh of relief when he rubs your arm with a bit of cotton and
puts his instruments away and goes on talking soccer with the
youngster: you get dressed again, fish two dirhems out of your
pocket, pay the man, leave the little cubicle, say good-by, and
go out onto the street: out into the sunshine, the light, the
street noises: with the joyous sensation of having been reborn,
of being alive again: an optimist all of a sudden: like everyone
who concludes (mistakenly) that he has a long, long life ahead
of him

trampling the dim light of day underfoot as you go up the
stairs leading to the second floor: the dark interior of a building
that has seen better days, doors with marquetry inlays, a
drooping fern in a green pot: a steep flight of thirty-six stairs
to climb before you find yourself standing in front of the invitation, in black letters on a white background: ENTER WITHOUT
KNOCKING: merely turning the doorhandle, thus automatically
setting off the cantankerous-sounding buzzer that keeps ringing
till you shut the door again and a profound, studious silence
falls over the place once more: a half dozen people, nearly
always the same ones, sitting, reading or meditating in the
various little cell-like cubicles, all alone with their thoughts or
their dreams: not to mention the drowsy old custodian: imbedded in his chair, as though expiating a fatigue that is
centuries old, a genetic bone-weariness inherited from dogged,

hard-working forebears: staring absently at the palms dotting the boulevard, languidly stretching their branches toward the sky: or clearing his throat and yawning in the nirvana of his devotion to crossword puzzles: as the neatly dressed little man in the gabardine suit devours every last page of the latest issue of *ABC* to have arrived from the capital: from the esoteric contributions of the Immortals (was one of the Three Kings of the Bible an Andalusian?), to the no less esoteric death notices of people who, alas, are not immortal (Pray to God for the soul of Don Abundio del Cascajo Gómez-Gómez y Orbanagochea, chamberlain of His Holiness Paul VI): and as the spinster prima donna with an umbrella beside her absorbs, with an ecstasy that greatly resembles a menopausal hot flash, chapter after chapter describing the expert maneuvers whereby the heroine of a best seller defends her virginity, *urbi et orbi*: all the regular readers, the habitués of the place are present, not to mention the mere occasional visitors, the chance seekers after knowledge: a vaguely middle-aged man consulting various volumes of a medical encyclopedia meant for laymen: a lady dressed in mourning, who is apparently passionately interested in gardening and floriculture: you tiptoe discreetly past them, bidding them an almost inaudible good day, and finally enter your solitary kingdom: the rich sedimentary deposits, the layer upon layer of the history of your very own native vernacular: a mother tongue, grave discourse by the soul of your country, flowing like a great river: a corpus slowly purified and polished by tradition down through the centuries: an admirable treasure: all collected here, from the first stammerings of the gloss of San Millán: a humble, tremulous prayer of a monk shut up in his cell like a diligent bee: the cry of a frail babe still in diapers: the Duero in its infancy, yet already quintessentially Spanish: fed by the wellsprings of a profound, passionate inspiration: winding its lonely way across the ancient, noble soil: a river constantly seeking, and finding, the course that best suits it: the robust octosyllable, the perfect hendecasyllable, the immortal sonnet; a powerful, abundant stream: narrowing at times and occasionally descending underground for a certain distance, bending back upon itself and meandering, but never ceasing to flow: from the *romancero* to Lope de Vega, from Lope to Federico García Lorca: and on to today's beloved poets: your cozy, frail, grown-up children, wrapped in swaddling clothes: overcome with amazement, joyous, smiling: dumfounded: holding the most intimate conversations with God: in a perpetual state of rapture: capital carefully preserved here behind glass cases: catalogued, arranged in the proper order, lined up in neat rows: on shelves within reach of your hand or accessible with the aid of a library ladder: a great long procession of geniuses, bound in paper or pasteboard or leather, with their impassive backs turned toward you: crushing you beneath the weight of their example: their heroism, their piety, their knowledge, their conduct, their glory: their countless noble acts and attitudes, worthy of the highest respect: a flowering of the most lofty human virtues: warriors, saints, martyrs, conquistadors: an inspired, transcendental, ecumenical gaze in their eye; their brows crowned with laurel or circled by a gleaming halo: perched on their marble pedestals, set before the common herd as objects of their admiration and models to be imitated: beneath the authoritative gaze of the Omnipresent: a purposely youthful likeness, the cheeks faintly pink: not a blush of shame, but rather a flattering job of retouching: in uniform, with a ceremonial sash and decorations: in those happy days of yore, officially abolished once conciliatory winds began to blow and the horn of plenty beckoned: those days when the defeat of his cronies failed to make him cautious and the salute with uplifted arm, imperial language, brown shirts and berets, patriotic songs, and emblems were the order of the day: sitting at your desk now, you survey, with a rapid, knowing glance, the vast perspective before you: the Spanish genius of

the *romancero*, the *libro de caballería*, the *auto sacramental*:
works rich in substance that are undeniably your very own
heritage: the fixed stars of the pure Hispanic firmament: of
the Spanish spirit rooted in the basic, enduring truths of an
entire people: the lineage of yesterday, today, and tomorrow, a
patrimony and titles of nobility handed down for century after
century by the most honorable and upright forebears: from
Indíbel, Seneca, and Lucan to the brightly gleaming constella-
tion of men who discovered the very essence of your historical
heritage, the barren, monotheistic landscape: Castile!: gray
plains, bony wastelands, bare crags bristling with rocks: dry,
hard, gnarled: vast, lonely, naked expanses: a homeland
oozing pus and grandeur through the cracked crusts of its
wounds: the collective work of an illustrious generation: that
of the First Philosopher of Spain and the Fifth of Germany, dispensing their lofty, sidereal teachings from the high shelf
housing their complete Hors d'Oeuvres: you are still dazzled
by the prodigious concentration of so many illustrious names in
so restricted a space: demigods, thaumaturges, or prophets:
the densest collection per cubic centimeter in the entire world:
you kneel before their statues, embrace them passionately:
if only some day you can get your name on the roster,
be put on the promotion list!: you are already drooling in
anticipation: playing the game, showing up in the right places,
writing admiring letters, organizing testimonial dinners!: a
brilliant future awaits you, spread out before your eyes like a
fan: imitating the masters, paraphrasing their works, basking
in their reflected glory, sharing their immunity!: strolling about
in the company of an illustrious cadaver, clad in the mantle of
virtue of an untouchable!: receiving gifts of flowers, incense,
garlands: being pampered, spoiled, cosseted!: donning an imposing mask!: pontificating!: overcome with remorse, hope,
doubts: adopting a long-range strategy, clever tactics: fre-
quenting cafés and salons, cultivating influential friends: re-

spectful, discreet, prudent: modest and retiring, heart beating fearfully: until the final apotheosis: election to the Academy, being awarded the Al Capone Foundation Prize!: settling down cozily to enjoy your dream life: being addressed by the title of Don!: floating blissfully along all by yourself atop your marvelous cloud: what's bred in the bone will come out in the flesh: genius and the appearance of genius, the more genius the more natural the appearance, and vice versa!: and your very own chair reserved for you at the Café Gijón: holding forth on mysticism, bullfighting, stoicism: on the Castilian concept of honor or the ten commandments of the perfect Christian gentleman: a national institution now, a living paradigm: the guiding light and mentor of younger, quintessentially Spanish generations: a valetudinarian slumping in your chair, with your hand on your heart: a high priest preaching to the awe-struck hordes of the vulgar: ah, my Spain hurts me!: as the little man in the gabardine suit turns a page of his newspaper and the *prima donna assoluta* with the umbrella sits there ecstatically devouring the story of how the heroine of the latest bestseller has managed to defend her virginity as stubbornly as the warriors defending the Alcázar in Toledo: walking over to the shelves of the literary section and making rapid, fruitful, stealthy probes, carefully hidden from the prying eyes of the others: seeking, amid sterile doubt, vigorous affirmation: Spain, under siege, alone with God: the authors with genius and the trappings of genius: visceral, noble, tough writers: fossils, crustaceans, all skin and bones: faithful to the inviolable constants of your spirit, the rich texture of your innermost soul: lofty Parnassuses, dense, magnificent anthologies: the sonnet, a virginal, perfect creature, zither and harp, the sweet-sounding violin carved out of mellow, melodious wood: climbing up to the top shelves with the aid of the little ladder running along a metal groove parallel to the floor: exploring the necropolis of bards and choosing a

stark drama of honor, by Calderón or Tirso or Lope, the latter
so rightly named since his verses are inevitably terribly flat[1]:
coming down to earth again and going back to your reading
desk with your rich booty: the custodian is yawning as though
trying to swallow the entire earth, his bulldog jaws gaping:
his eyes gazing at the green plumes of the palm trees framed in
the window: and when he closes his mouth, his face becomes
a mass of wrinkles and furrows, like some sort of clay structure
cracking apart: the reader consulting the medical encyclopedia
has mysteriously disappeared, and the lady clad in mourning is
silently leafing through her treatises on gardening: nothing to
the right, nothing to the left: you are free to move about as
you please: the books piled up on your desk serving as a
protective barrier between you and the custodian: who yawns
mightily yet again as you search in the left-hand pocket of
your jacket for the fateful, carefully concealed little pouch:
your meager capital: rapidly calculating the modest but en-
couraging range of possibilities: houseflies, ants, bees, horseflies: perhaps a fat, hairy spider or two: emptying the contents
out onto the oilcloth in a tempting pile: an insect hecatomb
such as has never before been recorded in history, which you
survey with a cold and resolute eye: reaching for the first
volume in the pile and depositing an ant and six flies inside it:
in the middle of the crucial scene between Cassandra and the
Duke: I could not love thee, dear, so much loved I not honor
more: suddenly closing the volume and crushing these seven
insects: very cautiously, however, so the custodian doesn't
catch you in the act: then opening the book and unhurriedly
contemplating the result, with the finical appetite of the
connoisseur: squashed flat, their guts spattered all over: indelible stains blotting the dramatic episode, contaminating it
with their sluggish, viscous flow: capes, inlets, bays: fantastic

[1] A pun on the name Lope de Vega. In Spanish, the noun *vega* means
flat plain. [Translator's note.]

geographical forms: islands, veritable archipelagoes: you select another volume, another somber drama: what lofty sentiments, what grandeur of soul!: the magnificent exchange between Diego Laínez and Count Lozano, going after each other hammer and tongs: discourse is dangerous, but it has never killed anyone afraid to die: a bee, eight flies, and bam!: not delicately fingering the fruit this time however: cautiously glancing into the next room out of the corner of your eye: a useless precaution: the reader of *ABC* is still ecstatically sipping the delights of its inimitable prose and the spinster with the umbrella is still heaving vague sighs: the custodian is still drowsing: the green light: the road is clear ahead: wandering through the monotonously unfolding landscape of Castile: grave, monastic, austere: past the endless fields of green wheat and yellow straw: concentrating all your attention on a middle-sized spider: eight eyes, four pairs of legs, two spiracles, pedipalpi, chelicerae: caught in the act, perhaps, of capturing a victim in these dark shadows: and you slam the pages shut, unable this time, however, to resist the temptation to have a look: the victim is forever immobilized on top of the delightful description of the tiny village huddling around its church steeple: you are amazed at your handiwork: terribly pleased and proud of yourself: and now you choose the paper-bound anthology of the thousand best poems in the language: the "Dos de Mayo," the resoundingly patriotic sonnet of Enrique López Alarcón!: you can barely keep from drooling as you place the massive corpse of a horsefly on top of it, and zap!: *consummatum est*: the perfect hendecasyllable is shattered, the grandiloquent tercet is blotted out: you stifle a triumphant cry *à la* Tarzan: tumultuous joy, exultation you are unable to contain, thereby attracting the attention of the custodian and brutally awakening him from his drowsy hibernation: his mouth gapes open in one of his troglodytic yawns, he stretches and walks over in your direction: allowing you just time enough to squash the last

corpses and assume a grave and serious mien as the man slowly
shuffles toward you, right foot, left foot, right foot: and now
he's peering out the window with unjustifiable apprehension
and venturing his usual daily comment on the weather: if this
norther keeps up, we'll have rain tomorrow, don't you think?:
you agree that yes, that's quite possible: and then, after making
certain that everything is in order, he yawns again, retraces his
steps, hesitates a second or two, and collapses in his chair:
ontologically welded to his seat: the time has come to make
your escape, and you return the books to their proper place:
those on the lower shelves first, and then the ones on the
topmost shelves, with the aid of the ladder: they are back now
in their vast tutelary pantheon: you climb down again and
stealthily thrust the little pouch in your pocket, with the
diaphanous, delicate sensation of having done your duty: you
cross the room again in the opposite direction, passing by the
old maid with the umbrella and the *ABC* reader with the
Bourbon profile: you eventually reach the door and the harsh
rasp of the buzzer is still ringing in your ears as you head down
the stairs

still clinging to your memory, like tendrils of a grapevine: those
verses of the Poet who, in his hours of solitude far from the
madding crowd, created, with grave, impenitent passion, a
dense, weightless beauty: a reality that has survived intact,
its radiance undiminished down through the years, transmitting
its redeeming signals to you across the centuries, guiding signs
that reach you even amid all the chaos, delivering you from the
deceptive labyrinth: from your daily wanderings amid the maze
of formless, spongy matter: not knowing where the truth lies:
in your sensory impressions or in your memories of the poetic
Word: wavering between the one and the other as you walk
along tracing hieroglyphs: immersed in the crowd, yet not a

part of it: following a different rhythm: subtly capturing the presence (the inrush) of signs that disturb (violate) the apparent order of things: brusque movements, sudden loud noises, angry gestures: small (dull) explosions of violence: an equation whose terms you are unfamiliar with, a script that you vainly attempt to decipher: as though lost in a dream that goes on and on without ever making sense: opening your eyes, waking up at last: JAMES BOND: THUNDERBALL, final week: passing by the terraces of other outdoor cafés, other travel agencies: Riff peasants, women with veiled faces, soldiers on leave: suddenly caught up in the flood of sound pouring out of a jukebox playing one of the Rolling Stones' top-ten records: a musical onslaught that grows fainter and fainter and finally dies away in the bright, tonic air, like a tiny rivulet emptying into the ocean or a well-organized charitable enterprise gradually swallowed up in the vast depths of anonymous suffering: dispensing its auditory favors to a few ears, and leaving the rest in their usual state of indigence: indifferent, moreover, to this sort of generosity: vendors of lottery tickets, shills, bootblacks: satellites orbiting around the bus station who earn the few pennies they live on from it: chasing after a fickle fortune that continually escapes their grasp and immediately slips through their fingers, fleeing their touch the moment they come within reach of it: or, if they are unusually lucky, according them a pale simulacrum of a smile: repair jobs that pay hardly anything at all, ridiculously meager tips that prolong their misery without alleviating it and give rise to a constant, unconscious, endemic feeling of frustration: amid hand baskets, string bags, and suitcases of travelers headed for Asilah, Tutuán, or Larache: sitting or standing or squatting on their heels, stoically accepting the capricious schedule of bus departures: as you walk up the street in the direction of the taxi stand, passing by the Cine América and the steps leading to Tenería: with the usual beggars at their post on each landing and the usual loiterers all

along the railing: an itinerary that you know by heart and
could more or less follow blindfolded: going off to the left along
the Tapiro, leaving the Café de la Terrasse behind you, and the
narrow alleyway barricaded by an imposing doorway bearing
the inscription: DON ÁLVARO PERANZULES, ATTORNEY-AT-LAW,
going on to Ben Charki, making your way along the wall that
surrounds the Hotel Cuba, and finally reaching the roofed-over
passageway and its dilapidated pinball machines: the Moorish
café, peacefully slumbering at this hour of the day: the lotto-
players have not yet appeared and the musicians' platform is
still deserted: the retouched photographs hanging on the wall
appear to share your nostalgia for the piercing notes of a flute
and the undulations of a young boy's body: a striking field
flower playfully and shamelessly playing hide-and-seek with a
scarf to the rhythm of the *rabel*: amid the aromatic odor
emanating from pipes and glasses: hashish and mint tea:
as the master of ceremonies draws numbered cards out of a
box and his assistant announces them in a loud voice: *tlata!*
achrá! set-tín! and you drink the strong-scented infusion and
slowly smoke your first pipeful of kef with the tacit, beneficent
approval of the stars: Pelé, Cassius Clay, Umm Kalsúm, Farid-
el-Attrach: who reign here in the place of Barrel-Shape: free
of the presence of your compatriots: an Arab, a pure Arab:
friend and crony of good old dependable Tariq: Ulyan, Urban,
or Julian: up above the little parapet that overlooks the sea and
the enemy shore: it's daytime and the sun is shining and it
would be pleasant to be out on it getting a breath of fresh air:
but you decide not to go up there and are content merely to
glance up at the little balustrade where you usually sit: seen
from below it looks thin and frail, supporting at this moment the
weight of two men in djellabas, who appear to be staring at
each other in rapt, mute contemplation: going on along the
Calle de Portugal, beneath the shabby dwellings imbedded in the
wall: lying in ambush for the reality hidden beneath a deceptive

coat of varnish: a message in code, intermittent signals that
come your way, demanding your entire attention, then disappearing immediately thereafter: a youngster walking along,
with a transistor radio in his hand, isolated from his surround-
ings by the thin harmonies of his portable music: enveloped in
it as though in a very subtle, personal atmosphere: a melody
that grows louder as the distance between you diminishes and
then is suddenly interrupted a few seconds before your paths
cross, replaced by the grave, self-important voice of the
announcer: ladies and gentlemen, you have just heard a selec-
tion from the ballet *Les Syphilides*, by Frederic Xopen: *Syphilides* or *Sylphides*?: it doesn't matter: the message has been
transmitted, and the herald goes on down the street with his
transparent musical halo, leaving you lost in a sea of proble-
matical conjectures: save a life, give your blood: why not?:
bottled and offered by Caritas, with the wheat and the conse-
crated wafers of the Pax Americana: napalm here, milk there:
with the smiling laying on of cardinalitial hands and sometimes
the benediction of the Pope himself: at the foot of the stairway
built into the wall, declining its invitation to climb its steep
heights: going on up the street instead, to the intersection and
the street that leads to the Zoco Grande: halting for a few
moments to catch your breath and then mingling with the
dense crowd: the absolute monarchy of the improbable: of
dubious sales and uncertain transactions: swarms of gestures,
a proliferation of voices, bargaining that attracts the usual
horde of curious bystanders who stand around the improvised
ring watching the ritual bout: entranced with this primitive
barter-economy universe, without the false embellishment of
gorgeous Hollywood technicolor: as in the films starring Maria
Montez and Jon Hall, with their multichrome markets straight
out of the time of Aladdin and Ali Baba: women squatting next
to a handkerchief or a little basket containing their meager
stock of merchandise that perhaps no one will buy: a tiny

bouquet of fresh mint, a dozen prickly pears, a bunch of dates: with their broad-brimmed woven-palm hats sheltering them from the sun: which is at its zenith now, proud and pleased at the lofty position it has reached: a red-cheeked goldsmith on high, beaming down on the vulgar and ridding them of their lice, as Quevedo might say: the blind patron charitably sponsoring all the faults and injustices of the universe: the sidewalks crowded with skinny men as silent as sleepwalkers, leaning against the wall in hieratic positions, staring into space: child beggars tugging at your sleeve and deafening you with their shrill, whining little voices: wandering shades, settled down in a dull torpor requiring the minimum expenditure of energy, waiting in vain for Charon's bark along the brackish swamp-waters of the Cocytus, which is blindly accelerating the natural process of decomposition: strong odors, acrid emanations that you eagerly breathe in with all the fervor of a catechumen undergoing a rigorous, demanding Orphic initiation: beyond the sphere of the meager, marginal benefits of the peninsular consumer society: outside the Spain that may well be prospering but is still mute: proudly proclaiming to your conceited compatriots that everything that is secretion, rottenness, carrion will be your chosen realm: rude caresses, a hard bed: expert love-making in the age-old manner of the Mohammedan he-goat: far from your saintly Spanish women and their zealously guarded sanctuaries: surprised by the sudden appearance of a beggar, like a ghostly apparition, painfully making his way toward you, summing up in his pitiful person the entire burden of human misery: his bare skull covered with pustules: one eye badly affected by conjunctivitis, as narrow as a buttonhole, and the other with a bright-blue doll's eye buried in the socket, the crazy, emptily staring eye of someone risen from the dead: a mythical Cyclops: a rachitic, sunken chest beneath a jacket in tatters: wide Arab pants, tied at the knee: bare legs, one of them shorter than the other, with an almost vertical foot, the naked toes of which barely touch the ground, as though he were walking on tiptoe: when he holds out his hand and you drop a few coins in it, your gesture suddenly strikes you as sacrilegious: alms to a king? the beggar goes on down the street, spinning like a top, his rigid foot, like the hoof of a goat, suddenly taking on the winged grace of a Pavlova or a Nijinsky: losing himself in the crowd with his sudden, swift beauty of movement as you slowly make your way up the steep street, lined with the first market stalls: trying your best to quiet your madly pounding heart: refusing all the suspect merchandise offered you, unmoved by the bustling, polyvalent activity of the vendors: fruits, vegetables, couscous grits being hawked with cries that assail your eardrums like sudden piercing stabs: as stylized, almost abstract mongrels search in vain for something to eat amid the garbage in the gutter and clouds of flies hover about and land on the mountains of pastries dripping with honey: black, hairy, sticky flies, more than enough to spatter the complete works of Lope: of the most eminent dramatist Spain has ever produced: the great *canard farci*, stuffed with watery Castilian dressing: a fleeting moment of nostalgia that suddenly brings you back to the Gilt-Edged Age and your shitty homeland: forcing you to recite the Prophecy of the Tagus to console yourself: *oye que al cielo toca con temoroso son la trompa fiera que en África convoca el moro a la bandera que al aire desplegada va ligera*[1]: all in one breath: and then, at peace once again, returning to your adoptive country: to the North African market with the Hollywood tinsel stripped away: continuing along the typically Tangerian Calle de la Playa: an outlying district of the city into which housewives dare to venture, in which the bartering takes on a slight tinge of European respectability: smells less strong, flies fewer in

[1] "Hark, the fearful trumpet-blast is proclaiming to the heavens
That in Africa the Moors are gathering around their unfurled banners
Stirring in the gentle breeze"—From Fray Luis de León's famous
"Praefecía del Tajo." [Translator's note.]

number: polished fruit, clean green vegetables, pastry protected
by a transparent sheet of cellophane: a commendable effort to
appeal to a wider clientele and attract the prudent middle strata
of society that fluctuate between the solid and the gaseous,
street vendors who have discreetly and stubbornly climbed the
social ladder and become tradesmen: speaking decent Spanish
and butchering French: ending up finally at the Zoco Grande
and its cluttered perspective: shops, stalls, bazaars, water-
vendors ringing their little bells, little groups of curious on-
lookers, the smell of grilled sausage and shish-kebab: making
your way among the sumptuous djellabas and suddenly stumbling on the Martian excursion bus: as huge as a whale with a
snout like a shark: with a glass roof and sides: sound-proofed,
air-conditioned, wired for Muzak: having momentarily dis-
charged its cargo of fat, sweating passengers: V.I.P.'s from
another planet come in search of autumnal adventures:
Lawrence of Arabia with Peter O'Toole: huddled around the
guide like a timid flock of sheep as they machine-gun the
esplanade with their Leicas and Kodaks and 16-millimeter movie
cameras: you stroll over, impelled by the same temptation
(though the pull is exerted in the opposite direction) to get a
closer look at the picturesque natives, and offer yourself (gratis)
the pleasure of pasting labels on them:
six bigwigs from the Bronx
ten furriers from Chicago
one gentleman farmer from Texas
a delegation of speleologists
two avant-garde music critics
a former married couple recently divorced
five war widows
who are standing there ecstatically taking in every word of the
meaty, fluent commentary of the extremely knowledgeable
guide: an Anglo-Saxon version of your own inimitable Castelar:

beautifully rounded periods, orotund phrases, with a patina of erudition both elegant and delightfully witty

fair ladies and good gentlemen, as you can see, Tangier is a wide-open city in all the senses of the word: it has been called the Land of the Dark Parting, because of the ambition of the Arab girls to become platinum blondes: Tangier is one of the world's few remaining pleasure cities: and no questions asked: the Zoco Grande, here, is good fun on market days: snake charmers, storytellers!: let us now sit outside the Café del Moro: on your right: drink mint tea to the concerts of Arab music: Eastern music!: its romantic mystery: real Moors: as well as your dear American friends: a favorite excursion is to Hercules' Caves where the hero-god lived: the cool *levante*, the Eastern wind!: the magnificent bathing beaches with such historic names!: Trafalgar, Spratell!

as itinerant vendors besiege the group with their array of deadly weapons: necklaces, earrings, rings, fezzes, post cards, branches of jasmine, copper articles: in accordance with the rules of a clever, patient politico-military strategy: the strategy of peasants who have become experts at modern guerrilla warfare: mercilessly harassing the outposts on the periphery before mounting their final victorious assault: astute disciples emulating the veterans of the Long March: in the optimistic, enthusiastic days of the Hundred Flowers Blooming: a tactic now thoroughly tested and perfected, the excellent results of which are obvious at first glance: Old World trinkets exchanged for American $$$$'s backed by the gold reserves of Fort Knox: retracing, in the opposite direction, the famous expeditions of your navigators of old: Spaniards debarking from Columbus's caravels beneath the awed gaze of the natives: this particular tribe headed, it appears, by a fabulously wealthy queen: the prime objective, at any rate, of the running gunfire: an imposing member of the D.A.R., straight out of a photo by

Avedon of a matron in evening dress, with a satin reticule and sash: attired on this particular occasion, however, in a seer-sucker suit, carrying a leather handbag, and wearing a pair of sunglasses, which despite their outsize dimensions do not ade-quately protect the lady's nose, which has been badly sunburned and is now peeling underneath the sheet of cigarette paper she has stuck rather precariously over it: beneath her mouth smeared with lipstick and her numerous chins her low-cut, scabrous, provocative neckline plunges downward, edged in a delicate, innocent ruffle that makes it all the more noticeable: breasts that threaten to collapse despite the rigid wall that holds them up and the sacklike cut of her dress, which gives no indica-tion of where her waistline is, falling in a straight line to her plump knees: with a fringe around the bottom: above chunky limbs supported by sandals with thick cork soles whose cut permits a scandalous display of toes: irregular, splayed, widely separated toes: with ten toenails lacquered a rosy red, like a bunch of ripe, tempting cherries: her entire person a vast synthesis of the outstanding virtues of a great people: the modern crusaders whose weapon is a smile: your saviors: ecstatically happy there amid the gnomes besieging her with their multiple extravagant offerings: look here: not expensive: souvenir: already having bought a red fez with a tassle and perched it on her head: already decked out in glittering jewels: in the half alcoholic, half sentimental euphoria of a person recently freed of petty complexes and inhibitions: by following the way of psychoanalysis or that other way: an easier and less taxing one, doubtless, in these proverbially sun-drenched countries where as yet there is very little industrialization and a more than sufficient supply of manpower: accepting with generous indulgence the exuberance of some youthful healer who may happen along: of some dashing young street vendor who, like his Berber ancestors, will adorn her and clothe her in beauty: a primitive, symbolic prenuptial rite, rich in affectionate promises, in passionate gestures: a branch of jasmine tucked in the plunging neckline of her dress: nice, very nice: in ecstasy when he plants yet another branch in the curly locks peeking out from the inverted flowerpot of her fez: wonderful: crowned with laurel and grape tendrils: wreathed in wild flowers: a veritable country garden: like a cow with a garland of blossoms on Saint Anthony's day: abandoning her to the fertile imagination of North African leprechauns, turning your back on the group and continuing on your way: walking past the displays of pastries, the shops of miraculous healers: mingling with the fluid mass of strollers heading toward Semmarín: stepping into the shadows of the first houses bordering the narrow little street without having yet made up your mind exactly where you will go from there: taking advantage of the quiet hundred yards that separate you from the place where the street forks: the other people on the street are slowly strolling along, peering into each shop window, and you will follow their example and simply saunter down the street too: you're free all day today, your time is all your own: you may turn off to your right if you so choose and amble along Tuajín with its jewelry shops, passing by the Pension Liliane and the Hotel Regina, the little street called Sinagoga, the second-hand furniture store: mirrors, sofas, hat racks, umbrella stands, the belongings of an aunt who's died, sold off by her heirs with an understandable sigh of relief: piled up in the middle of the street, doubtless feeling terribly lonely at having had to abandon their warm, cozy, dimly lit haven, full of folding screens, family portraits, Chinese teapots, and a vague smell of cats: exposed to the pitiless gaze of strangers, mercilessly abandoned in their old age: you turn down the tempting but deceptive prospect of going up Trinidad Abrines, knowing that it ends in a positively Venetian cul-de-sac, and instead continue on down Tuajín to Alejandro Dumas and the silent Calle de América: seduced once again by the romantic halo surrounding the old consulate and its drowsy deserted

garden in the inner courtyard: you must now either climb the
stairway built into the wall or fall into the trap of the Bastión
Irlandés: a blind alley that forces you to retrace your steps and
go back down the Calle de América and Alejandro Dumas,
which will inevitably lead you to the Calle del Horno: a narrow,
covered street, with the houses on either side so close together
they almost touch: the deliberate asymmetry of a capricious,
clever, persistent master architect: planes and surfaces that
neither Descartes nor Haussmann would understand: lines
and segments put together as though to prove an indemon-
strable geometrical theorem: you reject the welcoming shadow
of the Calle Bramel and the Calle de Sale: forced now to choose
between taking Khetib to Temsamani or going down Muley
Selimane to Colaço and Ben Charki: you continue on down the
Calle del Horno to the Callejón de la Sombra and then turn off
down Ksour: passing through the old red-light district where
you sometimes went with Tariq and made love with a Riff girl,
as wild as a mountain goat, her forehead decorated with tattoos
and her teeth capped with gold: deciding not to go by way of
the arch and the little fountain of Karma and choosing instead
the steep Calle de la Cruz Roja Española, which descends
abruptly and joins Ben Charki just a few yards lower down,
at its bottom end where it is narrowest: then rounding the
corner with the building that has a bat, a horseshoe, and a
curious head of a devil carved on the front of it: and then
finally stepping out into the blinding light of Tapiro: near
Álvaro Peranzules's, the Hotel de Cuba, and the Moorish café:
Cassius Clay, mint tea, the smell of kef: musicians sitting on
the platform, lotto-players: looking in vain for the fleeting
silhouette of the young male dancer: who is doubtless sleeping
at this hour: you stand there hesitantly at the intersection, and
finally decide to go down Almanzor: thus giving up the Mellah,
the Koran School, the itinerary that would lead you down Chorfa
de Quazán and Las Once to the Zoco Chico: today you choose

instead to walk along past the dry-goods stores and the spice market: the Calle Sir Reginald Lister and the Calle del Trigo: then you turn down Necharin, falling in behind a disturbing-looking woman: not veiled but gagged: with a coarse cloth covering her face from ear to ear: her dark glasses also remind you of the possibility of kidnapping and ransom, an idea that has doubtless entered your mind because of the posters plastered all over the city: JAMES BOND: THUNDERBALL, final week: following on behind her, the two of you passing through the musical tidal wave of an invisible transistor radio turned up all the way, playing the catchy melody of the schottishe "Madrid": walking beneath the arcades of the Calle de los Arcos till they turn right along Nasería and you turn left down Beni Arós: in the direction of the white mosque of Los Aisauas and its minuscule irregular-shaped plaza: at the precise moment that a band of little apprentice sorcerers, clad in tiny djellabas, make their brief, wraithlike appearance: chasing a fluttering rooster dripping great trails of blood: its head half cut off and turned back at an unbelievable angle: zigzagging along as though attempting to escape the fate that awaits it and un-wittingly moving straight toward it: you stop: its wings are beating furiously, and its tiny eyes are glazed with terror: as the officiants surround it to contemplate its death throes, a black mastiff bounds out of one of the nearby houses and licks up the crimson pools of blood with its slender, agile tongue: the neighbors stand about indifferently watching this spectacle and you turn your back to them to conceal your emotion: violence, inescapable violence: crossing your path at regular intervals: suddenly and unexpectedly: thus instantly destroying the illu-sion of order, revealing the truth hidden beneath the mask, catalyzing your scattered forces and your donjulianesque plans for invasion: a grandiose act of treason, the collapse of entire centuries: the cruel army of Tariq, the destruction of Sacred Spain: as you enter the Calle Chemaa Djedid, then Chorfa,

heading for the Calle de Baño: with the choice of going up to
Nasería and the little plaza with the fountain or going down
to Cristianos and threading your way to Sebu: losing yourself in the maze of the Medina: tracing with your footsteps as you walk (rather than dropping little pebbles or
crumbs to make the way back) a complicated pattern that no one
(not even you yourself) will ever be able to interpret: finally
splitting in two to tail yourself better, as though you were
another person: a guardian angel, a jealous lover, a private
eye: knowing that the labyrinth lies within: that you are the
labyrinth: the famished minotaur, the edible martyr: at once
the executioner and the victim: passing by the little café and
the Moorish bath, turning around and going back the way you
came, along Sus and M'Rini: taking Cristianos and turning
down Comercio: past the dim restaurants serving grilled
sausages and shish-kebab: declining the shadowy invitation of
Sekka and Abarodi: heading straight for Jayattin: the sun
visible now through the arch of the gate, like a joyous prelude
to the Zoco Chico: when you plunge into the sunlight, it is so
intense it forces you to lower your eyes: groping about like a
blind man, you locate the first empty chair and plop down in it:
not on the terrace of the Café Central: on the other side: right
next to the wall and well in the shade: surveying the usual
buzz of activity in this microcosm from your observation post:
a chair at one of the tables in the second row: less exposed to
the vendors persistently trying to force their wares on you, to
the beggars eyeing you expectantly and reproachfully: the
madman, strolling back and forth as usual, lost in his own
thoughts: his movements seemingly motivated by two ambivalent, contradictory impulses: frugality, a minimum of
gestures on the one hand, and wild extravagance, great sweeping
gesticulations on the other: standing at the entrance to
Cristianos now, between the terrace of the Café Tingis and the
Scheherazade Food Mart: with his filthy skullcap, his broken-

down shoes, his scarecrow's jacket: a vacant stare in his eye: as you call the waiter over and order a mint tea he suddenly starts moving, as though someone had wound up a spring inside him, walking along like a robot: with his arms swinging back and forth and his shoulders jerking, he walks past the terrace of the Central, the entrance to the Hotel Becerra, the combination tobacco shop and bookstore, the gate at the end of the Calle del Arco, the Bekali Abdeslam grocery store, the Café Tanger: then he suddenly halts in his tracks as though the spring had wound down: at the entrance to the old Spanish post office, next to the rusty letter box and the poster announcing JAMES BOND: THUNDERBALL: standing there a minute or two and then continuing on his way: without attracting the slightest attention: just another feature of the décor: the soldiers sitting on the terrace of the Tingis seem to be absorbed in a lofty discussion of certain strategical maneuvers of consummate importance and the long-haired hippies in the Central are fraternizing with the native girls by means of sign language: hordes of people pass by, in a rapidly flowing, continuous, heavy stream: middle-class Arabs in djellabas and slippers, Jewish craftsmen, delivery boys, fishermen, tourists: and now and again a restless Nordic type who sticks his head into the dark shadows of one café after another for a quick look around, fluttering like a butterfly from one terrace to the next with a fleeting, telltale wiggle of his ass: a siren on the lookout for tail, an elegant serpent with a deadly sting: the arty type, with dark circles under his eyes and thick silky eyelashes: a frequent guest, doubtless, at the Festival or Stephen's: greeting all his former playmates and on the prowl for new ones: young males with copper-colored skin and white teeth, with warm, sensitive, fickle hearts: usually without either a profession or a job: but easily approachable and understanding: he has no difficulty detecting them, thanks to the delicate intuition of the connoisseur, the instant flash of recognition of the veteran globe-trotter: a

Livingstone for whom Africa holds no secrets: a pilgrim and a frequent visitor, perhaps, of those homely but very convenient little facilities that Lenin generously dreamed of lining in solid gold: once world revolution had triumphed and man had been freed of his petty selfishness: paying dialectical, Hegelian homage to the zeal and the spirit of self-sacrifice of the practitioners of the cult: permanently installed there: on their guard, keeping a sharp eye peeled: contemplating the continual comings and goings of males dropping in to satisfy urgent calls of nature, on occasion lingering longer than necessary: hydraulico-contemplative: calculating with one quick glance, with electronic precision, the range of possibilities: the gap separating dull reality from the vivid color print: waiting for long anxious moments, which fortunately prove amazingly rewarding: like the modest architects of the Marshall Plan suddenly confronted by the unexpectedly vast dimensions of the German miracle: stupefied at the youthful vigor of such deserving lads: armed to the teeth and with no intention of laying down their arms: brandishing at any and every hour of the day or night the irrefutable proof of their never-failing, robust health: O tempora! O Moors!: conversing now with a red-headed spik-inglish, the sort who may just possibly be able to provide the proper introductions: hello-I-know-a-little-Spanish-Jewish-Moroccan-girl-boy, or perhaps even a swan of the sort that Tchaikovsky so admired, if one's tastes run to Leda-type fantasies: abandoning the hippie hangout and tagging along after the spik-inglish down Siaghin: the waiter brings your glass of tea, and as you wait for it to cool, a bumblebee buzzes over, hovers just above the edge of it for a moment, and then immediately flies away again: oh, if only you had with you the work of some untouchable!: a master of syntax, an eminent intellectual, a tauromatic genius: discoursing on awareness of self, the *en-soi*, the *pour-soi*: on Seneca, the Cid, a beloved burro named Platero:[1] opening the volume in the middle to attract the careless victim, to tempt the creature into landing on it to sip the nectar of its super-refined prose: metaphysical essences, ethical emanations: and bang! slamming it shut: a mine explosion, the sinking of the *Titanic*!: never once losing sight of it as it pretends to renounce its goal and engages in evasive tactics: flying in tight concentric circles, zeroing in closer and closer, intoxicated by the heady aroma of the infusion, finally daring to light on the warm, velvety mint leaves: remaining for a few seconds in this voluptuous Turkish bath and then swiftly taking wing again: as you sit there suddenly disturbed by the intrusion of yet another bumblebee, of the anthropoid variety this time, circling about you, sniffing around: a hairline mustache, a gabardine suit, glasses: a Bourbon profile, plump little hands: all the earmarks of that fierce tribe known as freelance reporters, who, rather than describing what they see, merely obediently repeat what they hear: with a vaguely familiar look about him: long-ago experiences as a crusader, unfathomable dynastic convictions: a real Colonel Blimp type: still a bit hesitant but eager to rid himself of his last possible remaining doubt: trying his best to catch your eye, and on failing to do so, installing himself at the table immediately adjoining yours, his very Spanish countenance turned in your direction, his eyes staring at you: one of your compatriots has left a newspaper on the table and you decide to pretend to be totally absorbed in reading every last word of it: 9:30 p.m.: semifinals of the high-school competition: 10:25 p.m.: illustrious Spaniards of yesterday and today: Lucius Anneus Seneca: 11:15 p.m.: special report on the passage of the Law for the Organization of: making a point of turning your back on him when he says to the waiter: I'll have the same

[1] The hero of a book of poems by Juan Ramón Jiménez. [Translator's note.]

as this gentleman: in a firm, thundering tone of voice, one last
vestige of imperial dreams that have come to naught: recipe:
¾ pound cooky crumbs, ½ cup powdered sugar, 6 egg yolks,
1 teaspoon cinnamon, 1 orange slice, 1 cup milk, sprinkling of
hazelnuts: feeling your ears, your back, your neck prick-
ling beneath his gaze, but nonetheless slowly and deliberately turning the page with a loud rustle: do you enjoy breathing the pure, fresh air of the great forests? do you enjoy
lingering on the banks of a quiet little stream trickling down
to the vast plains below, listening to the hum of bumblebees?
do you enjoy stretching out on soft grass, basking in the sun's
warm caresses? do you enjoy drowsing beneath the green
leaves of the trees, hearkening to the trill of the nightingale, the
song of the lark? do you enjoy peacefully contemplating the
crystalline depths of mountain lakes? do you enjoy rocking
your troubled spirit to sleep to the soothing rhythm of a babbling
brook? do you enjoy scaling mountain peaks and bursting into
joyous song once you have reached the summit? GUADARRAMA:
A SAFE INVESTMENT: CONVENIENT CREDIT PLAN: it's useless,
utterly useless: this *Homo hispanicus* simply won't give up: he
keeps clearing his throat and staring at you, clearing his throat
and turning his chair around toward you, feeling quite safe in
doing so, encouraged by your pretended total absorption in your
newspaper: he's rehearsing the whole conversation in his mind
now: working up his nerve to speak to you: and finally
addressing you
I beg your pardon
a living room with a fireplace, a completely equipped kitchen,
with formica cabinet tops and breakfast table, a matching
dining-room set, parquet floors, wooden door and window
frames, kerosene furnace and central heating, a bathroom with
a shower, a built-in toilet deodorizer, a bidet
I beg your pardon

A REAL BARGAIN: A DREAM COME TRUE
I believe we've already met
DAY-DATE ROLEX OYSTER: weight, 3.7 ounces, 18-carat-gold
band: automatic, antimagnetic, waterproof
I met you once in Paris, you were with a woman, your wife, I
believe
no
a young brunette, in the Latin Quarter or Saint-Germain-des-Prés
I believe you're mistaking me for someone else
searching his mind, close, very close to hitting the bull's-eye:
with the smile of a handsome young Spanish movie star of the
'40's: stupid and persistent
you were gathering information for an article
I assure you you're mistaking me for someone else
aren't you a journalist?
excuse me
you get up from your chair, walk right past him, forcing him to
uncross his legs: you pay the waiter for your drink, and cross
the room: yes, you're a journalist, all right: one with no talent
whatsoever: you've been one for years now: reporting on the
doings of your compatriots condemned to selling their labor as
though it were some sort of shopworn, unwanted merchandise:
bearing on their shoulders the weight of all the sudden accumulation of capital: underground workers laying the foundations
for the mushrooming suburban housing developments: or
on the doings of *nouveaux-riches* bourgeois suffering from
Antonioni-like neuroses, presumably liberated, but deep down
still pompous, self-satisfied, impermeable: all the flies of
Tangier would not suffice to blot them out, and yourself along
with them, their chronicler, their professional observer, their
photographer: with your mind still reeling from the shock you
push the little door open and enter the shadowy corridor, lit only
by a dim, niggardly skylight: a few yards from the nearly pitch-

black grotto intended for the relief of ordinary, elementary physiological needs: not lined with gold: prerevolutionary: practically invisible, though there is a certain sign pointing to its existence: the suspect damp trail trickling down the entire length of the corridor that has peeled the paint off the filthy walls covered with graffiti: penises with wings, round male spheres, a whole phallic artillery: fortresses that have suddenly surrendered, warm, hospitable tabernacles: accompanied by the inevitable polyglot glosses: cries of anguish or of passionate desire emitted by wretched, suffering human beings in the solitude of the act, resembling curious messages in bottles entrusted to the capricious flow of the tides: nocturnal entreaties, secret prayers inscribed in a hurried, furtive hand: with a pencil, a fountain pen, a ball-point pen, a pocket knife: addressed to the unknown god invoked by Saint Paul in his famous epistle to the Athenians: a god who refuses to hearken to them, or if he does, fails to answer them: for they appear again and again, inevitably exactly the same, in every clime, every latitude of the globe, in all such vitally necessary temples as this, in all such propitious places for meditation and reflection: would like to meet passionate woman charging no more than ten a night: or: *flic, 40 ans bien monté cherche jeune homme discret et vicieux avec chambre*: or: I fuck all girls from 7 to 75: or: *njab nnicq Kulchi nsa*: or the most sibylline, the most ambiguous message of all, inscribed in capital letters there before your very eyes: SPARE THE ROD AND SPOIL THE CHILD: at the edge of the omnipresent wet trail that suddenly fades away, only to come to the surface again in the cracks of the grotto: you reread it several times as you stand there with your legs apart, not daring to venture into this yawning, Cyclopean cavern, unbuttoning your fly: freeing the lowest buttons of the restraint of the decorous buttonhole holding them in bondage and groping about in an effort to determine the precise position of the indispensable instrument: called upon,

alas, to perform its most vulgar and simplest function: brought
out into the open at last: defenseless and flaccid: possessed of
all the tender vulnerability of your child poets: a state of affairs
that obliges you to lift it delicately with your fingers: and once
in position aiming it at the Elysian domain three feet or so
away: it proves reluctant at first, like a willful, badly spoiled
crown prince: but finally obeying, manfully and forcefully:
haughtily pumping out the yellow fluid until an anxious, plaintive voice reaches your ears from the shadowy depths below,
and an infernal shade, whom you have greatly discomfited as
it crouches there in a humiliating and painful posture, calls up
in an incredibly urbane tone of voice: hey up there, watch
what you're doing, I'm down here below you!: a mere item
of information, offered without the slightest trace of anger or
reproach: someone still squatting there, it would appear, from
the nature of his vague, neutral, successive utterances: ah eh
eh oh uff: shaking himself, perhaps, like a wet poodle: his
pride doubtless hurt, but still the soul of dignity: suddenly
interrupting your torrential outpouring: yet giving you sufficient
time to conceal the guilty party, to return it to its warm, idle retreat: incapable of voicing any sort of apology, you retrace your
steps, fleeing as fast as your legs can carry you: a Spaniard?
an Arab? a young man? an old man?: or one of those dwarfs
straight out of a painting by Velázquez whom you frequently run
into in the market place?: how in hell will you ever find out?:
in the Moorish hustle and bustle of the street, but having at the
same time returned to your childhood and its dreary pleasures:
twenty-five, twenty-six years ago?: you were nine years old (or
almost nine at most) and the image (whether invented or real)
is associated with a city, a country whose very name you would
prefer to forget: you will therefore erase it from your memory
and willingly accept the diverting, providential company of this
child: neatly dressed, despite the numerous cruel, adverse cir-
cumstances affecting his life: a clean pair of pants, a wool

sweater, plastic sandals: working off and on as a guide, a
messenger, a shoeshine boy, a perfect example of the scarcity
of regular jobs available to Tangerines
would you like to visit the Casbah?
I'd like that very much
I'll show you the way
leading you, with precocious self-assurance, down Marina, past
the record store and the souvenir shop, already at ease in his
new role as cicerone: showing you, with a vague wave of his
hand, the white walls of the mosque, the Kufic inscriptions
over the door
that's the mosque
what's it called?
the mosque
doesn't it have a name?
I don't know, it's very old
the youngster starts off again, with an eloquent scorn for all
things historical, and you tag along after him: an itinerary
that you know like the palm of your hand, but don't feel like
following alone today: pleased that his presence prevents the
usual disturbing soliloquy: the dangerous deciphering of the
messages that chance places in your path: down the street,
hugging the whitewashed walls of the *medersa*, in the blinding
shimmer of the sun's rays
are you French?
speak to me in Spanish
at the corner of Tenería he suggests visiting the terrace: the
usual loafers are sitting around on the edge of the parapet, in
rapt contemplation, and you lean over to look too: the
mirador towers over the roofs of the warehouses along the
waterfront, the docks of the fishing port, the solitary curve of
the jetty: overlooking the turbulent waters of the Straits, the
little boats crossing it, the cruel scar extending the entire
length of the opposite shore: or rather, a badly infected open

wound: a mere blur in the distance: inspecting it with the delirious gaze of the great Mutanabbi: waves galloping like stud stallions toward the opposite shore: the victorious armies of Tariq: a count whose honor has been outraged: your native land, the target at which the rusty battery of cannons of Bordj-el-Marsa, right there beneath your feet, are aimed: two drowsing eighteen-pounders abandoned there in the redoubt built long ago by Muley Hasán: a battery the youngster also looks at, glancing out of the corner of his eye, trying to catch some sign of approval or interest on your face

the port, he says

and what's that over there?

Spain

and that?

two cannons

what period do they date from?

very old: they don't work any more

that is the end of the conversation, and you continue on your way: not via Dar Barud, however: you immediately turn into the Calle del Huerco, threading your way down this very narrow little street: as dark and as long as a tunnel, with a few little glimmers of light here and there, and a strong smell of tannin from the nearby leather workers' shops: the youngster walks on just ahead of you, not saying a word, his hands in his pockets, turning around only to warn you against stepping into a pile of dog shit or slipping on a treacherous banana peel: politely greeting every adult he meets in his own language: on reaching Hach Mohamed Torres he turns to the left and falls in step beside you: he asks you for a cigarette and tucks it behind one ear: you reject the dim possibility offered you by the Calle Abarodi, pass by the Hotel Xauem, the Hotel Andalus, and come out at Cristianos, which you follow as far as the little square of Ued Ahardan: a tradesman in a white djellaba is sitting in the doorway of his shop guarding the entrance to

his establishment and the youngster walks over to him and kisses
his hand: but divining your craven misgivings, he does not
invite you in to see his shop, and when you say good-by to the
man and go on off down Sebu, the only thing the boy says is:
he's a good man: and although you faithfully follow the rules
of the game, pretending you're a foreigner who doesn't know
his way around, he stops you from going on to the Fuente Nueva
and leads you off to the right, up Ben Raisul: a steep climb,
up a flight of steps usually jammed with tourists coming from
the Casbah: for the moment, however, it is deserted: and the
place has the peaceful air of craftsmen working silently and
diligently: little apprentices holding the loom upright in the
middle of the street, master weavers tirelessly threading the
shuttle back and forth in their tiny little shops, like patient,
busy arachnida: terrestrial arthropods, with chitinous shells,
rather undeveloped cephalothoraxes, and huge, bulging abdo-
mens: two spiracles and six nipplelike processes with minute
orifices which extrude the threads for the trap: carefully and
swiftly weaving a treacherous web: dry silk for the center and
the radiuses, sticky wet silk for the spiral: never moving from
their secret hiding places at the edge, but immediately aware
of what is happening all along the web, thanks to a slender,
supersensitive warning-thread: the moment the apprentices
touch the loom they are caught fast and their every effort to
free themselves is useless: the weaver witnesses the whole
desperate struggle through the eight eyes that give him stereo-
scopic vision: he might readily pounce upon his victim and
gobble him up: but he bides his time: the youngster has a
premonition that the end is near and tries to escape his fate
but merely becomes more hopelessly entangled in the web: the
weaver is in no hurry: he has a cold, implacable look in his
eye as he slowly creeps up on his unfortunate prey, step by step:
he still might spare his victim's life, magnanimously give him
his freedom, were he so inclined: but he does not care to do so:

instead he delicately inserts his poisonous chelicerae in his little victim's body, injects his own digestive juices into it, dissolving the softest parts of it and slowly sucking them out: then he deposits his eggs in it and spins a cocoon around them: and after several months (when spring comes!) tiny spiders emerge from it and subsequently undergo a series of changes: not genuine metamorphoses, however: in order to propagate themselves over a wide area these tiny spiders catch hold of a thread and allow the wind to carry them along: swinging back and forth like Mowgli in *The Jungle Book*: from one trailing vine to the other: smiling, air-borne creatures, resembling thistledown or delicate iridescent soap bubbles: and meanwhile the bones of the apprentices scattered along the edges of the stream are a dramatic testimony to their tragic fate: stark white, picked clean, without an ounce of flesh on them: mounting the steps now that lead to the sanctuary named after a legendary Mohammedan hermit and to Barbara Hutton's mansion: passing by future victims holding the threads of the loom and master weavers squatting on their heels tirelessly plying their shuttles: weaving together red and blue threads, yellow and black threads, to form the spider web that traps and immobilizes only very young victims, mere children caught in it at a very early age and thereby condemned for the remainder of their lives to hard labor that pays almost nothing: a ladder with innumerable rungs stretching from childhood to adulthood, from apprenticeship to the title of master craftsman, from the realm of the insect to the realm of the arachnid, a ladder laboriously mounted step by step: threading your way among them with your young cicerone, lightly brushing the tomb of the Mohammedan hermit as you pass by, stopping to catch your breath at the landing at the top of the steep flight of stairs known as Sidi Hosni: the hippie café with the garden on your left and farther up the café that you habitually frequent: a peaceful sunny place, with two large plate-glass windows affording an incomparable view of the city: the place where you smoke kef and lose yourself in dreams every day, but it is still too early to do so today, as you are well aware: so you give up the idea of dropping in there and instead follow your guide up the Calle Amrah to the Plaza de la Alcazaba and the mirador: turning around from time to time as you climb higher and higher to have a look at the city below: the youngster halts too, and when you begin climbing again, he quickens his pace, as though in a hurry to reach the top: as you go through the gate in the wall the piercing wail of Arab music assails your ear-drums: the excursion bus full of Martians is parked beneath the walls of the prison and the group of tourists has formed a circle around a snake-charmer: an old man with dark skin, dressed in a djellaba, with a turban atop his head, squatting on a mat playing a primitive reed flute: the ophidian (a cobra? an asp?) appears to be asleep: but suddenly, as though in answer to a prearranged signal, it assumes a defensive posture, rising up almost vertically, its head thrust forward: weaving back and forth as though about to inject its venom, apparently fascinated by the rustic piping of the snake-charmer: the defenders of your threatened way of life are capturing the scene with their Kodaks and their movie cameras and hailing the old man's prowess with squeals of admiration as he picks the snake up, wraps it around his neck, and then immediately rises to his feet to garner his rightful homage: with a solemn, stern expression on his face: resembling that of General Pershing as Clemenceau pins the Grande Croix de Guerre on his chest: meanwhile his assistants pound their drums and the guide asks for volunteers to pose with the snake wrapped around their necks: a moving impromptu speech, worthy of an electoral candidate: don't be afraid (pause): there is no risk whatsoever involved: the snake-charmer is here to prevent the danger: a remarkable souvenir, ladies and gentlemen (ex-pectant pause): that will amaze your dear friends in Minnesota

or Colorado: I myself, your most humble servant, will pose with
you, of course: you don't believe me? (dramatic pause): ah!
I was certain you'd trust my word: here we are: how many?:
one? two? three?: how about you over there, Miss?: would
you like to pose too?: there's nothing forcing you to: two
volunteers are quite sufficient: the fair lady and the good
gentleman: the two of them detach themselves from the group
and march fearlessly forward to win fame and glory: you recognize them immediately: one of the bigwigs from the Bronx,
with a straw hat and a bow tie, and the D.A.R. straight out of a
Richard Avedon album: with her red fez and her ridiculous
sandals, but no flowers: they have been removed, alas, by a
pious hand: she is very much the *grande dame*, a smiling dema-
gogue: standing rigidly at attention as the old man picks the
snake up very carefully and cautiously drapes it over her
shoulders: are you ready? yes, she's ready: for the grand
finale, the apotheosis: a great lady of the turn of the century
with her boa: the same scene as every other day, but this time
it is going to end differently: some outward provocation?: a
sudden fit of rage?: both things at once?: nobody knows, and
probably no one ever will know: but the fact remains that the
snake suddenly awakens from its lethargy, begins slowly writhing along on its scaly belly, and coils itself like a noose around
the woman's bejeweled neck: its flat, triangular head weaves
back and forth in a hypnotic rhythm: its piercing eyes, like
two tiny pinheads, with transparent eyelids, relentlessly track
her every movement: its forked tongue grazes the little sheet
of cigarette paper that barely covers her peeling sunburned
nose, and suddenly it opens its flexible hinged jaws that allow
it to swallow huge-sized prey and buries its hollow fangs,
situated in its upper jaw, in the woman's round, plump cheek:
the other members of the group stand there, open-mouthed with
amazement, watching the edifying spectacle: a morality play,
a fabliau, a Flemish altarpiece, or a medieval allegory: Poti-

phar's wife, with the red fez atop her head and the ridiculous
sheet of cigarette paper stuck over her nose, and the Levantine
serpent, with a zigzag stripe down its back, no longer coiled,
and therefore twisting and turning to conceal its lascivious head
from view: slowly infusing the poison stored in the glands in
its head: enveloped in a halo of terror and awe, in the very
subtle sacred zone that slowly advances, like a blind man feeling
his way with his cane, casting its inescapable anathema,
imposing its imperious interdict on everything that falls within
its purview: endless minutes, fleeting instants?: impossible
to say: the reel has stopped turning: a stop-motion frame: or
rather a piece of statuary: figures carved in stone or chiseled
in bronze: hours days weeks months years: and then the final
collapse: Potiphar's wife tries desperately to keep her balance:
her sunglasses appear to grow larger and larger as vertigo
overcomes her, as though the very earth beneath her feet were
giving way: she turns round and round, staggers forward a
few paces, reels back, and finally sinks to the ground: her
vast bulk as she lies there supine mindful of a temple sadly
fallen into ruins: her mask has turned black, and a fetid,
nauseating liquid is trickling out of her mouth: there is not
the slightest possible doubt: the poison is fatal: parents and
friends stand by helplessly watching her writhe in the throes
of death: ill-omen vultures wheel in helicoidal spirals above
the corpse and the sinister African gnomes of the Zoco Grande
pounce upon it and strip it of its jewels and baubles: with
obscene irreverence, they lift the skirt of her dress and urinate
in the sanctuary: the unexpected arrival of a hearse disperses
the fascinated crowd that has gathered and puts an end to
this macabre Happening

the sovereign arbiter of mountain peaks and the ocean strand,
as the Poet would say: greeting, with a feeling of relief, the

diffuse presence of the sea separating this shore from the other and guarding your adoptive country against the painful, poisonous scar: you mingle with the tourists and the natives leaning on the balustrade looking at the view: Cape Malabata, forbiddingly bare, hostile to any sort of domestic vegetation: the foamy, tossing waves: the Algeciras ferry slowly heading toward the entrance to the port: directly below you, at the bottom of the steep cliff, the tide is out and a group of youngsters are playing soccer on the wet sandy beach: to your right, an old man in a burnoose is lost in thought, his eyes scanning the enemy coast: less than three hours by boat to reach the vaguely outlined, looming bulk of Gebal-Tariq, and then dashing on to Guadalete and forcing your brothers to strike their proud colors forever: you search in vain for your guide amid the idlers taking in the view of the Straits: he has disappeared without charging you a cent and without bidding you good-by: as swiftly and suddenly as he first appeared, with a radiant smile on his face: causing you to wonder whether he ever really existed or whether he was merely a figment of your most untrustworthy imagination: in any case, he has left you to your own devices again amid the chaos: under the guardianship of this sun that beams brightly and warms and corrupts and rots: the one certainty, omnipresent today: a lustful goat, a lubricious satyr: its rays shimmering on the whitewashed walls of the prison and the Tribunal as you slowly cross the square, walking past the snake-charmer and his musician assistants: all of them inactive at the moment, having perhaps been overcome with the lethargy of the snake by contagion: bright dirhems and francs are lying on the ground all around the mat, and none of the snake-charmer's helpers seems to be in the slightest hurry to pick them up: the cetacean, on the other hand, has emerged from its torpor and is emitting clouds of exhaust fumes: the Martians have settled down in their soft, comfortable seats and are being lulled by the soporific strains of a Gershwin tune:

having recovered from her death and profanation, the D.A.R. matron is leaning out one of the side windows, with her cigarette paper over her nose, her red fez, and her sunglasses: waving at the natives, electoral-candidate-fashion, her arm laden with charm bracelets up to the elbow: silver coins stamped with the effigy of the Emperor Franz Joseph, or Maximilian and Carlota, which tinkle delicately as the bus starts up: it backs up and blocks your path and then sits there panting for a few moments: then the driver straightens the wheel, puts the vehicle into first gear, and it takes off in the direction of Riad-el Sultán: the tourists, the guide, the clouds of exhaust fumes and the Gershwin tune disappear with it: there is nothing barring your way now: the street leading to Bab-el-Assa is clear again: the place where in the old days punishment was meted out to malefactors: beatings by the alguazils that began the moment the condemned criminals stepped out through the portals of the Tribunal: along the brief stretch between the Plaza de la Alcazaba to the stairway that descends to the Arab quarter: beneath the shade of the dwellings built into the wall: hurrying through the gate and dashing down the half-dozen stairs that separate you from the café: delivered from the sun once more: in the cool, sheltering shadow: surrounded by the familiar faces of the habitués of the place, who offer you their hand and then courteously raise it to their heart: exchanging customary polite formulas with them: not in Spanish but in Arabic: happy to forget for a few moments the one last tie that forever binds you, despite yourself, to your native tribe: the marvelous language of the Poet, the linguistic vehicle most appropriate for treason, your beautiful native tongue: the indispensable weapon of the renegade and the apostate, at once magnificent and devastating: a sharp-pointed (insidious) weapon that drives off (exorcises) the African army and increases (whets) its irresistible appetite for destruction: taking your usual seat next to the windows: looking down on the hippie café, the garden of the Frenchman, the tomb of the Mohammedan hermit, Barbara Hutton's mansion: contemplating at your leisure the hallucinatory geometry of the city: cubes, dihedrons, parallelepipeds, prisms: buildings riddled with tiny openings, the minarets of mosques, tile roofs with looping decorative motifs: a weird conglomeration: the design, the construction, the overall appearance of it: groping your way about as you enter a porous, calcareous reality entirely foreign to both the laws of logic and European common sense: lengths of cloth as brightcolored as flags, burnooses and djellabas flapping in the breeze, the solemn, majestic voice of a muezzin summoning the faithful to prayer: the image of a grove of palms in the middle of the desert, surrounded by sand dunes as gently rounded as the breasts or the hips of nubile young girls: verdant foliage around the edge of the spring: ritual dances and holiday merrymaking at Aid-el-Kebir: the owner of the café has brought you a glass of mint tea and you slowly inhale a puff of smoke: when you open your eyes, the apprentice guide is there in front of you, staring at you with a reproachful expression on his face

I've been looking for you, he says

I thought you'd abandoned me, you answer

I didn't leave you alone for a single second, he replies

his voice sounds very familiar to you, and his distinguished air intrigues you: a thin, frail young boy: huge eyes: pale white skin: not the slightest trace of a beard profaning his softly rounded cheeks

you're dressed very elegantly, you say to him

my mother's got lots of money, he replies

how come you're carrying a book bag? you ask him

I'm on my way home from school, he answers

as he stands there with his elbows leaning on your table, you gaze at his profile through the delicate swirls of smoke: picturing him doing his homework for his Natural Sciences class or absorbed in trying to solve an impossibly difficult problem: a

diligent, conscientious student: adoring his mother and in turn
adored by her: admired and cherished by his professors and
his classmates
would you like a drink? you ask him
no thank you, he replies, I'm supposed to meet someone
who's that? you ask him
a man, he replies: the night watchman at a construction site
near where I live: he has a pet snake he shows me when I go
visit him: one he's tamed: he's a snake-charmer
the same one who was in the square a while ago? you ask him
yes, that was him, he answers
why did you try to run away from him then? you ask him
I didn't want him to see us together, he answers: he's terribly
jealous: if I disobey him, he beats me
well, in that case why do you want to go see him? you ask him
I don't really know
his face vaguely recalls an image that you try in vain to summon
up from the depths of your memory: a long-forgotten memory
of the city, the country whose name you do not want to
remember
the moment I spied him I hid under that woman's skirts, he says
what woman? you ask him
the one with the red fez, he answers: I hid under her skirts
till he went away
and what are you going to do now? you ask him
the snake is waiting for me, he replies
wouldn't you like to stay with me for a while?
the youngster stares fixedly at the birds hopping about in their
cage: swift and agile: deftly balancing on their perches: their
tiny heads darting this way and that: their piercing eyes
transfixing you
they're stoned, he says
how can you tell? you reply

see how they're moving about? he answers: a little kef has been
mixed in with the seeds in their food so they'll sing better
the boy stares knowingly at the little birds hopping about in the
cage: and suddenly you are certain you recognize him: a
quarter of a century ago: a part of the city with quiet, almost
dead-silent streets, bordered by shady gardens and huge
mansions: iron fences topped with spikes, walls bristling with
broken glass on the top
where are you going? you inquire
look at my back, he says
who in the world did that to you? you ask him
I have to go, he says: I'm in a hurry
wait a minute, you say
I can't, he answers
please, you say: I think I know you: your name is
so long
melting into the fumes pouring out of the vial: behind the
domino-players and the kef-smokers dozing on the platform: the
birds hop about, dart in and out, swing to and fro, fly round
and round: aerial vertebrates with bodies covered with feathers,
their anterior appendages transformed into wings, warm-
blooded, completely developed double circulatory system:
suddenly become giant birds: falcons and hawks: rapacious
birds of prey, as swift as hurricanes: sharp, curving beaks and
talons, heavy, enfolding wings: wheeling in huge flocks above
the city, as in Hitchcock's film, plunging it in panic: scandaliz-
ing the heavens with their sudden torrent of raucous screams:
soaring to great heights and then swiftly diving on their prey:
the chaotic city appears to be on the point of rebellion: its
geometry is becoming more and more threatening: you will
therefore close your eyes and shut out the vision of the Spanish
church and the Protestant cemetery, the half-deserted beach, the
blank façades along the Bulevar Pasteur: as the African sun

licks your eyelids and the aroma of the tea in the glasses mingles with that of the kef in the pipes: a fruitful, pleasant drowsiness: swift spiralings of light: sunflowers turning in dizzying circles: concentric and eccentric waves: splinters that light up, sparkle a few seconds, flicker, and go out: a heliocentric, dissociative, vibratory motion of lines and curves, ellipses and hyperbolas: a solar spectacle that falls into tatters: a succession of words that come pouring out, which you clumsily attempt to grab by the tail as they rush past you

GIVE

BLOOD

BOND

ROD

CHILD

dashing up the stairs and darting into the Calle Bab-el-Assa: passing beneath the octagonal minaret, heading down the dark, winding Calle Ben Abu in the direction of the Tabor Español and the dramatic spectacle it has to offer today: pursued by a horde of beggars at your heels: surrounding you, tugging at your sleeve, threatening you, whining at you, attempting to block your path: my liver again: already past seventy: her health, so many worries: very nice, very quiet people: one a handyman, the other making a living as best he can, the third one trying to get his passport: almost nothing this time: a hundred dirhems: feeling their expectant gaze, avoiding being trapped by their clever ruses and tricky stratagems: once past Bab-el-Marxán, you walk downhill in the direction of the Hebrew school and the Calle Italia: munching a sausage-and-pepper sandwich, mingling with the crowd waiting to get in: admiring as you stand in line the stills of the hero of today's film and his exquisitely depraved, infinitely desirable leading lady: the two of them lazing on a beach beneath coconut palms, embracing each other in a white convertible: chewing on your sandwich without really wanting it till you reach the head of the

line, purchase your ticket, enter the theater, grope around in the
dark for an empty seat, and plop down in it: the gilded splendor
of nights in the Antilles, the ephemeral domain of His Majesty
the King of the Carnival and his cortege: floats shaped like
swans or pearl oysters stuffed with fake nymphs and bogus
Tritons: blacks unable to contain their riotous joy, their tooth-
paste smiles baring teeth as gleaming white as their peasant
blouses: penitents clad in monks' habits and hoods embroidered
with Pythagorean symbols: a cross between the stern Brotherhood of the Blessed Death of Christ and the clan that metes
out death (blessed or otherwise) to the natives of Mississippi
or Alabama (by way of police dogs, the hangman's knot, or
tins of gasoline): expert lynchers, members of the devoutly
Christian Ku Klux Klan, possessed by the devil of the tropics,
music: their bodies swaying in time to the high-pitched wail
of flutes, their hips and shoulders wiggling to the furious rhythm
of bongos: drifting this way and that, obeying the unpredictable
attraction of an entire zodiac of radiant floats: statuesque
Venuses with feathered headdresses, with fan-shaped trains,
draped in skimpy bits of taffeta and frothy lace: the crowd
throwing handfuls of confetti, treacherous, lewdly writhing coils
of *serpentin*: as the parade with its brotherhood bedecked with
dazzling signs of the zodiac and its gleaming asteroids passes
by: disappearing amid the crowd, leaving a little winding trail
of blood behind: they're coming! they're coming! but the night
has no counsel to offer, and the delirious crowd throws them
off the track: the natives are downing rum, the mulatto girls
in their carnival costumes are blossoming like flowers: the
drummers in the steel band are pounding furiously, as though
announcing that Judgment Day is at hand: the black girl's
breasts bob and bounce, her bold ass wriggles madly: greedy
red lips, ready to swallow down all the salt of the earth in one
gulp, with pagan voracity: turning his head to watch the
nocturnal procession snaking along the street toward him with

its nebula of comets, satellites, stars, and moons: the herald
of the glad tidings that ring joyously in his vigilant ears: the
parade's coming! the parade's coming! you can hear the
trumpets blaring now!: pressing his hand over the wound with
manly courage to keep the blood from trickling out and hastening on: amid musky-smelling blacks and their passionate
women whose hips quiver like custard: syncopated movements,
the precursors of horizontal jousts, the preamble to expert,
perfectly executed croupades: in the dark recesses of propitious
colonial dwellings: fortresses surrendering, eager lips, fire-
breathing snakes: still fleeing as fast as his legs will carry him:
the parade is passing beneath arches adorned with gleaming
white statues of goddesses of wisdom and gods of war:
triumphal arches where Fame is flourishing its great trumpet!:
luckily managing to slip down an alleyway just as armed men
elbow their way through the crowd, following his trail with the
keen noses of hunting dogs: men with bloodhound faces, deprived by heaven's decree of the Apollonian perfection of Anglo-
Saxon countenances: the Central European or Mediterranean
type, with the one unmistakable, telltale trait that betrays the
half-breed: hats pulled down around their ears, disturbingly
bizarre finger rings: finding their way amid the dark shadows
thanks to that sixth sense characteristic of suspect peoples
difficult to rescue from ruin, even with floods of dollars and
napalm: on the languid island inhabited by simple-hearted,
lovable, gentle blacks: a sumptuous décor of palm trees and
ornamental plants: at the entrance to a swank nightclub, part
jungle and part aquarium: adjusting the knot in his tie with
the haughty air of distinction of the perfect gentleman: not a
single wrinkle in his impeccably tailored suit or his custom-
made shirt: handsome, nonchalant, with an aura of irresistible
sex appeal: totally self-possessed: striding imperiously across
the room to the calypso band decked out in baroque uniforms:

with the sound of moaning and panting, locomotives whistling, champagne bubbling in the background: as the mulatto girl whirls round and round the stage, overcome by the contagious, epileptic frenzy of the drums: her brassière barely concealing the volcanic eruption of her breasts, her little triangular island of satin indicating, unmistakably, the precise location of the treasure-trove: fifteen men on a dead man's chest, yo ho ho and a bottle of rum!: the rough sea chanties of freebooters, the imperishable magic of Robert Louis Stevenson!: her torso writhing, her hips swaying: in slow, persistent, dialectical, rotary motions: a corkscrew or a propeller: in the limbo between being and nonbeing: the epicenter, the bottomless navel, the recruiting post for the human legion!: pleading for masculine help with parched lips, provoking a sudden flux of blood with her frenzied eyes: accompanied by the musical erection of a throbbing Negro rhythm, the repeated muscular contractions apparently bringing on orgasm: taking the blow and enduring the torture with the heroism of the defenders of Numantia: waves and floods of water that increase and multiply, crash down, inundate, penetrate, penetrate: suggestive hypotheses that converge on the focal point of the dogma and crystallize to announce the glad tidings: it's coming! it's coming!: a beatific vision at the end of the dark night of the soul: the saint's spirit has ascended to heaven and the snake is *in situ*: a hallelujah chorus on the hills and mounds of Venus: accompanied by the vibrant hosanna of the musicians, pounding furiously on their drums as the pursuers station themselves around the edge of the dance floor: brandishing short, deadly blades and forcing him to seek refuge among the dancing couples: welcomed by the woman's apocryphal smile: are you horny, man? or some similar phrase which she pronounces in English and you translate into Spanish just a moment before you close your eyes and begin having a marvelous dream: a

short one? a long one?: how can you possibly tell?: when you
wake up, you are at the bottom of a turquoise sea: on a prairie
of gently waving seaweed, amid the swirling eddies that the
fleeting silhouette of the frogman has left in its wake: giant
sponges, umbrella-shaped jellyfish, solitary, motionless sea
anemones, with a dark, shadowy resemblance to flowers: dense
schools of fish brush his palmiped feet, pale, blue-green, gelati-
nous algae spread their languid locks, distracting his attention,
so that he fails to see a lazy, deadly, lurking shark: the great
rounded zeppelin-like hull of the boat passing overhead slowly
blocks out the light: the ocean becomes a vast grotto and the
sudden proliferation of greenery is reminiscent of the fleshy
thickening of stalactites in the kingdom of the Night, of Dreams,
of Shadows: your frequent readings of Virgil: a female sanctuary, the dark realm of Pluto!: swallowing the last few mouth-
fuls of your sausage-and-pepper sandwich and then resolutely
arising from your seat: obliging those sitting in the same row
to stand up to let you past: groping your way to the door:
no more than a crepuscular glimmer of light: dim, faint,
flickering: making your way through the usual milling horde
waiting outside to get into the movie theater: and at that
moment unexpectedly encountering the Great Figurehead: a
stern jawline, a Bourbon nose, a neat hairline mustache that
looks like the diacritical mark over n's in Spanish: the quintessential incarnation of your tribe, of the omnipresent Effigy,
by the grace of God: enthroned everywhere: above the teacher's
platform in classrooms, struck on copper coins: staring at you
like a rude bat: dressed in black from head to foot, arms outstretched like the acrobatic Christ on the cross hanging in the
middle of the wall: forbidding, enormous: hey there, you!:
cutting off all possibility of escape and pointing into empty
space with his menacing ruler: you're not going to get away
from me today

the Great Figurehead hands you a rectangular card that reads
DON ÁLVARO PERANZULES, ATTORNEY-AT-LAW, and falls into step
beside you, elbowing his way through the crowd with typical
Spanish arrogance: his facial features are noticeably larger in
size than the norm, and all his joints creak painfully with each
step he takes, like ill-fitting sections of a suit of armor: night
is falling, and the abandoned fortress of twilight is suddenly
invaded by clouds
we Hispanos who live far from our native land ought to get
together from time to time, he says in his deep, solemn voice:
we risk being swallowed up by the invertebrate African masses,
don't you agree?: our duty to bring our influence to bear on
other peoples: one of our oldest historical traditions: a poetic
imperative: an aggressive ecumenical spirit: the transmitters
of eternal values
Don Álvaro expresses himself in very pure Castilian Spanish,
and tightening his grip on your arm, he drags you off in the
direction of one of those typical Madrileño cafés, every corner
of which is illuminated with blinding neon lights
a very distinguished establishment, where I spend all my
evenings: a meeting place for real Spaniards, upright men who
follow the straight and narrow path all their lives, sustained
by a deep feeling of peaceful certainty, of tranquil self-assurance,
of serenity unassailed by doubts: holding themselves resolutely
aloof from everything that is vulgar, ignorant, and disordered:
men of few words in their everyday intercourse with others, but
capable of raising their voices and ascending to loftier heights
of eloquence and rhetoric: haven't you ever been there?
no, you answer
well, you must come: we must continue onward and upward,
raise our sights: view life as service, obey every order that we

are given promptly and cheerfully, be masters of our ship and captains of our soul

without once letting go of your arm imprisoned in his iron grasp, Don Álvaro plunks you down on one of the stools along the bar and settles down comfortably on the one next to yours, with each of the various articulations of his bony carapace cracking in turn: the features of his mask have meanwhile grown even larger, now forming a massive, solid structure, much more akin to the mineral kingdom than to the vegetable

two *ballons* of red wine and chick-peas for two, he orders: frugal repasts, abstemious habits: an ascetic, militant view of life: eternal essences!

his stern gaze lingers on the fleeting silhouettes passing by on the street: burnooses, djellabas, veiled women: a blind man being led by his young Lazarillo, vendors of hazelnuts, almonds, and peanuts

an invertebrate people who will never amount to anything, he says: and as for us, will to empire, manifest destiny: Spanish grandeur and glory ruling the ocean waves!

he downs his claret in the wink of an eye and the chick-peas disappear one by one down the man's gullet: having thus devoured his own fair share, Don Álvaro finishes yours and then sits back with a smug, satisfied expression on his face, picking his front teeth with a toothpick

do you ever read Seneca? he asks you

no, you reply

you really ought to: we must do away with complacent, pedestrian attitudes: force reality to obey the categorical imperatives of the spirit: to submit to a hierarchical, vertical order!

Don Álvaro's face is aglow with inspiration, and his height and his physical dimensions continue to increase, but suddenly he halts in mid-sentence and turns his head: you too turn about to follow his gaze, and spy a young goatherd tending his little flock: a thin, blond-haired, barefoot Riff with a stick in his hand, watching over his meager movable property, encountering the greatest difficulty herding his flock down to the end of the street through the long lines of people queued up outside the movie houses: the terrified animals huddle together, and two baby goats frantically circle about their mother, trying unsuccessfully to latch on to her teats: when the goatherd and his flock finally disappear from your field of vision, Don Álvaro leans down, picks up a goat turd, raises it to his broad nostrils, and ecstatically inhales the odor emanating from it

it's a *capra hispanica*, he says: here, have a whiff of it!

you do your best to get out of his reach and scramble off your barstool: but it's no use: Don Álvaro shoves his huge hand right under your nose and forces you to smell the dark, already solidified substance which he is holding in the palm of his hand, which he keeps displaying and then concealing, like some precious object, with alternate pronations and supinations of his wrist and palm

ethical emanations! he exclaims: metaphysical essences! Gredos, Gredos!

excuse me, you say: I have an appointment on the Bulevar Pasteur and I'm afraid that

haven't you ever been to Gredos?

no, you've never been there

that's a shame, he says

why is that?

the remote recesses of Gredos are more or less the very bowels of our heroic, mystical Castile!: the umbilicus of our mountains, at an altitude of more than six thousand feet!: the *capra hispanica* is the incarnation of our purest essences, didn't you know that?

I'm terribly sorry, but it's getting late, and I really think

The *meseta*, a vast horizontal plain, rough and rugged Castile!

you've finally managed it: you've fled your barstool, the typically
Madrileño café, and the pervasive presence of the Great Figurehead and run, on and on, down Lucus in the direction of
Tadjinia and Fuente Nueva: no, toward Abdessadak would be
better: allowing you to turn immediately to your left and take
refuge in the formidably intricate, baffling labyrinth of Ben
Batuta: but you are still on Lucus, amid the barbershops and
the clothing stores, the craftsmens' workshops, the second-hand
bookshops: then down Sebu and Cristianos, heading for the
promiscuous tangle of shops in the Zoco Chico that will be your
salvation: or perhaps down Romah: beneath the dark inaccessible arcades that lead to the human river flowing up and
down Almanzor: though you do not reject the possibility of
retracing your steps and going down Gzennaia, past the drowsy-
looking pottery shops: thus returning to your original starting
point and mingling with the crowd of James Bond admirers
waiting in line: still wandering down Lucus, pondering the
secret motives impelling you to follow this tortuous itinerary:
your pursuer has vanished into thin air and all you can see at
the other end of the street is the little goatherd and his humble
flock: but at this very moment an old man heads your way,
sitting astride an ass, and you will follow him to the right, trying
your best to stop panting, to walk along slowly and calmly, step
by step, reliving your rather dull memories of previous strolls in
this vicinity: the shish-kebab place, the little plaza with the
fountain, the dim café full of kef-smokers: waiting at the intersection as the old man chats with a crony in the dim light of a
street lamp: deciphering their conversation in an arcane
dialect: and then each of them kisses the other on both cheeks
and the burro grudgingly moves off toward Nasería: on and on:
through the concerted chaos of the city: an ideogram straight
out of the Koran, a subtle maze of lines: opinions voiced by
alfaquis, maxims uttered by imams: hordes of the faithful
silently flocking to the mosque for evening prayers: and since

the old man has disappeared from sight, you will be obliged
to continue on alone: blindly groping your way: at the mercy
of your balky, pedestrian inspiration: to the right, to the left?:
following attentively the trail of signs through the deserted
street, catching, to your relief, a glimpse of a hand stealthily
pointing to a door, a vestibule, a short corridor with peeling
plaster: going in as far as the little table fulfilling the function
of cashier's desk and the tiny public cloakroom: all for the
modest price of three dirhems (service included), payable (paid)
to the obliging Pluto who addresses you in French and insists
that you deposit your limp (unworthy) wallet there: you are
now standing on the threshold of the Mystery, at the mouth of
the infernal Cavern, in the middle of the dreary empty space of
what is reputedly the world's most formidable break in the
earth's crust, a yawning crack leading to the kingdom of
Shadows, Dreams, and Night: an illustrious Aeneas suddenly
abandoned by the Sibyl: a damp Virgilian lair permeated by a
faint, subtle smell of seaweed: moving forward very cautiously
across the smooth polished tiles in the dim light, in the air
electric with tension: amid swirls of vapor that blur the contours of everything about you and transform the assembled
Moors into viscous, ductile, frightening submarine fauna:
spherical visages like puff-fish, arms like octopus tentacles,
empty, dead eye sockets: through room after room with sweating walls, full of swirling miasmic clouds of effluvia: no, not
toward the frozen horror of the victim stripped naked, of the
futile scream of terror, of the weak, defenseless gesture: beings
reduced to nothing but a heap of bones, human cattle crammed
into freight cars, one atop the other, and then eliminated further
down the line, for hygienic reasons, for the peace of mind of
the pure-blooded race of the elite: cartful after cartful of bodies,
about to be dumped into the voracious maw of the common
grave: no, no, no: here it's to purify oneself: of lust or of
greed: of nutritional or perhaps seminal excesses: enveloped

in a nebulous penumbra that seems to become thicker and
thicker as you proceed farther and farther into it: a bath of un-
reality that shatters planes, blurs contours, and permits no more
than the vaguest glimpse of disjointed, fleeting images: bodies
standing, sitting, lying down: motionless or engaged in the
most arduous gymnastics: robust genitals: taut tendons and
sturdy nerve fibers: firm, white musculature: hunting for a
niche to shelter you and finally finding one: your back leaning
against the marble, your legs stretched out in front of you:
breathing a vast sigh of relief: you're alive! still alive!: not
in the protean kingdom of the flaccid and formless, of obscene
creeping flora, of filthy outpourings of the inorganic: but instead contemplating smooth polished surfaces, successfully
contriving to avoid flabby, unnecessary excrescences of flesh:
without Rhadamanthus, without Tisiphone, without Cerberus:
the ritual ablutions now made, the sacrificial offering presented:
on the broad plain with its delightful meadows and rustling
forests, the kingdom of the blessed: shades exercising in the
palaestra, testing their strength in manly sports, wrestling on
the soft golden sand: craters of red-hot lava, burning geysers
wherein the eternal Pompeian seeks and finds a sudden, exquisite, voluptuous death: Tariq! Tariq!: the recognition of
human brotherhood!: the epiphany of the Word: as the sweat
runs down your body as though you were being cleansed with
bucket after bucket of water, and little by little you sink into
a salutary languor: immersing yourself in the marvelous verses
of the Poet slyly inciting you to commit treason: to besiege
language, to snap off roots, to violate syntax, to wreak havoc
on every hand: only a few steps away from the tempting
Straits: ready to cross them now: nodding your head, and closing, yes, closing your eyes

part two

Flatus voci and gesticulation

—AMÉRICO CASTRO

penetrating deeper and deeper: wandering farther and farther into the quiet, cottony atmosphere, by way of the twisting, turning paths of the urban labyrinth: as in the hall of trick mirrors at a fairground, unable to find the exit, with the rubbernecks standing watching outside on the sidewalk laughing their heads off every time you take the wrong turn: paying to become an object of universal derision: finally managing to make your way out, amid scornful taunts and jeering laughter, with a rather sheepish, embarrassed look on your face: you spy Tariq walking just ahead of you and quicken your pace in order to catch up with him: dressed in his tiger-striped djellaba, his cat's eyes gleaming, the ends of his handle-bar mustache curling up to a fine point: the streets are deserted now, the light from the street lamps makes both of you cast giant shadows, thereby suddenly causing your own reality to appear precarious and threatened: isn't the echo of your foot-falls perhaps too loud?: dwellings are piled one atop the other like architectural scale models made of pasteboard, and the night sky dotted with clouds looks like a theatrical fly painted by an amateur: fake, fake: characters in a novel not yet written, both of you mere fictions: doubt is your only certainty, yet you follow him, and will continue to follow him without a word of protest: to the left first, and then to the right, and then even farther to the right, to the café crowded with men, in the perfumed warmth full of the aroma of mint and kef: but no announcer calling out the lotto numbers and no sound of dominoes clicking: no Cassius Clay, no Pelé, no Umm Kalsúm, no Farid-el-Attrach: motionless, silent, attentive, almost hypno-tized spectators: faces that stand out sharply against the shadowy background as you thread your way among the chairs, heading for an empty table at the back of the room: with two glasses of mint tea and a pipe to share in front of you: held spellbound, like all the rest, by the little lighted box: the atavistic voice of the blood, the transcendent, ecumenical

message!: along with millions upon millions of your countrymen, united as one with them in blissful communion: entire
Spanish cities and their great tangle of antennas, holy families
gathered around the sacred table, Papa, Mama, and all the
kids!: gratefully receiving the eloquent decrees of the oracle
as though they were manna from heaven: a provocative commercial for a brand of brassières, the snow-white virtues of an
amazing new soap: the ubuesque, ubiquitarian version of the
events which each day shake the shadowy, tottering modern
world to its foundations and make your country an enviable,
envious oasis of peace, harmony, and prosperity: seas of auto-
mobiles, arteries teeming with neon signs, skyscrapers thirty
stories high whose towering bulk dwarfs the minuscule statue
of Cervantes!: Hollywood studios at Almería and Hilton hotels
at Motilla del Palancar!: transformations that are admittedly
spectacular, but which in no way alter the eternal essences of
your country's soul: the quintessential spirit of Seneca that is a
part of your very bones: dazzling Alpine splendors in the
mountain peaks of Gredos and the Ku Klux Klan during Holy
Week: as the oracle in starched collar and plaid tie broadcasts
cryptic news reports that cross the Straits of Hercules, reach
the shores of Africa, and enter the Moorish café by way of the
little magic box: a blond Sibyl with jutting breasts at his side
now, the smiling herald of the Omnipresent and his heir-
pretender: the modern theory of mass media adapted to the
nation's most peculiar idiosyncrasy!: in a comfortable salon
now, with soft upholstered armchairs, the unexpected preamble
of a gathering of far vaster dimensions: row upon row of
children's faces that appear and disappear as Tariq fills the
bowl of the pipe and passes it to you: a quarter of a century
ago?: more or less: children seen in blurred outline, sternly
herded by the master of the flock into a compact mass beneath
his sheltering wing: still clad in black from head to foot,
bearing not a royal scepter but a threatening ruler: images of

a city whose name you would like to forget, questions and answers whizzing like arrows, exploding like a dazzling display of fireworks: Natural Sciences today: Geology, Zoology, Botany
the distinctive features of diptera
a single pair of membranous wings, balance mechanisms, an oral sucking apparatus, lower lip in the form of a tube, a complex metamorphosis
the morphology of the scorpion
an arthropod with crablike pincers and an abdomen tapering to a sharp point, highly developed pedipalpi, four pairs of stigmata, a chitinous carapace, air-breathing spiracles, a poisonous stinger
arachnids
terrestrial arthropods with a chitinous carapace, a not very highly developed cephalothorax, a large, rounded abdomen, six processes with numerous tiny tubes emitting the strands out of which its web is woven
biology of the snake
when approached, it adopts a defensive posture, supporting its body on a flat coil, spreading its hood, and thrusting its head forward
particular features of the viper
a flat triangular head, a forked tongue, flexible hinged jaws that allow it to swallow large prey, a divided lower maxillary, hollow poisonous fangs
important characteristics of the
a carapace composed of thick horny polygonal scales
spiny?
probably
chelonian or saurian?
a heart with two auricles and one ventricle, short lateral appendages, skin covered with scales, scutella, or plates
a colored print representing different varieties of?
leaves

cordate?
buckwheat
dentate?
nettle
digitate?
chestnut
verticillate?
madder
printed by?
Hallweg, Bern, Switzerland
scale?
1 : 1,000,000
the other details of the room are of no interest: neither the
lamp, nor the ashtray, nor the red notebook with the multiplication tables, nor the little folder of cigarette papers: so you will
proceed directly to the lab session
amid the other students in lab aprons, grouped around the table
on the platform where he (the Figurehead?) is holding up the
glass jar, making certain that the lid is tightly screwed on: a
thin, transparent circular receptacle some twenty centimeters
in diameter, with a wad of soft yellow cotton in the bottom:
speaking in his usual persuasive, didactic tone of voice, perhaps
watching closely for the first clinical signs of terror on his (the
child's) face: signs that would still be imperceptible to the
inattentive or superficial observer: as the calm pupils of his
classmates' eyes observe the minuscule battleground and the
heroes of this modest little drama: the motionless scorpion and
the grasshopper that is trapped in the jar with it and desperately
attempting to escape, trying to get a purchase on the smooth
glass wall of the jar, falling to the bottom, trying again, and
falling again: fascinated perhaps (as he himself is) by the
rigidity of the ringed segments, the sudden raising of the
pincers, which remain erect, poised and waiting, like cranes in
a port prepared to unload cargo: instinctively turning his eyes

away, refusing to watch the implacable, horrible sight: the childish faces crowding around the jar and the ineffable smile of the man who witnesses the desperate and futile struggle of the insect with seraphic calm and grabs him (the child) gently but firmly by the neck so as to force him to watch, to keep his eyes wide open as the scorpion finally seizes the grasshopper in its pincers, curls its stinger around, and plants its poisonous dart in its victim as he (the child) suddenly turns deathly pale and falls to the floor in a faint

I'm not hurting you, am I?

no, not in the least

breathing a sigh of relief once he steps out onto the street again: not into the sun, the light, the hustle and bustle of an African street: into the old Spanish quarter, laid out by the generous compass of the land-surveyor: iron fences topped with spikes, walls bristling with broken glass, romantic gardens, a faint scent of lime trees: a hushed, dreamlike universe: winding paths, reflecting pools, summerhouses, wicker chairs, pots of hydrangeas, croquet wickets, mah-jongg counters, silver teaspoons: morally uplifting reading, faded copies of *Signal*, old tennis courts overgrown with weeds: villas only recently occupied once again by their owners, in the happy days of rationing and falange handouts: and right in the middle, the youngster, who now appears to be quite a few years younger

what youngster?

the same one who came to see you in the café a few minutes ago: the diligent, conscientious student, who adores his mother and in turn is adored by her, who is admired and cherished by his teachers and classmates: a thin, frail youngster: huge eyes, pale white skin: not the slightest trace of a beard profaning his softly rounded cheeks: doing his homework for his Natural Sciences class or absorbed in trying to solve a difficult problem: amid damp, moss-covered villas with their canopied entrances, their statues, their lightning rods, their weather vanes, their little cupolas: amid the usual wistarias, mimosas, geraniums, rose bushes, morning-glories: up to the rusty iron grille and the English garden where the faithful old governess has laid out a tray with a cup of chocolate and tea cakes on it, and is reading aloud, for his edification, the exemplary tale of Little Red Riding Hood and the big bad wolf

oh, Mama!: what delicious little cakes!: are they for me?

no, my darling Little Red Riding Hood

you know how fond I am of them!

they're for your granny: she's sent word that she's not feeling well

not feeling well? what's the matter with her?

I'm sure it's nothing serious: but I want you to go see her and take her these cakes and this little jar of butter

yes, Mama: I'll go right away

put them all in this little basket and take it to her as quickly as you can

what (he) is really listening to is disjointed bits of a conversation going on in the garden next door

at the end of the street

the one on the corner?

the one they're never going to get around to finishing

the one where the black marketeer lives?

it seems to me I saw him once

a big tall bruiser?

with a bushy mustache and a scarred face, like an Arab?

they came here during the war

and what about the woman?

she's the one that sells flowers

the one who hangs out in that bar?

yes, she's always drunk

I know the one you mean

she goes there with him?

didn't you know?

, after dark
how dare they do such a thing!
it makes shivers run down my back just seeing him
tell me all about it
it's been going on for two years now
the shameless hussy!
and he drove her out: whipped her with his belt
why did he do that?
it was just last summer
good heavens!
that's exactly what happened
and then what?
the other day he was standing in the doorway and when I
passed by
I simply can't believe it
yes he hypnotizes them
what about her?
let me at least catch my breath, darling
we were in
her son?
I don't remember
a little boy, with an enormous head
feeble-minded?
yes, he can't even talk
his son?
nobody knows who the father is
I know she runs around with
come on, tell me everything you know
don't be so impatient, I was just about to give you all the details
one time, in front of the flower stall
with his mouth open?
as though he were trapping flies
the sin of
and then they broke up and he

nobody knows who the father is, I tell you
oh, I see!
yesterday afternoon
that same man?
at her place
no, she wasn't home
do you know what he did?
come on, tell me everything
he walked straight over to the kid and pissed on him
what!
yes, that's precisely what he did
he pissed on the kid?
they were right there and they say that
did he cry?
no, he has no idea what's going on around him
well, it's a good thing he doesn't
did they see him?
yes, with his pecker right out where everyone could see, and
then he buttoned up his pants and went away, as calmly as you
please
and what did they do?
oh come on, darling, what could they possibly have done?
as the faithful, devoted old governess continues reading in her
didactic tone of voice
knock, knock!
who's there?
it's Little Red Riding Hood, bringing you cakes and a jar of
butter from Mama
and then (he?) stealthily slips down underneath the spotless
tea cloth on the table, leaving the chocolate and the cakes
untouched, and cautiously makes his escape down the block:
relentlessly pursued by premonitions and desires: running
through the deserted streets with pounding heart: barricaded
gardens, mansions lying in ambush, damp vegetable smells, the

muffled melodious sigh of the wind in the myrtles: fleeing to
the entrance to the construction site and there anxiously invoking the appearance of the night watchman and the child, the
chastiser and his victim: cranes and jackhammers covered
with canvas, dreary empty scaffoldings, useless bare iron rods:
and amid the buckets of tar and the sacks of cement the night
watchman's shack: spying through the cracks between the
horizontal planks, listening to the dull thudding noises, quite
possibly heavy panting, echoing in the darkness: nocturnal cat
fights, the roaring of wild beasts in heat, the arduous copulation
of carnivores locked in silent combat, slowly devouring each
other, inch by inch, with languid delectation: meanwhile
desperately trying to glimpse the torpid silhouette of the
humiliated idiot boy: stunned? hydrocephalic? his mouth gaping open foolishly?: not there at all, far away: as (he?)
fumbles with the bottom buttons and frees them of the restraint
of the decorous buttonhole holding them in bondage: aiming
the thing at the Elysian domain three feet or so away: reluctant
at first, as though wanting to be coaxed: but finally obeying,
manfully and forcefully: haughtily pumping out the disdainful
yellow fluid until an anxious, plaintive voice comes up from the
shadowy depths below, and an infernal shade, greatly discomfited as it crouches there in a humiliating and painful
posture, calls up in an incredibly urbane tone of voice
hey up there, watch what you're doing, I'm down here below you!
the faithful old governess wets her fingertips with her tongue,
turns the page, and clears her throat slightly
come in and close the door, you're letting a cold draft in
what shall I do with the presents Mama gave me for you?
put them on the mantelpiece and come lie here beside me, please
yes, Granny
vainly peering through the cracks between the planks, lips
brushing the wood, inhaling deeply the heavy, disconcerting odor
of their lair: without noticing, poor innocent little thing, that

the panting has ceased, that the savage beasts are no longer devouring each other, that a huge fat lady has silently opened the door, and in perfect focus square in the middle of the screen of the little box, is stealthily creeping toward (him?): clapping her enormous hands on his shoulders and bursting into laughter I've caught you!

increasing the pressure of her fingers, forcing him to look her straight in the eye

what was it you were trying to get a peek at?

nothing

you're a liar, a dirty little liar!

the woman who sells flowers? she's wearing a red fez with a tassle on top: her mouth smeared with lipstick: the neckline of her dress low-cut, scabrous, provocative: breasts that threaten to collapse despite the rigid wall that holds them up: despite the sacklike cut of her dress, which gives no indication of where her waistline is, falling in a straight line to her plump knees: above chunky limbs supported by sandals with thick cork soles, her toes peeking out of them: Mrs. Potiphar! Mrs. Potiphar!

did you see the snake?

no, I swear I didn't

liar

I didn't see a thing

you wanted to see how it gets inside, isn't that right?

no, no

do you know where the grotto is?

no!

right here!

grabbing his head with one hand and raising her skirt with the other: forcing (him?) to enter the Virgilian cavern: leaving the mons Veneris, the lips, the hymen, the clitoris, and the vaginal opening behind and working his way into the narrow oblique passageway leading to the pelvic cavity and wandering about every inch of the anterior and posterior face of it, as

well as its upper and lower edges and extremities: before crossing the isthmus of the uterus and entering a vast cavity in the form of a pear turned bottom side up, creeping into the Fallopian tubes and their meandering loops lined with a soft, vibratile epithelium, advancing along this visceral tube that gradually becomes wider and wider, finally flaring out into a receptacle shaped like the bell of a trumpet: a sort of flower or large ear possessed of fringelike hairs, the function of which is to suck in the ovum at the moment of dehiscence and propel it toward the uterus by means of subtle peristaltic contractions: finally reaching the ovary: a pinkish-white, almond-shaped structure, which becomes congested with blood during menstruation and turns gray at the menopause, the surface of which is smooth during puberty and later becomes rough and wrinkled and covered with scars, an organ made up of a fibrous central stroma and a firm, white outer sheath: suffocating, drowning did you have a good look at it?
yes!
do you know what it's called?
no
well, go ask your mama!
holding her sides laughing as (he?) runs as fast as his legs will carry him across the temporary board walkway, and still on-screen, flees down Necharin and then Arcos, turns to the right along Nasería, and runs on along Palma, Chemaa Djedid, Chorfa, and Baños: feeling quite safe in the complicated labyrinth of little streets, yet suddenly meeting him face to face: suitably dressed for the occasion: an overcoat that is just a bit shabby and missing several buttons, the collar pulled up around his ears, the pants legs of his worn-out trousers drooping, his feet shod in pitifully misshapen tennis shoes: heading (his?) way with a grave, tortured smile on his face: his right hand groping for his (?) with respectful alacrity: my mama, poor thing, the same as ever: slowly wasting away: over seventy

now, health failing, lots of worries: her head aches constantly:
she can hardly eat a bite, poor dear: a little bit of bread in the
morning and a bowl of *jarira* in the evening, and even that's
too much for her: as though it were Ramadan: and aspirin too,
of course: twice a day, with a few swallows of water: from
the mosque to the house, from the house to the mosque:
meditating and praying all day long: for her children: for her
relatives back in her village: a bit pressed for money, it's true:
decent jobs always so hard to find: but they haven't lost their
faith in God: as (he?) escapes round the corner, hugging the
brick wall around the vacant lot down the street
as meanwhile (he?)
then walking across the leafy grounds of the school and taking
refuge in the church: beneath the supporting timbers with a
luxuriant proliferation of gilded volutes and floral motifs:
columns and capitals, grilles and altarpieces, the heads of
winged angels, little carvings of writhing demons: the usual
assortment of horrifying Grand-Guignolesque props: plaster
arms and legs, crutches, locks of hair, bullfighters' capes, prosthetic devices: a collection that greatly enhances the rhetorical
effect of the sermon being delivered by a priest well aware of the
combined powers of a terrifying stage setting and the anguish
and tortures which the spoken word is capable of inflicting
and the unfortunate young man succumbed to the lure of the
sirens: he plunged of his own volition into the mire: the
pleasure lasted no more than a few moments: but the first
breach was opened in the bastion of his purity and little by
little all his strength, all his physical vigor, all his spiritual
energies will trickle away through this breach: his iron will
collapses: he puts his lips to the edge of the cup to sip the
nectar and does not notice the poison at the bottom: oh, if only
he could imagine his heart, his poor heart, still generous and
pure, turned to a chunk of hardened lava: courage, nobility of
spirit, patriotism, filial piety, pride, chivalry, heroism giving way

to indolence and dissipation: a young tree, just beginning to
blossom, whose leaves wither, whose branches rot: there are no
more buds or foliage or flowers: its trunk has suffered a mortal
blow, and its vital sap is trickling out drop by drop
(the sidewalks full of skinny men, as silent as sleepwalkers,
leaning against the walls in hieratic postures, staring into space
a woman wrapped in a worn, threadbare length of cloth,
squatting on her heels next to the wall: a mute reproach or a
mute question)
you are doubtless familiar with the story of Pandora, that
woman possessed of a marvelous beauty: as her dowry, she
brought her spouse a magnificent gold box, and when the latter
opened it, pain and misery and sickness flew out and spread
throughout the earth: my dearly beloved young flock, forbidden
pleasures are like this gold box that appears to contain a
splendid treasure: but woe to the imprudent hand that dares to
open it!: there is nothing that so predisposes the organism
to consumption as sin: like an insatiable leech it sucks your
blood, fades the rosy bloom of youth on your cheeks, extinguishes
the joyous sparkle in your eyes: a dread disease that even those
researchers in the very forefront of science confess they are
powerless to cure: the body of the sinner becomes covered with
pustules, he suffers constant wracking headaches which give
him not a single moment's respite: little by little the telltale
signs of his affliction manifest themselves, on his skin, on his
eyelids, in his intestines: he is tormented by insomnia despite
his desperate craving for sleep: he is helpless in the face of
disease, and is overcome by all sorts of physical ailments: in
the most acute phase, his palate is pitted with sores: very often
the cartilage of his nose rots away and his face is permanently
disfigured: he looks like a ghost: his joints become very brittle
(as the old man gets the sharp instrument out and refills it and
I'm not hurting you, am I?
no, not in the least

but breathing a sigh of relief when)
nonetheless this is no more than the first step on the path to
doom: we have not yet reached the bottom of the mire: there is
a law of physics according to which a falling body does not fall
at a uniform velocity: rather, the velocity of a falling body
accelerates as it approaches the abyss toward which it is being
attracted by mysterious telluric forces: this law of gravitation
applies not only in the physical realm, but also in spiritual
life: the soul has its own insidious tendencies, its own perverse
inclinations: as we begin to give in to temptation they begin
to impel us, with a more and more irresistible force, toward the
obscure abysses of sin: lion cubs are gentle creatures until
they see blood: but at the very first bite, they are transformed,
they become savage beasts: my beloved sons, famished dogs,
bloodthirsty wolves lie hidden in the depths of your nature as
fallen creatures: don't offer them food, or they will sink their
fangs in your flesh and drink your pure, fresh young blood
(it flutters about awkwardly, dripping great trails of blood
a black mastiff bounds out of one of the nearby houses and
licks up the crimson pools of blood with its slender, agile
tongue)
according to the ancient Greeks, Prometheus stole fire from
Olympus and in order to punish him, the gods chained him to
a rock in the Caucasus: an eagle came every day and pecked
out his liver: but his liver grew back again every night, and the
next day the eagle would come back again: perhaps the horribly
painful sight of the adolescent sufficed, in and of itself, to kindle
the flames of lust
(hey up there, watch what you're doing, I'm down here below
you!
his pride doubtless hurt, but still the soul of dignity: suddenly
interrupting your torrential outpouring: yet giving you sufficient time to conceal the guilty party, to return it to its warm,
idle retreat: incapable of voicing any sort of apology: you re-

trace your steps, fleeing as fast as your legs can carry you: pursued by a horde of beggars at your heels, tugging at your sleeve, surrounding you, threatening you, pleading with you, trying to block your path

fleeing their viscous gaze, avoiding being trapped by their sly tricks and clever stratagems

once past Bab-el-Marxán, turning into the steep street that leads down to the Casbah)

in the National Museum in Berlin there is a very moving painting on exhibition: at the foot of a precipice, amid towering, jagged peaks, a raging torrent flows: a bridge spans the abyss: a bridge that becomes narrower and narrower, until finally it is no more than one thin plank: a young horseman with flaming cheeks and burning eyes is crossing it: he is heedless of the yawning abyss below: his eyes are riveted on the seductive, provocative figure of a lascivious woman on the other side: Death is there at his side, with a cold, ironic smile on her face: holding in her hand an hourglass, the sands of which have almost run out: the horseman reaches the wooden plank, and rides on farther and farther: in a moment he will fall, he will be plunged into the abyss below, where the gaping jaws of the Avernus await him

(as Potiphar's wife dances with her red fez and her necklaces: her torso writhing, her hips swaying: in slow, persistent, difficult rotary motions: a corkscrew or a propeller: in the limbo between being and nonbeing: pleading for masculine help with parched lips, provoking a sudden flux of blood with her frenzied eyes

waves and floods of water that increase and multiply, crash down, inundate, penetrate, penetrate)

travelers returning from South Africa speak of a peculiar species of snake that hypnotizes birds by its gaze: the reptile merely stares fixedly at the bird, and although the poor creature beats its wings frantically and hops from branch to branch, it is

unable to resist, it cannot tear its eyes away from
(the American tourists stand there mesmerized, watching the
edifying spectacle: a morality play, a fabliau, a Flemish altarpiece, or a medieval allegory: Potiphar's wife with the red fez
atop her head and the ridiculous sheet of cigarette paper stuck
over her nose, and the gray-colored serpent, with a zigzag stripe
running down its back
or rather a piece of statuary: figures carved in stone, chiseled
in bronze
the ophidian (a cobra? an asp?) appears to be asleep, but
suddenly, as though in answer to a prearranged signal, it
assumes a defensive posture
turns round and round, staggers forward a few paces, reels
back, and finally sinks to the ground
lift the skirt of her dress and urinate in the sanctuary)
you have surely read, my beloved sons, how carnivorous plants
trap their prey: the unsuspecting insect alights on one of their
hairy leaves and is immediately caught like a fly on the sticky
surface of a strip of flypaper: the voracious leaf then curls
round it and immobilizes it with these hairs that are coated
with a sweetish nectar: when the plant opens again a few days
later, there is nothing left of the hapless insect except a carapace
stripped absolutely clean
(instinctively turning your eyes away, refusing to look at the
implacable, horrible sight: the childish faces crowding around
the flask and the ineffable smile of the man as he witnesses the
insect's desperate, futile efforts to escape and grabs you gently
but firmly by the neck so as to force you to watch, to keep your
eyes wide open)
during vacations you have perhaps also observed the behavior
of arachnids: when the victim touches the web, its every
attempt to extricate itself merely worsens the situation it finds
itself in: the harder it struggles, the more desperately it seeks
to escape, the more firmly trapped it becomes: the spider silently

contemplates this frenzied struggle, these frantic, panic-stricken movements seemingly exciting it: it might readily pounce upon its prey and finish it off once and for all: but it bides its time: the insect has a premonition that the end is near and tries desperately to escape, but merely becomes more and more hopelessly entangled: the spider is in no hurry: it has a cold, implacable gleam in its eye as it slowly creeps up on the unfortunate insect: it might spare its victim's life, magnanimously grant it its freedom, were it so inclined: but it does not care to do so: instead it slowly inserts its chelicerae in its victim's body, injects its own digestive juices into it, and still without killing it, but on the contrary attempting to prolong its agony, it slowly dissolves all the soft parts and sucks them out

guilty, guilty!

dressed in a sanbenito, a gag over your mouth, a duncecap, a bunch of faggots, a crown of flames on your head, a white scapular: or naked, barefoot and bareheaded, with a green cord around your neck and a green candle in your hand: beneath the supporting timbers with a luxuriant proliferation of gilded volutes and floral motifs: columns and capitals, grilles and altarpieces, the heads of winged angels, little carvings of writhing demons: the usual assortment of horrifying Grand-Guignolesque props: plaster arms and legs, crutches, locks of hair, prosthetic devices: on the screen of the little box, beneath the reproachful stare of myriad pairs of Peninsular eyes, prostrate before the Virgin's niche

a wooden mannequin with moving joints, clad in a blue and gold mantle, its heart pierced with pins, like a seamstress's pincushion: in her arms, the Child, a doll with natural red hair combed in Shirley Temple corkscrew curls, clutching a toy sword in its hand

the face of the Virgin is both puffy and emaciated: the thick streaks of red plaster on her shining cheeks resemble trickles of blood

is she weeping?
yes, she's weeping
why?
because of you
an unworthy explorer of the cavern of Potiphar's wife: a
torturer of the innocent idiot boy in the making: your sins
aggravating the pain of her already tormented soul: plunging
yet more sharp-pointed pins in her grievously afflicted maternal
heart
praying, praying

>My beloved Mother
>Aqueduct of divine graces
>Queen of heaven and earth
>Advocate and refuge of sinners
>Immaculate daughter of Joachim and Anna

on the bright flat grassy plain bathed in sunlight where the
blessed gambol and romp about, sing in chorus, and engage
in sports
the paradise promised a select minority of the chaste and
continent
you are chaste, thus saved for all eternity
amid white lilies and dark crimson roses
redeemed, joyous
until a cruel hand intervenes, tugging at your sleeve, and a
voice asks you, in an Arab dialect, for a light
n'chal?
baraka-lau-fik
brutally awakened·from your dream, you open your eyes

the studious, tense faces of children have vanished from the
screen, and along with them their youthful scientific and
mnemonotechnic emulation of their master: the oracle and the
sibyl are now sitting chatting in the ultra-modern office of a

technocrat, and Tariq silently passes you the pipe: the little
stalk of mint is dripping a last few drops in your empty glass:
the café owner brings you another, and the warm odor of the
tea blends harmoniously with that of the kef: the blurred
faces of your neighbors are suspended in mid-air in the dim
shadows: as intent and motionless as masks: gleaming feline
eyes converging on the little screen, on the alert for new message
of transcendent importance from the other side of the Straits:
modern marketing techniques for the promotion of your imperishable values: cars, soaps, detergents, household electric
appliances of domestic manufacture?
the oracle expounds his very Spanish theory in carefully
modulated tones amid the solitary splendor of his soundproof
office: a literally self-effacing man, he conceals himself behind
a Roman bust with the head of an old gypsy: the look of a
proud eagle, the network of capillaries of a bullfighter, Flamenco-
style sideburns
Seneca?
yes, Seneca
that is to say, his portrait in the Prado Museum
if not a gypsy's head, then that at any rate of a retired *torero,*
standing on the threshold of old age
listening
it used to be said of the famous Lagartijo[1] that he talked like
Seneca, and Nietzsche called Seneca the toreador of virtue: as
for Manolete, his life and his art, his entire career, his philosophy
so eloquently summed up in the proverb what's bred in the bone
will come out in the flesh, are fed by the eternal springs of
the Senecan tradition at its purest: the family line of Seneca,
resembling a river at times disappearing underground like the
Guadiana, at times meandering across the land at surface level,
at times swelling to a mighty, majestic stream, has never died
out in Spain: the stoic acceptance of the fate of the nation is

[1] A celebrated matador of the beginning of the century.—*Tr.*

the prime trait characterizing the Hispanic attitude toward life:
the Hispano conceives of history as a slow process of self-
purification, a never-ending ascetic exercise in self-perfection:
in the depths of the Iberian soul there is an indestructible
residuum of stoicism which, acting in intimate conjunction and
perfect harmony with Christianity, has taught the men of the
Meseta to suffer and endure: it has made them a breed with a
rough, dry, gnarled look about them, a breed of solemn, sober
men, perfectly adapted to the region's inclement skies and
harsh climate: the landscape itself, that great vista so dear
to our hearts, seems to be permeated with ethical and stoic
emanations, as the masters of the generation of '98 so rightly
observed, immortalizing this land in pages cast in a silken,
fluid, solemn, reflective style of expression, with a sort of stern
tenderness that would appear to have been bred into their very
bones
Castile, Castile!: moments of ineffable serenity in which
History and a radiant Nature are conjoined: in the distance, the
towers of a cathedral stand out against the horizon: a bell
tolls: then silence descends once again
we who are mere atoms of eternity see opening before us the
mysterious, boundless vistas of ages to come
the endless road across the plain stretches out before us: as far
as the eye can see everything is flat, uniform
villages that proclaim their beatific happiness at living outside
of History: arcades, a little shop with a cloth curtain at the
door, a modest country inn, an ancient palace with a coat of
arms carved in stone, the jalousies of a convent
a concert of bells, like a symphony in a wasteland: groves of
motionless pines along a roadway: a solemn, monotonous procession of dark oak trees: scattered poplars, which in their
infinite solitude learn to live a profound, intense life
steep bone-bare mountain cliffs bristling with sharp rocks:
hills covered with scanty patches of weeds, where the only

flowers are rough thistles and naked branches of broom
an infinite expanse, where man, though he does not lose his
way, feels suddenly dwarfed and humbled, amid these vast dry
fields that vividly remind him of the great barren stretches
within his soul!
the voice-off commentary has ended, and the Gregorian chant
of the monks, and the guitar solo: you are in the café again
Seneca?
here he is once again, standing there life-size, draped in his
toga, stern-faced, lean, and spare, exactly like his statue in the
Louvre
a Latin writer, of course, but nonetheless a purebred Spaniard
whose Iberian lineage goes back many generations: a philosopher of bullfighting and the bullfighter of philosophy, as one of
his compatriots so aptly described him: a member of that illustrious line of thinkers that has continued on down to Lagartijo,
the Stoic, and Manolete, the Pythagorian: Lagartijo sowed in
his heart the forever incorruptible seeds of stoicism: Manolete
implanted in his mind the will to remain faithful to supreme,
absolute, unquestionable values: a love for the calm, quiet
gesture, the silent, meditative attitude, a grave demeanor, and
extreme reserve in his dealings with others
but let us turn now to his origins and his epiphany: as in the
case of Christopher Columbus and other great historical figures,
a number of cities claim the honor and the privilege of having
been his birthplace: recent studies by our historians prove
beyond the shadow of a doubt, however, that he was born in the
center of the Peninsula and not on the periphery, and today we
may state without fear of contradiction that he first saw the
light of day in the remote fastnesses of the Sierra de Gredos,
amid towering rocky crests and peaks, close to the stars: that
is correct: Don Álvaro Peranzules, better known today by his
pseudonym, Seneca, was born in the Sierra de Gredos, of a very
upright family with the purest of bloodlines

his father, Don Álvaro Peranzules Senior, was a man of average
stature, with a bald, prominent forehead and eyebrows spaced
far apart that made his gaze appear both stern and animated:
a methodical, austere, pious man, he had been appointed In-
spector General of Prisons and by the age of fifty was the author
of several very fine collections of poems: his daily habits
never varied: on Saturdays, he would repair in the late afternoon to the church of San Millán and fervently purge his soul
in preparation for Sunday communion: at nightfall he would
return to his austere residence and call together the members
of his family and any visitors who chanced to be present to
recite the Holy Rosary together

his mother was possessed of that gentle, transparent grace that
is the hallmark and almost the appanage of Castilian beauties:
a perfect oval face, and sad, pensive eyes: on reaching adulthood, Isabel la Católica always chose to accouter herself in the
style of noble matrons of bygone days: her dress, that is to
say, was old-fashioned in the very best sense of that word, for
her conception of dignity and modesty did not exclude an
admirable elegance of comportment: thoroughly self-disciplined,
possessed of an intense spiritual life, she bore up under the
rude shocks that fate inflicted upon her with a serenity and a
strength of character that we might be tempted to describe as
stoic were it not for the fact that they are perhaps more
accurately described as typically Spanish

in Gredos there was a school staffed by upright, humble, devoted,
self-sacrificing teachers, and it was in this school that Seneca
received his primary education: at this period in his life,
Alvarito was thin and frail, with huge, bright, inquisitive eyes:
a conscientious student, willingly fulfilling all the duties, however painful they might be, imposed on him in the name of
educational discipline: at the same time, however, he was a
delightful, lovable child, with a lively, happy, outgoing disposi-
tion which made him naturally inclined to perform those

meritorious deeds that are the sweet perfume of the flowering years of childhood

onscreen: gracefully draped in a toga, with a bullfighter's sword in his hand, crowned with youthful laurels, little Seneca feels an insatiable thirst for immortality and is eager to bridge forever the gap between temporal being and eternal being: he picks a caterpillar up off the road and places it along the edge, thus preventing its likely death beneath the shoe sole of some absent-minded passer-by: he props up the stem of a flower drooping in the summer heat: he puts out crumbs of bread for starving birds: he gently but firmly fustigates two scandalously immodest flies locked together *ex commodo* in fulminous, sonorous copulation: he recites brief ejaculations in Latin and prayers rich in indulgences, the approximate total of which, with expenses deducted, adds up to the astronomical figure of 31,273 years: as a consequence: fifteen souls in purgatory are relieved of their spiritual and corporeal punishments according to the most faithful and most obedient calculations of the I.B.M. machine, and there is even the possibility that a mentally retarded child or a Mongolian idiot may be rescued from limbo: a result that completely discredits even the most optimistic projections, and the name of the future philosopher hence becomes famous in all the villages and towns of the region

his lively curiosity, his obvious intelligence also arouse the admiration of his teachers: Alvarito answers, swiftly and correctly, every one of the questions put to him by the panel of examining professors in the course of his orals, and he receives the excited congratulations of his teachers and fellow students

I am alive, I am active, I do as I please, I neither toil nor spin, I hop up and down, I'm never still

a squirrel!

he's small, hairy, very gentle: so soft-looking you'd think he was made of cotton wool, without any bones

Platero!

an animal inhabiting the Pyrenees, with a red crest, which once
it has confessed and taken communion, attacks man
a Hispano!
I live without living within myself, and aspire to such a lofty
fate that I die because I do not die
a hen!
very good: perfect: a score of a hundred: in record time his
name is on everyone's lips and soon attracts the attention of
Lagartijo
the celebrated Stoic sends him to the bullfight school at Alcalá
de Henares, so that he may be initiated into the philosophical
principles underlying tauromachy: little Seneca rapidly learns
the passes required for philosophical duels in salons, and clutching his hard-won diploma in his hand, he transfers to the taurine
University of Salamanca: there Manolete is teaching his unforgettable lessons in bullfight poses and miming, his quintessentially Spanish doctrine of impassibility: his motto:
what's bred in the bone will come out in the flesh: audacity,
heroic force of will, a scorn for material possessions, stubborn-
ness, intransigence: a peaceful faith, unclouded by doubts:
serene submission to the will of God
the more genius, the greater the appearance of genius: the
greater the appearance of genius, the more genius: inspired by
the terse ideology of Manolete, Alvarito carefully fabricates an
impermeable, hermetic image of himself for the public: a
dermatico-skeletal structure, articulated like a suit of armor:
at the same time his facial features acquire a granitic hardness
that makes him stand out from the mass of students less gifted
than he and spreads his fame as a youthful teacher and master
to the farthest corners of the land: his mask soon becomes both
an indispensable point of reference and a popular center of
pilgrimage: persons of every age and condition hasten to it and
religiously contemplate the various sections of his bony armor,

his frozen stone features: the Hispanic essences are manifest:
the national soul has found its symbol: Alvarito is now Don
Álvaro Peranzules Junior and little Seneca is now Seneca the
Great, the celebrated, immortal Figurehead
the Figurehead, that's correct, the Figurehead
sitting behind the rector's desk strewn with papers and books,
an austere Kierkegaardian crucifix with arms outstretched above
the bedside lamp projecting its immense shadow on the rug:
stern-faced, lean, and spare, slowly spreading his cape and
executing an unsurpassable series of *manoletinas* and *pases de
pecho* which provoke the awed surprise, the seraphic ecstasy of
the multitudes from one end of the Peninsula to the other:
acknowledging the delirious applause with a stereotyped rictus,
raising his hand, that most unusual hand, unlike any other,
which might have been painted by El Greco, to the general
region of his heart
oh, my Spain hurts me
or in the midst of the tumultuous battle, his spirit of chivalry
and his Christianity, now perfectly fused, become as one, talking
to his son on the phone, raising his voice, reaching supreme
heights of eloquence and rhetoric.

SENECA JUNIOR: oh, Father! why send me to my death?
SENECA SENIOR: we owe our lives and our fortunes to the
                  King;
                  but honor is the patrimony of the soul and
                  the soul belongs to God alone
SENECA JUNIOR: I have boundless trust in thee yet am I still
                  sore afraid
SENECA SENIOR: if I, thy father, so order thee
                  wilt thou dare refuse?
SENECA JUNIOR: it is rightly said
                  that life is but a dream
SENECA SENIOR: yet all these are but notions

that feed imagination's fears: and fear of
the dead
is a most base fear

SENECA JUNIOR: I am in such peril
that, since death is inescapable,
I believe that honor dictates
that I suffer and die in silence

and his fame continues to spread, overshadowing and eclipsing
that of his teachers, attaining unprecedented proportions, becoming the national emblem: aided by his inseparable companion and assistant, the illustrious Dr. Leech, he subjects his
country to a carefully administered series of therapeutic blood-
lettings and purges which after several decades restores its once
dangerously threatened health: the Hispanos understand him,
since they believe in the proverb that has it that he who loveth
chasteneth and thereupon give him ample proof of the truly exceptional affection and devotion they feel for him: the patient,
evolutive method of shaping reality is repugnant to your
Seneca, who is eager for evil to disappear here and now, instantly, thanks to his power and will alone, who would have the
entire universe obey the categorical formula he pronounces:
matter, the corporeal, physical bodies in general, obey, or ought
to obey, the dictates of the spirit: should they refuse to obey,
it is then necessary to force them to do so, through violence,
penitence, or the punishment of oneself and others: discipline,
purges, bloodletting: *profluvium sanguinis*: the judicious elimination of red cells and a severely limited, strict regimen

and now the invalid who has been ill for centuries is slowly
recuperating and taking his first steps around the sickroom,
expressing his eternal gratitude for Seneca's zeal and the
empirical remedies of his assistant: and the Hispano bows,
reverently and eagerly, to this royal *I*, whose strength, energy,
ability to rule with an iron hand, and superior qualities of
character are obvious to him: the color photograph of the

philosopher is prominently displayed in all public establish-
ments and government offices, and countless cities, villages,
districts, public squares, boulevards, and streets are named
after him: children are christened with his name at the
baptismal font and his effigy is stamped on coins: his ascension
is literally irresistible, and despite the obstructive tactics of his
enemies, Seneca receives well-nigh unanimous recognition and
support throughout the world: he introduces new concepts and
new bullfight passes, establishes schools of tauromachy and
sets up chairs of philosophy: he fights in the bull ring and
crosses dialectical swords at the Seville Feria, receives prelates
and dignitaries, visits the Sierra de Gredos to breathe in the
ethical emanations, and engages in lengthy conversations with
his old friend the *capra*
on the other side of the Straits, along the backbone of Castile,
in the sierra six thousand feet above the Meseta, they are
climbing up to the great shelf of rock that supports the crag of
Almanzor, contemplating the imposing spectacle of the amphi-
theater that surrounds the great lagoon of Gredos: the very
bowels of Iberia, soaring peaks of silence, oblivion, and peace!:
reciting in chorus frontier ballads, sonnets by Lope de Vega,
and *autos sacramentales* by Calderón: a stentorian declamation
that echoes and re-echoes in these lonely mountain fastnesses:
they then recall memories they share, nostalgic reminiscences
of historic events that take them back to the sunny, happy days
of long ago when they were valiant young warriors: bound each
to each by the virile fraternity of arms and letters, by their
profound, visceral loyalty to the Universal Salvation Movement:
after a deliberately modest repast, they clink glasses full of
Spanish wine and willingly allow themselves to become so
carried away by emotion that tears fill their eyes
do you remember?
those were real men for you!
long live the Legion!

and then the dirty bastard
yes, behind the hill
and me with the machine gun
we really gave it to those mother-fuckers!
ha ha!
we made mincemeat out of 'em
we killed 'em like flies
tac, tac, tac, tac!
oh, those were the good old days!
his soul expanding with the breath of eternity, swelling with
the timeless sap of History, your Seneca returns to the city and
its trials and tribulations, to urban traffic jams and the deafening
roar of this world, transfigured like the Beatles after their
spiritual retreat in India: journalists, photographers, interviewers from the radio and television networks surround him
and plague him with countless questions, all of which he
answers with the greatest dignity, intelligence, and poise: as
the great Figurehead, his features have an impassivity and an
austerity that is most exceptional, and the mucilaginous, invertebrate mass of his supporters and followers are overcome with
admiration: they crowd around in swarms, like bees, to gather
the nectar of his words: Seneca executes a couple of bullfight
passes, founds a new dialectical system, organizes night-school
classes and correspondence courses in immobilism and hiera-
tism, and having triumphed over all odds and attained an international apotheosis, he hints that if some day in the far-distant
future he should vanish from the scene, Senecism, his Great
Work, must continue
the very thought of his retirement or his disappearance from the
scene naturally causes a shiver to run down the spines of his
disciples, and people of every age, class, and condition again
surround him, and with great moans and sobs assure him of
their unswerving loyalty
one after the other, preceded and followed by guitar music and

taurine *pasodobles,* they now parade across the hypnotic little screen

A FAN FROM ANDALUSIA

I'm thinkin' of telegraphin' him to tell him I got down on my knees and prayed to the Blessed Virgin to make him change his mind: the way I look at it, she's got no reason atall to leave him in the lurch at this stage of the game, seein' as how she's given him a helpin' hand his whole life long: he just can't throw in the sponge and leave us flat like that: me and all the millions of guys who watch him with eyes as big as saucers on afternoons when there's a *corrida:* he's tops in our book: it'd be a catastrophe for us ordinary folks if he quit on us: we wouldn't have a thing left to live for

A POET FROM MADRID

my poetry is essentially intimist verse: that is to say, it is by and large inspired by emanations from the depths of my being, by my conception of the world as shaped by my own personal experiences, by the joy I find in savoring my own self: it is a sort of continuous dialogue that I carry on with my soul, which sometimes discusses my queries at length, and at other times remains stubbornly silent when I try to coax an answer out of it

do you intend to vote?

certainly

do you care to say anything further in this regard?

my vote will be an unqualified YES

A LADY NOVELIST FROM THE PROVINCES

what are you really like? let us suppose that you are one of your own characters whom you must describe

I am feminine, sensitive, passionate, sincere: and also very absent-minded: to the point that I don't even watch where I'm going when I walk down the street and keep stumbling over things: once a man whispered a flattering remark as I passed by, and I turned around and went back and asked him: what was that you said, sir?

do your characters believe in God?

yes, but they have doubts: they wrestle with their consciences and suffer

are you going to vote?

certainly: I adore Seneca: he's a divine man, simply divine

AN ACTRESS

I keep my figure by eating nothing but lettuce and being chaste

how would you define your philosophical position?

I'm a stoic through and through

will you fulfill your duty as a voter?

Seneca fascinates me

A VOCAL TRIO

romancero, auto sacramental, libro de caballería!

the Cid, Manolete, the Meseta!

mysticism, tauromachy, stoicism!

Seneca, Seneca, Seneca!

the charismatic invocation is on everyone's lips: all over the country, Hispanos hasten to the polls to reaffirm, with the whole world looking on, their incorruptible spirit of patriotism and their unswerving devotion to the person of the philosopher and his doctrine

the voting is by universal popular suffrage, a tumultuous affair, but at the same time marked by one of those tender, human, touching incidents so revealing of the Spanish spirit, both because of its spontaneity and because of the humble unpretentiousness of the persons involved

when Seneca appears at the bar of El Chicote, those present burst into enthusiastic, heartfelt, indescribably moving applause

a woman well advanced in years approaches him and shouts at the top of her lungs: blessed be thy mother!

a woman in labor manifests her irresistible desire to vote and is transported *ipso facto* to the voting booth in her precinct: the blessed event takes place as she is returning home, and the parturient gives birth to an adorable Hispano and expresses her joy at becoming a mother by shouting *viva Seneca*

a bride and groom present themselves at their respective polling places immediately after the nuptial ceremony, dressed in their wedding costumes: we've said *I do* in church, and we're now repeating our vows: we promise to love, honor, and obey Seneca and stoicism

a touching ballot is cast in Precinct Number 44, in the heart of the city: beneath the rectangle bearing the word YES in capital letters are the handwritten words: I am voting for Seneca because he is the incarnation of our purest essences and corresponds perfectly to the eternal coordinates of our History

a ballot cast on the ethereal heights of the Sierra de Gredos reads: yes, yes, yes, for all eternity

I am writing the YES on my ballot in my own blood, a disciple of Dr. Leech proclaims

at Madrigal de las Altas Torres another voter also stamps his ballot YES and signs his name in blood

I was given a seven-year prison sentence as a convicted epicurean, but I am voting for Seneca: YES to the greatest guy in all of Spain!

in the pure blue sky of Madrid, skywriting planes trace enormous YESES to the ontological continuity of Senecism

everyone votes for Him

gypsies

cloistered nuns

soccer players

octogenarians

invalids

the physically handicapped

helicopters from the U. S. Strategic Air Command unfurl a giant portrait of him overhead and rain down thousands of coins bearing his august Effigy: groups of devout women, urged on by zealous sisters in nun's habits, chase after them and catch them in mid-air with incredible swiftness and dexterity: breathtakingly bold, battle-hardened Falangist roosters joyously crow to celebrate the advent of eternal spring in Spain, and angels stand guard, sword in hand, at the gateway to the paradise that looms before your eyes, forbiddingly difficult to enter: the transparent visage of the Omnipresent is superimposed upon a display of bright fluttering flags as the muted strains of the national anthem played by a brass band are heard in the background: unforgettable, truly unforgettable!: surrounded by emblems and symbols: the lord and master of all Hispanos: beyond question immortal when the magic screen blacks out and falls silent, the hypnotized habitués of the café blink sleepily and rub their eyes

Tariq passes you the pipe again, and you are about to take another puff

soaring falcon, noble Poet, come to my aid: bear me aloft to the realm of more luminous truths: one's true homeland is not the country of one's birth: man is not a tree: help me to live without roots: ever on the move: my only sustenance your nourishing language: a tongue without a history, a hermetic verbal universe, a shimmering mirage: a lightning bolt or a scimitar: the Word freed after centuries in bondage: the illusion of the bird who flies into the canvas to peck at the painted grapes: language-as-transparency, language-as-reflection, witness that is worthless, sound and fury, signifying nothing: a wrecking yard, rusting junk on the outskirts of the great city: a verbal Guadalajara, a river of excrement that befouls without fertilizing, stinking, useless garbage: speeches, programs, platforms, lies couched in lofty language: simple words for simple feelings:

genuine affections, straightforward convictions: yours, Julian:
in what language can they be cast?: the extreme language of
extreme passion, a gorgeous orchid that hypnotizes, that weaves
a fatal spell: forbidden desires, illicit emotions, blinding betrayal: close your eyes, shatter the shadowy screen with a swift
thunderbolt: its Cyclopean eye is endeavoring to freeze you in
your tracks, to turn you into a sightless statue of salt:
imagine the scar dripping its poison on the opposite shore: a
vast, dreary country irrigated by the waters of the prophetic
river: accursed be your pleasure, cruel rapist!: gaze upon this
swollen womb and its countless progeny: the stoic philosopher
and his dauntless partisans: look at the lot of them, imbedded
in their chairs, clad in their impermeable gabardines, clutching
their cigars, their mustaches delicately curved, their hair as
glossy as their highly polished shoes: standing there drooling
outside the inaccessible cavern or the gratuitously well-rounded
excrescences: the seamy, virginal seraglio that is a cliché in
the libidinous subconscious of the Hispano!: as the bootblack
kneeling at their feet ministers to their soles and their souls,
acting out the stoic motto "the voice-of-the-people-is-the-voice-
of-truth" with the ethereal-musical conviction of a Paganini
directing Beethoven's Fifth: a man whose sustenance is filth
and chick-peas, a messianical worshiper of the chains that en-
slave him: flee them, Julian, take refuge in the Moorish café:
safe from your own people, in your African land of adoption:
base treason blossoms slowly here: the viper, the reptile, the evil
serpent that rips its mother's entrails to shreds at birth: your
smooth belly is untainted by the infamy of the umbilical cord:
life and death are commingled within you in the most meticulously measured doses: surrounded by benevolent presences,
amid spirals of sweet pungent smoke, savoring the communion
of a glass of mint tea: kef, the crafty ally of your passion for
destruction!: the caressing flight of your wings traces a splendid,
somber halo round about the opaqueness of language, the en-

slaved Word is freed, its architecture becomes fluid, the wretched word awakens and carries out the implacable act of treason: in a deserted district of that city whose name you would like to forget the youngster is coming home from school with his book bag over his shoulder: a thin, frail boy: huge eyes, white skin: not even the shadow of a beard profanes his softly rounded cheeks: you see, there he is, the scene, as old as the world itself, is repeating itself once again: the piercing chords of Arab music accompany the ancestral rite: the boy fascinated by the asp, and you, Julian, creeping toward him in the darkness, as stealthy as a Nubian domestic slave: but wait: there is no hurry: you will carry out your treasonous deed: your stubborn serpent is patiently awaiting the revenge it has planned for centuries: the breath of austere Castile, the land of grim-faced, solemn, taciturn men!: simple, chaste love relations, spouses coupling in tedious, dull procreation: the pruning by castration has been total, and your fury knows no bounds: the passive seraglio will joyously welcome the asp, the robust cobra will supplant the feeble idea, as limp as a lettuce leaf: winged serpents are escorting the army of turbaned liberators on the march: their voices are ringing out now: hark!: in that harsh land, the scourge of free men, intelligence and sex will flower

part three

The Moorish warriors were all clad in silk and cloth of many colors that they had taken as booty, the reins of their horses were as blazing bright as fire, their faces were as dark as pitch, and the handsomest of them all was as black as an iron cooking pot; their eyes shone like torches; their steeds were as swift as leopards and their horsemen much more cruel and dangerous than a wolf on the prowl in the night amid a flock of sheep.

—ALFONSO X EL SABIO: *Crónica General*

. . . Africa, which suddenly let loose its serpents from one end of Spain to the other, submerging it beneath yet another deluge of people.

—SAAVEDRA FAJARDO: *Corona gótica,
castellana y austriaca*

for some time now, in the windows of shops and on the walls of houses, little rectangular signs, written in French, invite the people of Morocco to participate en masse in a noble humanitarian endeavor

DONNEZ VOTRE SANG: SAUVEZ UNE VIE

the appeal pursues you, haunts you like an obsession, and this very afternoon, just as twilight is descending

(shadows ordinarily favor your dark designs)

you will present yourself at the designated location and patiently await your turn in line

(as a precautionary measure, you are wearing dark glasses and a grotesque false mustache)

the donors exchange banal remarks in quiet voices and you will remain on your guard, painfully tense

you must steal in without anyone's noticing, and the slightest sign of excitement or nervousness might betray you

your face will take on the compact hardness of rock and your eyes will stare into space

when the nurse winds the rubber tubing around your arm and plunges the hypodermic needle in one of your snaking blue veins, you will breathe a sigh of relief and satisfaction

(you are not in Tangier but in Spain, and the blood that you have craftily come to donate is certain to infect your tribe)

not spirochetes: the rabies virus

a mad dog has bitten you, and you will add to the thick liquid in the flask

(a necessary precaution since in this particular case it does not usually spread infections)

a few threads of saliva

(events have taken place in the following sequence: you are lying stretched out on the mat, attentively watching the hieroglyphic dance of the drugged birds when suddenly you notice that the mastiff has unexpectedly appeared: his coat is black and curly, his tongue pink, his eyes yellow and gleaming: his member quite short and tapering to a sharp point, and his muzzle ecstatically breathing in the fragrant smoke of the kef pipes: his movements are supple and harmonious: no one seems to be paying any attention to him: the floor is strewn with decapitated roosters, and he is slowly sniffing their delicately palpitating entrails: something tells you that danger is close at hand, but you feel incapable of making the slightest move: the animal's fangs glisten like polished steel daggers, and with no warning he sinks them in your flesh with brisk precision: not the slightest pain: on the contrary: the keen, acute perception of the paranoid or the invalid, as the blood flows out down below, sinful and rebellious: like an amber sea of freely moving, unattached coilsprings: an ordinary slender length of rubber turning and twisting, suggesting a pleasingly curved, comfortable style of architecture)

the nurse will not notice your sly stratagem and will thank you for your donation in a voice trembling with heartfelt emotion

you will modestly acknowledge her flattering remarks and deliver an eloquent impromptu speech in reply

(there is a choice assortment of different models to be found in the library on the boulevard

epic, dramatic, poetic, etc.)

safe now from any and all reprisals, you will calmly await the result of the furtive inoculation, and witness the slow but fatal course of the disease

(the medical textbooks currently in use ordinarily distinguish three phases: during the incubatory period, the person infected with this disease experiences intermittent abnormal sensations: itching, irritation, sudden burning stabbing pains: these symptoms are followed by the onset of a period of melancholy during which the victim feels extremely sad and depressed: he begins to gasp for breath and is overcome with acute free-floating anxiety: the slightest effort to swallow liquid, light that is too bright, or even the mere thought of drinking bring on such

painful spasms, such severe choking sensations that he flees
in terror at the very sight of water: his face contorts with pain,
his features contract, his limbs tremble, he shivers from head
to foot: these acute reactions make it impossible for him to
take a single drop of water: crises of this sort recur sponta-
neously, at shorter and shorter intervals, accompanied by con-
vulsions and a sharp rise in temperature: between attacks, the
patient is subject to severe fits of delirium, and often is obsessed
by thoughts of suicide: he becomes extremely agitated and
overexcited: he is unable to lie still: he gets up out of bed,
paces about the room, bumps into the walls and the furniture,
hurts himself, and lets out furious howls: his lips tremble and
he foams at the mouth: he attempts to flee the room, to force
the door open, to throw himself out the window: he gets back
in bed, thrashes about frantically, rips the bedspread, the
sheets, and the blankets to pieces, bites everything within his
reach: after a few hours, his entire body is bathed in viscous
sweat and a whitish froth appears at the corners of his mouth:
paralysis gradually sets in, and in the majority of cases death is
due to asphyxiation)
once the text has been read, you will solemnly hand down your
decree
any person who contracts rabies will be locked up in a room
until dead
there is no known remedy and the outcome is inevitably fatal
after the victim's demise, the aforementioned room will be
hermetically sealed, along with all the objects the sick person
has used, and will not be used again until thoroughly disinfected

one's homeland is the mother of all vices: in order to be cured
of it as rapidly and completely as possible, the best remedy is
selling it, betraying it: selling it?: for a mess of pottage or for
all of Peru, for a great deal or for almost nothing: to whom?:

to the highest bidder: or giving it, as a gift filled with poison, to someone who knows nothing about it and does not care to know anything: a rich man or a poor one, a man who is indifferent or one hopelessly in love: for one simple but sufficient reason, the pleasure of betraying: of freeing oneself of that which identifies us and defines us: of that which converts us, against our will, into spokesmen of something: of that which pins a label on us and fashions a mask for us: what homeland?: all of them: those of the past, the present, and the future: large or small, powerful or miserably poor and helpless: selling one's homeland into bondage, an endless chain of sales, an unending crime, permanent and active betrayal
selling Chaldea to Egypt
Egypt to Persia
Persia to Sparta
Sparta to Rome
Rome to the Barbarians
the Barbarians to Byzantium
Byzantium to Islam
becoming totally absorbed in this exciting game in which all sorts of winning combinations may turn up, and reaping some measure of profit from every operation: economic, physical, spiritual: or, in the end, for the sheer, gratuitous pleasure, the heady satisfaction inherent in the act in and of itself: solemn treason, joyous treason: premeditated treason, spontaneous treason: overt treason, covert treason: he-man treason, pansy treason: liquidating everything, putting everything under the auctioneer's hammer: history, beliefs, language: childhood, landscapes, family: refusing your identity, starting all over from zero: a Sisyphus and at the same time a Phoenix being reborn from its own ashes: a slightly stronger dose of kef than usual will suffice: and an intense, glowing, propitious animal heat: Tariq is there beside you and you suspect that you spy the implacable gaze of the tiger in the depths of his eyes

convinced of the urgent and imperative need for treason, you
will set up more and more recruitment and enlistment centers
join me, you warriors of Islam, you Bedouins of the desert, you
instinctively cruel Arabs!: I offer you my country, invade it,
sack it, plunder it: its fields, its cities, its treasures, its virgins
are yours for the taking: destroy the tottering bastion of its
personality, sweep away the debris of its metaphysics: collective
animal aggression is what is needed: whet your knives, prepare
to bite: may your seditious serpent rise up to its full height, a
proud royal scepter, imposing its tyrannical rule with silent,
inscrutable violence: a host of sumptuous, lyrical images
suddenly invades your mind: stucco festoons, plaster lacework,
mazes of stalactites, fragile columns, expletives of exquisite
tilework: arabesques, Kufic inscriptions, Neshki letters: mou-
charabies, wrought iron door latches, mosque lanterns: secret
gardens, patios enclosed within whitewashed walls: palm trees,
a fountain spray of green branches:dunes, a familiar landscape
your armies will henceforth be made up of cruel faces, briefly
glimpsed or seen in dreams: shepherds from Tenira and Mulay
Busselham, miners from Laarara Fuara, fellahs from Suk-el-
Tlata and Laghouat, huge strapping men from Oujda and
El Golea
the ends of your turbans flutter as you gallop on: see the scar
dripping poison on the other shore of the sea: the rich treasure
that awaits your horsemen
our boring, worn-out symbols are lying in a heap in a dusty attic:
plush lions, castles built of sand: tangled ribbons, tapestries,
coins with faces stamped on them: flags, coats of arms, the
national anthem played by a brass band
our glorious figures and national ephemerida provoke politely
stifled yawns, affable, discreet smiles: Trajan, Theodosius,
Hadrian!: Pelayo, Guzmán el Bueno, Ruy Díaz del Vivar!

the prodigious rate of industrial growth, the glorious consumer
society have undermined traditional values: Agustina, the
heroine of the War of Independence, serves hotdogs in an air-
conditioned government-run tourist hotel: the little drummer
boy of Bruch who helped save a nation chews spearmint gum
and smokes Benson and Hedges cigarettes
we have held our arms up, fingers together, palm extended
heavenward for so long that our bones have become as heavy
as lead and, alas, have fallen, in accordance with the law of
gravitation
Alto de los Leones, the epic of the Alcázar, the siege of Oviedo,
the cruiser *Baleares*, the Red jails, the Civil War battlefields
have forever disappeared from sight behind a very urban décor
of service stations, snack bars, international banks, billboards,
espresso places: feeble, uninspired political ideas: indifferent,
spineless, overcautious attitudes: effete intellectualism
the breathtakingly bold, battle-hardened Falangist roosters who
once joyously announced the advent of eternal spring in Spain
are dead now: in our comfortable, downy-soft paradise, the
angels who once waited sword in hand at the gates are today
recovering from terrible hangovers after a night on the town
drinking whisky and manzanilla
hearken to my words: the Meseta of our ancestors, the invincible
sword of the Cid, the white steed of Saint James: you will not
encounter the least resistance: the mask weighs heavily upon
us: the role we are playing is a false one: our lungs gasp
desperately for air: hearts beat faster, pulses quicken, bodies
eagerly await your pent-up virility: do you still doubt my word?
listen to me: it is the safest possible gamble: the effects of my
heinous crime will continue to be felt eight centuries from now:
it is written in the stars, as your prophets and holy men know
full well: unending disorder, general corruption, a sudden,
deadly, devastating epidemic!: the premonitory signs are

multiplying and the turbulent waters of the Straits are now as smooth as a quiet pond: the crossing presents no danger whatsoever: disembark!

you will step off Tariq's swift vessel onto your fateful native soil and take over as leader of the over-all operations

you will disguise your savage, untamed warriors as Hispanos and order them to mingle with the crowds at bullfights and soccer matches

you will occupy churches, libraries, military barracks, the monastery of Yuste, San Lorenzo del Escorial, the Cerro de los Ángeles

you will liberate the mosque of Córdoba, the Giralda, the Alhambra

you will raze the palace of Charles V in Granada

you will install your harem in the gardens of the Retiro

you will encourage apostasy by Christians and conversion to Mohammedanism, and spread Koranic propaganda

when the wretched Peninsula develops several focuses of infection and its physical resistance is greatly weakened, you will mount the final brutal assault

at the head of the Moslems of your harka, armed with the keen-bladed weapons of treason

thanks to a handful of illustrious men: masters universally cherished and admired and respected: diviners and speleologists who explored all the hidden veins and seams and wellsprings of your soul: detectors of essences that have existed for thousands of years, tracers of family lines that go back generations: famous men, models of civic uprightness: theoreticians of *la razón vital*, precursors of Heidegger: defenders of a noble civilization fending off barbarism: Hispanicizing Europe, Europeanizing Spain: contemporaries of Proust, but introducers of

D'Annunzio and Maeterlinck: pilgrims visiting the grave of Don Quixote, exegetes of the ancient *romancero*: champions of a fierce Iberian particularism, of the unique, privileged destiny of Spain: denouncers of the old status quo, and creators of a new one; an incomparable group of stylists, artists, and craftsmen of language: the possessors of unexceptionably modern cultural baggage, always carefully enveloped in distinguished, beautifully rounded periods: authors of delightful essays, disseminators of historical erudition, subtle oracles of the Spirit holding forth in the rarefied atmosphere of elegant, quintessentially Spanish gatherings: heralds of arcane sciences inaccessible to the profane, which they felt it their duty to transmit to the good people of their country in order to remedy their countrymen's intellectual poverty and incidentally assure a normal consumption of the output of an entire century of academicians: proud, grave, austere, unyielding patriots: zealous guardians of the truth, locking it up inside a new, patented Ark of the Covenant: statues on pedestals, draped in their rector's togas, their brows wreathed in a graceful crown of laurels: paladins of the Cid, of Seneca, of Platero: of the intimate, typically Spanish linking of stoicism and tauromachy: ardent supporters of genetics and the laws of heredity: an obviously valid explanation of the perpetuation down through the centuries of certain indelible ethnic traits: of the firm roots of the Spanish spirit in the eternal verities of the race: of the Hispanos' indubitable descent from Tubal, son of Japheth and grandson of Noah: of that Guadianesque, subterranean line that extends from Sagunto and Numantia to the epic of the Alcázar of Toledo: restorers of the Celtiberian-Visigothic-Castilian continuity: a sturdy species of eminent hikers, exploring every plain and mountain peak and valley: very Hispanically opposed to time-is-money, common sense, the dread contagion of logic: visceral enemies of Baedeker and the sleeping car, pillows, and bathrooms: of railroads, the flush toilet, and the telephone: rallying round the aristocratic banner of fidelity to every sort of elite: possessed of a dermatico-skeletal, crustacean soul: a bony carapace on the outside and bony flesh inside: faithful to that handful of thaumaturges endowed with a delicate artistic sensibility and a profound intellectual absolutism: sharing a profound Platonic mistrust of the idea of democracy: thanks to them and their luxuriantly proliferating epigoni, the monopolists and bankers of today's vigorous prose, you will be able to identify and traverse the various regions of the fateful Peninsula, the various landscapes gloriously immortalized in their writings

you stealthily make your way across barren, arid Castile, seared by the summer sun, lashed by winter's bitter-cold blasts: keeping a sharp eye on the quiet countryside, absorbed in thought: the quaking aspen along the riverbank, the late spring: the bare hillsides, the rustling elms, the tall poplars, the drowsy oaks
the Angelus rings out, note by note, like beads of a rosary: a concert of church bells amid the solemn silence of the ages: the days slip by, each exactly like the other: repetition, the foundation of happiness: sacred tradition
it is midday: the mist rising from the ground veils the landscape: everything is blurred and indistinct: the colors are so soft as to be almost invisible
a sere, naked land, where the mineral holds dominion over flora and fauna: a crystal-clear, bright-blue sky, vast plains, ochre-colored hills with deep clefts and fissures: desolation, spiritual drought, wandering flocks of sheep, an itinerary leading nowhere
the road is endless, stretching as far as the eye can see: steep

crags: bald peaks: tall straight poplars: a grave, monotonous
procession of dark oaks, their foliage a sempiternal, somber
green
humble, modest villages, steeped in a history half as old as time:
a square bordered with arcades, an old man sitting in a doorway,
palaces with the coats of arms of a hundred noble families, the
jalousies of a convent, weightless footsteps in an alleyway
the ruins of the fortified castle of Mota: a dove on the bell-
tower: the cathedral clock slowly striking the hour, the bells
of the Tribunal of Soria
you walk on: you cross the Tormes: the bridge of La Segoviana:
the steppes of the upper Duero: the water-mills of Zamora:
Salas de los Infantes: the gray walls of Olmedo
you stop to contemplate the poplars along the riverbank: the
wind dies down in the grove of oaks: the water wells up in
abundance, from springs far below the surface: twilight descends and the tenuous autumn light gives the craggy, barren
landscape a rather anchoritic air
the melancholy tinkle of sheep bells can be heard in the distance: a shepherd boy is singing: close at hand, the bees, the
hermitage, the river gorge, the roar of the water eternally
rushing through the deep canyon
hiding in a little grove, at the edge of a little rustic trail, you
survey for the last time the points marking out the rigorous
coordinates of this dead-still landscape: a motionless stork,
a bare elm, a chaste oak, a few gnarled scraggly bushes: a
little old lady astride an ass passes by and says good afternoon:
your fierce burst of laughter dies away in the conventlike silence
of twilight
too many oaks, eh Julian?: too many elms, too many poplars!:
what's to be done about this damned plateau?: all this barren-
ness, all these bells tolling stir the fires of rebellion in your
heart: leave the beaten path once and for all: this place is a

pesthole: can things go on this way? patience, bide your time
let's see if some way can be found to remedy all this

gallop, you handsome stud, gallop, don't lose heart, you who
are God's chosen creature and the son of the Thunder, mounted
on your white Dioscuran steed, descending through the air at
the speed of light, Iago Matamoros, bearing the ineffable white
insigne, the great shining sword in your hand, the nemesis and
scourge of all Islam, the very spirit of Spain, astride your
charger, armed with a trusty blade, just as you are portrayed
on the tympanum of the cathedral dedicated to you, a shrine
visited by thousands and thousands of pilgrims over the
centuries, following the nebulous Milky Way in their sandals,
in armor, with their scallop shells and their pilgrim's staffs, the
oldest tourist route in the world, ladies and gentlemen, with its
panoramic vistas and historic sites, its excellent hotel accommo-
dations and its gastronomical specialities, among them the
celebrated *coquilles Saint-Jacques*, all at unbeatable prices:
galloping across the land and through the air to the other shore
of the sea in order to lend Cortez a hand and coming up against
the natives of Cholula, Texcoco, and Tlaxcala, slaughtering them
in droves, then kicking and beating and prodding the rest of
them into founding three Royal Tribunals in Mexico, plus eleven
bishoprics and a Universal College of Arts and Sciences granting
master's and doctor's degrees, so that there may be master-
printers of books in Latin and in Romance and the Indians may
learn how to work iron with hammers and files and weave silk
and satin and taffeta and make sculptures rivaling those of
Berruguete and Michelangelo: flying swiftly and surely through
the air to countless battlefields, hovering in the sky above in
great sweeping circles, amid choirs of angels singing antiphonal
hymns and Hispanos who have fallen to their knees in humble

devotion, awaiting your messianic gifts and favors, oh you
Hispanos, a wretched breed, alas, eaters of chick-peas, as hard
and compact as rocks, drowsing and dozing, an unfortunate
people, you Hispanos, hostile, alas, to progress and new techniques: and yet withal the hammer of heretics, so hail to the
brownshirts, eternal crusaders
(the area chosen for the metamorphosis and the historical
decharacterization has been carefully reconnoitered: you have
with you topographical maps and weather tables: to sum up, in
a few brief words: the designated sector, to be referred to as
Area H, extends from the northwest slopes of Moncayo to the
Guadarrama, Gredos, and the Sierra Cabrera: within its perim-
eter are rocky wastelands, arid plains, humble little rivers
and brooks: church bells toll the Angelus and sober thoughts of
eternity seem to gush forth from the earth: the landing strips
for the fumigation and pruning teams will be indicated by blue
markers: a Decca Radio transmitter will be set up in the center
of this sector to dispatch back-up helicopter teams: the helicopter transporting the vegetable species adapted to the new
climatic conditions will fly at an altitude of ten thousand
feet and a speed of three hundred miles per hour: once the
weight of each shipment has been calculated, simultaneous
parachute drops will be necessary, and as the terrain is rough,
they must each be encased in foam rubber: the parachutes and
the boxes being dropped are to be coated with a phosphorescent
substance so that they may be recovered more easily: all helicopters will keep tuned to a frequency of eighteen megacycles:
any questions?
no questions
the harkis adjust their white turbans and leap into the saddle:
their fiery steeds whinny with joy, as though they could already
smell the blood)
gallop, yes, gallop, you slender horseman, at the head of your

verbose, gesticulating horde, an invincible warrior, an apostle of chick-peas: your elegantly aristocratic patronage cannot stave off disaster: Hispanos have lived past their time and are now hollow, useless men: fencers without foils, they wave their arms and bandy words about with the violence of men crossing swords with an entirely imaginary adversary: their diet of chick-peas has paralyzed their minds and since this staple causes flatulence, it has aggravated their age-old natural tendency to lose all power of reason: gallop, yes, gallop, across this fateful wasteland where nothing is stirring: an enemy who is stronger than you is cleverly covering up his tracks: craftily gliding across the stone, a cautious, stealthy, treacherous snake, the powerful weapon of Julian: its flat triangular head weaves back and forth in a hypnotic rhythm: its piercing eyes, like two tiny pinheads, with transparent eyelids, watching intently: gallop, yes, gallop, spurred on by the voices of the multitudes stuffed with chick-peas shouting in chorus: down with intelligence, may the dangerous new art of criticism be invented far from our shores!: as the famished serpent prepares to attack, to rear up and strike its prey, injecting it with the fatal liquid that will slowly spread throughout its victim's body and inevitably bring on death: raising itself up vertically on a flat coil, it slithers upward over the belly and thrusts its head forward: hard, imperious, stubborn: not a conquered dragon: a sly, creeping, crawling conqueror: the distilled essence of savage Arab vitality: gallop, yes, gallop, across that land that exists only as a dim memory: the son of Jupiter, a celestial herald: your blinding, gleaming white apparition no longer works miracles: the die has been cast, your fate foretold: yes, gallop, gallop, toward the fog-shrouded myth you emerged from at the wrong moment: gallop, gallop away, and leave us in peace you will now proceed to carefully eliminate every last trace of the fateful landscape

the intensive, methodical operations of the warriors of your harka will first bring about the immediate destruction of its typical flora

> down with you, rustling elms, chaste poplars, dark majestic oaks!: your mystical aureole is fading: your leaves are suddenly turning yellow, a secret, shameful disease is poisoning your sap: your bare felled trunk totters and falls: you are now nothing but vegetable skeletons, charred stumps, sad remains doomed to combustion and decay: you need not expect any elegy from me: I rejoice at your ruin: let the bards of the steppes celebrate your demise in tearful sentimental verses: your heart knows no pity: your only response will be a burst of derisive laughter: growing tired of lopping off branches and chopping up trunks, you will aim the yellow stream of your disdain at their mutilated corpses

fleeing the vegetable disaster by way of little rustic trails and paths, you will maraud and plunder round about the villages and cause their church bells to fall silent

> down with the ringing and pealing of village church bells, rustic tollings of the Angelus, traps baited with the sweet, false promise of the eternity of the soul!: your stupid clangor makes us brutish: the hour of justice has struck: your magnetic lightning bolt will destroy the belfry of the church, and its collapse will sow death and desolation: storks and martins will perish: little old ladies sitting in the sun with shawls over their heads will be crushed to death: farewell, servile bells: I shall use your henceforth harmless metal to mint coins: the hammer will stamp the memory of your visit in bronze: a witness to your vengeance for all time to come

above the monotonous, endless plain, above its bare, stark organic

contours you will heap up masses of clouds that will cause a
sudden, violent change of climate

farewell, arid plateaus, barren wastelands, parched
plains: the ethical emanations have dried up: your
nakedness will cease to nourish the obscene metaphysics:
cumulus, nimbus, cirrus, stratus clouds will forever veil
the sky: the vegetation will hereafter be that of a rainy
region: fallow land and stubble fields will once again be
green: stands of grain, vegetable gardens, and orchards
will carpet the fertile plain: a network of canals will
facilitate this ludicrous transformation: where once
there was a wasteland, there will henceforth be polders:
within this sodden, soggy setting, cows will graze amid
tulips

the bald peaks, the rugged crags, the rocky buttes of your
mineralized universe that has no water will also soon experience
the effects of your chemical aggression, and they too will shortly
become part of the Nordic landscape, full of humming factories
and industrial plants

disappear, you limestone peaks, you bare, stark sierras,
you fatally contaminated Meseta!: the schist will soon
be covered with new species of plants, beautiful soft
prairies: the sere yellows and the somber grays will turn
to bright greens: water will well up everywhere:
marshes, pools, ponds, lagoons will quench the poet's
nauseous spiritual thirst: may he choke, strangle, drown:
may his belly harbor frogs: may his soul engender toads:
may his grotesque body drift on the waters and become
food for leeches

on the way back home, you will meet an old woman mounted on
a humble ass, and gratuitously attack her, with the greatest
severity and cruelty

the animal is small and hairy and soft, panting as it
walks along, as though it had come a long way: you

will feed it with one hand as in the other you clutch a
razor-sharp knife and slowly sink it into its throat: the
blood will spurt out, thick and crimson-colored: the
animal's shoe-button eyes, like two shiny black crystal
beetles, will gaze at you pleadingly: you will stab it
once again, in the abdomen this time, and its intestinal
matter will leak out in little trickling coils, like a
ridiculous *serpentin*: the little old woman will attempt
to intervene and will suffer the same fate: her delicate
viscera are a pale pink, like the ribbons birthday presents
are tied in: a little girl will snip them with her scissors
and make a jump rope of them: the donkey and the
old woman will die: the little girl will develop a fatal
case of rabies
the re-creator of the world, a bone-weary god, on the seventh day
you will rest

in Madrid, one night toward the end of July, the clock of the
Puerta del Sol strikes eleven: cars breathe their last along
the Avenida del Prado, and inside the Chicote bar, the famous
philosopher Seneca, the idol of the people, is receiving heady
compliments from the intellectual elite when suddenly Tariq,
your robust crony, grabs you firmly by the arm and drags you
to the watchtower of Bab-el-Assa, a marvelous vantage point,
and then removing the roof tiles of the houses in one fell swoop
as though they were layers of puff pastry, he suddenly discloses
the meat filling inside: the great city and all its many human
species of thinking vermin
corporation presidents on their knees worshiping an I.B.M.
machine, one-time crusaders who today are arthritic, and obese
bureaucrats absorbed in reading the Official Record: shop
clerks who are the proud possessors of television sets and cars,
soccer fans, bullfight aficionados: Sunday afternoon explorers

of the Sierra, tamed factory workers and proles, devotees of
rock and admirers of Elvis the Pelvis
looking in the direction that his finger is pointing to, you will
be able to make out old people who have outlived their time and
young people who are outdying theirs: great throngs of living
corpses walking around, cautiously obeying the traffic signs:
women of every sort, all of whom reject the pricks as limp as
lettuce leaves offered them by Spanish males and dream of Arab
serpents and the leisurely, sumptuous feasts they offer
at various places in this city with no roofs, children and
adolescents are diligently applying themselves to learning the
principles of stoic philosophy, to memorizing the tables of
angelic choirs and hierarchies, the exploits of Isabel la Católica,
the virtues of your Vertical Labor Unions
at literary gatherings and cocktail parties, in arty cafés and
elegant salons, men of letters are carefully tending the flame
of the brightly glowing Torch of Generations: sons, grandsons,
great-great-grandsons of the giants of '98, bards celebrating the
immutable flora of the steppes, the Hispanic essence that has
stood the test of centuries: statues who do not yet have a
pedestal, but are already masters of the art of tauromachic
miming and posturing, already possessed of the austere genius
and appearance of genius of Senecism: patiently climbing, rung
by rung, the ladder festooned with laurel, lavishly pouring on
the charm: if you quote me I'll quote you, if you praise me I'll
praise you, if you read me I'll read you: an original, quintessentially Spanish method of criticism founded on an age-old
primitive economic system, tribal barter!: poets, novelists,
playwrights chasing after third-rate prizes, a grant from the
Al Capone Foundation!: plaiting garlands of flowers for each
other, offering each other the loftiest paeans of praise, penning
the most orotund panegyrics, resounding rhetoric that is always
inappropriate and unfailingly insincere, save when they employ
it to attack each other in reciprocal raging fury: long-pent-up

vengeance that can no longer be contained, and inevitably is unleashed upon the outlaw and the exile: the immortal vicious Spanish temper, your one true reality!

half a league away, the representatives of the government information service are allowing their pens free rein and hammering the keys of their typewriters in inspired frenzy

"The fiery chargers of Phoebus had just appeared on the rim of the crystal-clear heavens when, awakened by the melodious morning song of the birds, the philosopher Seneca . . ."

"Those who had the great good fortune of being at Seneca's side during the ceremonies opening the Eighteenth International Exposition of Chrysanthemums were witnesses of an episode so moving that it bordered upon the sublime: detaching herself from the double row of admirers, a darling little girl three years old ran to meet the philosopher and with a graceful bow presented him with a fragrant bouquet of flowers which . . ."

"At 11:17 a.m. today, the great Seneca threw the window of his study open, and leaning pensively on the sill, whistled with incomparable mastery the opening bars of the march from *The Bridge over the River Kwai*, amid the applause of the stoics, who, as is their wont, were eagerly awaiting his appearance in order to . . ."

in a vast and luxurious auditorium in one of the new Ministries a valiant disciple of Dr. Leech's, wearing four stars on his sleeve, explains to the large distinguished audience that has gathered there that never in the history of humanity has there been a more perfect example of stoic perseverance than that offered by the endless phalanx of dauntless bloodletters who for century after century have taken it upon themselves to improve the circulation of Hispanos, admittedly sending many of them to their graves, but purging the rest of their bloody excesses in order that they might live in relative peace and calm, and proposes that

the nation officially offer its homage to the maximum blood-
letter, to the immovable philosopher, as eternal as the rock of
ages: the great Seneca
in the comfortable sitting room of the ultra-dynamic Club Index,
the cultivated and highly respected director is holding forth with
great intelligence and wit on the subject of the typically Spanish
virtues of chick-peas: the cornerstone of your social institutions,
the basis of your instinctive love of herding and being herded:
where the Frenchman would say *cherchez la femme*, the Hispano
would say *cherchez le pois chiche*: the chick-pea of all sizes and
descriptions: none of your hollow noodles or puffy soufflés:
fancy European concoctions that look very appetizing but leave
you still hungry: rather, the plain, homely, straightforward,
compact national chick-pea: the epicenter and the motive force
of your glorious conquests in the Americas, Flanders, and Italy:
the sustenance that builds strong, austere men: the source of
sweet sedative emanations and sturdy spiritual fibers: your
country has been, is, and will forever be a vast patch of chick-
peas: and your national symbol, the hero with the profoundest
of Iberian roots, of the finest Senecan stock, Don Chichote de
la Mancha
finally, having grown as tired as you of spying on the enemy
from the incomparable vantage point of the Casbah, your
Crippled Devil will glue the puff-paste roofs back on and allow
the meat filling inside, the city and its many scurrying species of
thinking vermin, to rot a while longer

a horse could easily get lost in the dense jungle of this bushy
mustache: and so could you, even more easily, as you proceed
on foot at a leisurely pace, wandering, dreaming, exploring the
highways and byways: bravely making your way through the
wild, bristling brush: a happy parasite of this hirsute forest:
as yesterday, as tomorrow, as always: tangled foliage that your

compatriots do not even know exists: thick vegetation with upright stalks, clinging vines: rugged, savage flora, brambles,
briars, creepers: stopping to rest in them without fear of
suffocating: frankly and unashamedly: these tangled thickets
and thorny patches belong to you: you will therefore enjoy
them and seek refuge in their thick fur: soft, sheltering mountains where you would like to stay forever!: yes, like Mowgli:
far from the meticulously barbered civilization of the Hispano:
in the hairy, impenetrable jungle, inhabited by fierce wild
beasts: agile, lithe, wary, flexible fauna!: sharp fangs, smooth
muscles, retractable claws: anarchical and barbarous prose,
the very opposite of your carefully kempt style, your anemic,
prim and proper, overrefined writing: and as you clear a way
for yourself through the underbrush, you will blaze new trails,
invent new itineraries, discover new shortcuts, breaking away
altogether from the official syntax and its attendant procession
of dogmas and interdicts: a heretic, a schismatic, an iconoclast,
a renegade, an apostate: violating edicts and rules, tasting the
delicious forbidden fruit: the rough, wild forest of Tariq: his
bushy black beard, his dazzling, flashing smile!: a wild, rugged
landscape you joyously roam about in and hide in: ordinarily
without a care in the world, but preoccupied today by the nearby
presence of a hominid there in the curly hide, jauntily whistling
a melody from Chopin's *Les Sylphides*: you will tiptoe over
that way and spy a philosopher with the face of an old gypsy,
squatting on his heels, draped in an immaculate toga, his brow
wreathed in a crown of laurels: to doubt is to affront: it is
Seneca, in person!: his countenance stern, austere, solemn,
exactly like the bust of him in your museum in Madrid:
absorbed at the moment in a slow and painful task, doing his
utmost to bring about expansion in an inferior region, humming
the celestial leitmotiv the while, as a fitting anticlimax: strain-
ing his voice in what might well be the triumphant apotheosis of
his effort until finally he raises his head, discovers your indis-

creet presence in the vicinity, and still squatting in his humble, painful position, warns you

hey, watch it, there's somebody here!

and although you mutter an apology and discreetly turn your back, you keep eavesdropping on his succession of vague, neutral utterances: expressions of satisfaction or of anguish: or possibly both things at once: after a few moments during which you are unable to resist the temptation to take a further peek at him, the humble squatting philosopher heaves a gentle sigh and with his toga-draped dignity still intact, he leans over to lovingly contemplate his work, the tender fruit of his entrails: it is hidden from your view by arborescent bushes, but apparently sufficient and satisfactory according to his lights, for he now struggles to his feet, leaving behind the end product of his mighty exertions to fulfill its fecundating destiny, though not without first covering it with rustic foliage: he then stoically turns around to confront your gaze and a grave, anguished, forced smile appears on his lips

although a philosopher, I am sometimes forced to yield to imperative natural needs, if you know what I mean: the same was true of Saint Augustine and the Church Fathers of old: and even of the angelical Saint Thomas Aquinas: a pious legend has it that he composed his loftiest works in this very posture:

Seneca gives a vague apologetic wave of his hand, and since you say nothing in reply, he continues his discourse in an emphatic tone of voice

it was at a similar critical moment that I myself composed some of my best epistles to Lucilius: the famous one on intemperate desires, for one particular instance: do you remember it?

no, you do not remember it

that's a shame, he remarks: in it I utterly demolish the hypotheses of Freud, Marx, and Friedrich Nietzsche: I suppose you know that the latter was a syphilitic?

no, you were not aware of that fact

well, I assure you it's true: and tertiary syphilis, at that! lingual chancres, and ramifications in the bones and the intestines: incurable, kid: his intimates say that he used to gnaw his fists and bang his head against the walls: his tragic end was the inspiration of the ode I wrote that got me elected a corresponding member of the Spanish Academy and also won me the Al Capone Prize: do you have any idea how much it was worth to me? no!

well, listen to this: I pocketed half a million pesetas, would you believe it!: even after the last devaluation, that's nothing to sneeze at: and then there's the prestige, the popularity!: television, press conferences, the whole bit!: not to mention all the broads that came flocking around: they practically ate me alive: married women, old maids, even a couple of virgins!: I admit I had to take an occasional bottle of tonic to get back in shape, but I had myself a high old time, let me tell you!: there was one chick especially, a redhead, with tits as big as grapefruit, who just wouldn't let me alone: she really went for my apple in a big way, if I do say so myself!: a real ballbuster, that kid, as crazy as they come: If I left her alone for one minute, she went plumb out of her mind: she'd smother me with kisses and bite me: a sad case, I swear: look, I've got a picture of her right here

the man pulls an old, beat-up leather wallet from his pocket and takes a colored photograph out of it: a girl dressed in a miniskirt and a flimsy tight-fitting blouse that shows her firm little round breasts underneath

I took this snapshot myself, at the foot of the Eiffel Tower: barely eighteen, and a real tigress in bed: an honest-to-goodness French girl: very clean, with nice manners: if you'd care to measure how much oil she's got in her lamp, I'd be glad to introduce her to you: it wouldn't be any trouble at all: she lives right here in the neighborhood: twenty-five dirhems a lay, fifty for the whole night: what do you say, fellah?

no, you're a bit hesitant, and on noticing your reluctance to take him up on his offer, he grabs you by the sleeve and keeps insisting, meanwhile taking more photos out of his wallet and spreading them out before you in a fan: a deck of cards with pictures of scantily clad girls on the backs, in seductive poses on a red velvet sofa

if the French girl isn't your type, I also have a little Spanish one: a real volcano!: this brunette here: not a day over twenty, and a really hot piece of ass: I'll make you a special price: only thirty duros

you continue to clear a trail for yourself through the dense foliage, and he follows right at your heels, still insisting, begging and pleading and trying to block your path

a Jewish girl?

a Moroccan girl?

petite fille?

fraulein to fuck?

allora, ragazzino innocente?

without your noticing, the two of you have arrived at the edge of the forest: at the very tip of the handlebar mustache: Tariq's wrinkled cheek dilates to exhale the puff of pipe smoke, and the pimp, being lighter than you, is knocked backward and lands up on the floor of the Tangier café alongside a pile of cigarette butts: his toga and his crown of laurels have fallen off and he is now a pitiful, heart-rending sight to behold: his stiff, jerky movements seemingly motivated by two ambivalent, contradictory impulses: frugality, a minimum of gestures on the one hand, and wild extravagance, great sweeping gesticulations on the other: a filthy skullcap, broken-down shoes, a scarecrow's jacket: staring into space, a part of the décor, attracting no one's attention: when one of the smokers at the next table turns his head to follow your gaze and notices him, the denouement is sudden and unexpected: with no sort of prefatory remarks or explanation, the man will cross the distance that separates them in one leap: his huge, dark, phantomlike shadow will circle about for a few moments above the head of the skinny beggar, and then without violence or hatred, but rather quite the contrary, aseptically, carefully, he will step on it, crush it beneath the weight of his felt slipper

in the old, inhospitable library that you visit every day, you have patiently compiled evidence of the abuses of the Word: what a cancerous, useless proliferation, what creeping, parasitic excrescences!: words, hollow molds, receptacles that echo emptily: what microbe has sucked out your pulp and left only the skin?: your apparent health is a deceptive mirage, a clever illusion: constant careless decanting from one century to the next has destroyed your vigor: the light source surrounding you with a gleaming halo no longer exists: the star that emitted it died ten thousand years ago: it is time to hand you your death certificate: your obvious servility and docility support the theory that you are an infamous race: sly pimps, respectful prostitutes, ever ready to sell yourselves to the highest, most dirty-handed bidder: simony is your bread and butter: voracious, tentacular, jellyfish-like, you increase and multiply there on the paper, stifling the truth behind the mask: how long will your tyranny continue?: the noble sentiments that you pretend to serve are rotting in the refuse heap of history: eclogues, patriotic odes, sonnets imbued with quintessential religious fervor!: love, into the garbage can: love of country, into the garbage can: gods and kings, into the garbage can: may pigs root and wallow in this pestilential sewer: the sea is choked with stinking corpses: give up all these books, let them all fall to dust: poems, spiritual eructations, flatulent rumblings of the bowels: how many Parnassuses to put under the auctioneer's hammer, how many Academies to sell off at bargain prices: down with flower gardens, flower garlands, flower

gardening, flowers of rhetoric: the time has come to root out
the quackgrass: the Word is dead and in your ears there rings
the intoxicating summons to action: remember, Ulbán:
violence is mute: to pillage, to destroy, to rape, to betray, you
will not need words

before going on with the bloody razzia, you will consult one last
time the books neatly lined up on the shelves, searching for the
definition and the ten commandments of the perfect Christian
gentleman

> "The Christian gentleman is essentially a paladin defend-
> ing a cause, an avenger of wrongs and injustices who
> roams the world, subjecting all of reality to the rule of
> supreme, absolute, unconditional values.
> "The Christian gentleman is courageous and intrepid. He
> fears only God and himself. Sustained by a calm sense
> of certainty and security, by a serene, dauntless, un-
> troubled spirit, his entire life is directed toward a single,
> clear-cut goal.
> "Because he is a Christian and a gentleman, the Christian
> gentleman conceives of death as a dawn and not a
> twilight; far from fearing it, he will accept it joyfully,
> for he sees it as the gateway to eternal life.
> "The Christian gentleman feels in his soul so passionate
> a desire for immortality that he impatiently awaits the
> end of his brief life on this earth. Unlike other souls
> who seek to reach the infinite by the slow path of the
> finite, the Christian gentleman aspires to reach the very
> heart of the divine essence in a single leap."

four centuries of Castilian dust look down upon you from the
dusty shelves of the library: the book falls from your hands and
you return the fly-spattered volume to the limbo from which
you imprudently removed it: it is closing time: the custodian

rewinds his watch, and casting a sidelong glance in your direction, stifles a cavernous yawn
hurry, Bulian: you must meet this extraordinary gentleman

in the narrow streets of some dead city forever ennobled in the solemn, serene, most pure writings of that enlightened group of thaumaturges and prophets who miraculously appeared on your soil around the year of grace 1898 A.D., you will have no difficulty finding the domicile of the perfect Christian gentleman and will have a long leisurely chat with him: a house built of the same stone as convents, with a rusty grille and a niche for swallows who in the course of their migrations proclaim their beatific joy at living outside of history
passing through the massive door of the vestibule, you will enter a country kitchen, with a blackened hood over the hearth, just above the burning coals of the fire, and a humble set of dishes on the mantelpiece: the only light in the room is that from a little window with a balcony: after having warmed your hands, numb from the cold, at the fire, you will go on into the next room: a small room whose only furnishings are a rough esparto-grass mat, a crude bed of bare wooden planks, and a night table with a crucifix and a sturdy wooden coffer that dates from the Crusades on top of it: a man sitting on an austere straight-back chair with a rush seat is reading verses by Calderón and Lope de Vega: his stern, lean, untroubled countenance reflects the solemn grandeur of these barren regions: but at the same time it hints at the existence of a cool subterranean spring hidden far in the depths of his flinty heart
Don Álvaro Peranzules will receive you with the proverbial lofty pride of men of his caste: his look of hauteur is clear proof of his noble Visigoth ancestry and his four plump fingers incontrovertible evidence of his descent from Old Christian stock on

both sides of his family: what's bred in the bone will come out
in the flesh, he tells you: genius and the appearance of genius:
the more genius the greater the appearance of genius, and vice
versa: and amid the very Hispanic fauna of figure drawings,
figurines, and figure studies, you admire his impermeable,
hermetic Figure: the purest sublimate, the most quintessential
distillation of the genius and the appearance of genius of his
race: not so much a personification as a mask: an exemplary
mask amid the banal multitude of shoddy masquerade costumes
and flimsy disguises: not so much a mask as a figurehead,
whose features have been chiseled by the passing years into a
set, stereotyped rictus, the fixed grin of a skull: an enormous
figurehead, just above the prow, below the bowsprit, facing into
the wind, braving the storm, as unmoving as a statue, impassively observing the formless, pointless existence of hominids
who have no mask, of the invertebrate anonymous masses, with
no cothurni, no pontifical rictus, no purple toga, no silver
sandals: a figurehead around the clock, twenty-four hours out
of twenty-four, appearance and the appearance of genius preserved in 180-proof alcohol: he has difficulty moving in his
bony armor, the joints of which creak with every step he takes:
a cross between a mammal and a medieval warrior: his head
a helmet: his forehead a visor: his chest a cuirass: his hands
gauntlets: his legs thigh-pieces: his feet sollerets: symbioti-
cally fused with his mask, imbedded in his armor: his facial
expressions and his gestures are as rigid as a robot's: the hardness of his shell is reminiscent at times of the carapace of
crabs: at other times his hieratic pose and elegant dress suggest
a wooden mannequin, a dressmaker's model: Don Álvaro en-
thusiastically demonstrates for your benefit the appearance
befitting his genius and the genius befitting his appearance, and
then suddenly the frozen features of his mask become even
more stony and he recites in a gravelly voice a crustacean sonnet,

with a bony morphology and a calcareous syntax, selected from
one of the collections of fossils on the shelves of the library
on the boulevard

> In the stately pavan of the universe,
> I bear on the solid pommel of my sword,
> a scarlet cross that proclaims
> my noble Castilian lineage.
> I drape a crimson cloak over my shoulders,
> I curl my mustache upward, Burgundy-style,
> and my starched white ruff stands out stiffly
> beneath my curly white locks.
> I have a hundred lancers fighting in Flanders,
> a thousand serfs on the slopes of the Andes,
> kettledrums and a pennant, a gibbet and a bodkin,
> a count's demesne in a mountainous region,
> a friar to shrive the countess,
> a hundred greyhounds, ten pages, and a castle.

what lofty ideals! what noble sentiments! what fervent patriotism! amid smiles and polite murmurs, you are taken on a visit
of the count's demesne in a mountainous region with the pages,
the greyhounds, the friar: Don Álvaro discusses the future
Poles of Promotion and the marvelous Department Plan with
you, and announces on the local radio network an annual
increase in per capita income amounting to 3.82 per cent:
apprentices clad in tiny djellabas weave the web that will inevitably imprison them: a Riff woman, wearing a veil that is so
thick it is almost a gag, silently pleads for help and the friar
hears her confession: you are approaching the summer residence of Don Álvaro Peranzules: a great bulk of a fortress with
stone watchtowers and crenelated battlements: great windows
with mullions and arches and ogives in Late Gothic style have
been let into the faces of the fortress: your host now recites
a fiery patriotic sonnet and the rule for the agreement of
participles as set down in the latest edition of the grammar of

the Royal Academy: with his glasses firmly perched on his
nose and a little ruler in his hand, he quizzes you on epenthesis
and synaeresis: the zeroes pile up, millions of them, in your
thick schoolboy's notebook: the Hispanicism of Seneca, the
Quixotism of the Cid, the Senecism of Manolete: in a barren,
arid landscape once more, profoundly rural, intimately rustic:
the old elms, the somber peaks, the gray mules: the pious,
humble, early-rising village church bells of mystic, militant
Castile, of gentle, humble, simple-hearted Castile: a peaceful,
serene land, an august dream in stone: the gentleman then
recites, in intoxicated tones, the poem "It takes a heap of livin'
to make a house a home," as the dogs fling themselves on mal-
contents and tear them to pieces, and the friar blesses the
corpses: you have now entered the apartments of Don Álvaro's
daughter, and taking advantage of a moment's distraction, you
convey yourself behind the arras: Isabel la Católica is a woman
of average height, of pleasing physical proportions, very fair-
skinned and blond, with blue-green eyes and a frank, gracious
gaze: she is generous, expansive, rigorously just, cheerful: she
endeavors to discover the guiding principles of life in books and
conversation with scholars: she hears Mass daily, and observes
the canonical hours: she is learning Latin in order to pray and
has as good a grasp of it as the most erudite humanist: her
father has taught her the love of God: to safeguard her honor
and be scrupulously faithful to her word: to aid the helpless:
to be dignified and truthful, chaste and continent: to recite the
Angelus three times a day and to venerate Saint Millán and
Saint James, two saints on horseback, heralds of Castile's poetic
mission and its crystal-pure will to Empire
Don Álvaro continues his discourse on the Hispanic heritage and
the rules governing the use of prepositions, and meanwhile
behind the curtain that so handily conceals you, you spy on his
daughter, ready to leap into action: the lights in her apartment
slowly fade, and when they go out altogether, the wench's

toothsome body is plunged into dark shadows that tempt your
greed: but a shaft of light suddenly rescues her from darkness:
dressed in a nun's habit, the young lady is devoutly reciting
her prayers, kissing the crucifix above her prie-dieu, and
telling the beads of a rosary: loud-speakers turned down low
discreetly playing a Rolling Stones hit: "Time Is on My Side," or
perhaps "It's All Over Now": the little nun rises to her feet
with a sigh, and turning her back to her audience, unzips her
soft habit: and immediately black silk pajamas come into view,
with the sound of moaning and panting, locomotives whistling,
champagne bubbling in the background: loving you, loving you,
my lord and master, is my constant delirious dream: I am sick
with love, but do not want to be cured: a pure, crystalline,
passionate, perfectly modulated woman's voice, tenderly chiding
the figure in a precarious, uncomfortable position, urging him
on, but with no success apparently: offering herself to him,
body and soul: her life, her honor, and her sacred fortune:
as the Rolling Stones go on singing and the sound waves increase
and multiply, crash down, inundate, penetrate, penetrate:
innocent hands distractedly keep time to the music, and pairs
of feet mechanically imitate them, tapping out the beat:
unbelievable: the young lady's movements begin little by little
to obey the mad cadence of the music!: she first unbuttons
the jacket of her pajamas, then slips the pants off, attempts
to cover her nakedness with her arms, gyrates round and round
the stage, making pleading gestures and letting out prudish
little gasps: her tempting-looking navel is clearly visible in
her smooth, tan belly, the color of sherry aged in the keg,
her buxom breasts wriggle suggestively beneath the auspices of
her lace brassière: her mesh stockings are held up by flowered
garters attached to her panty girdle, and with a candid rotary
motion of her fingers, she removes her hose, thus revealing the
incomparable perfection of her soft, shapely limbs: long legs,
but not spindly ones: open like a compass, firm and round, her

COUNT JULIAN : 139

thighs converging on the half-glimpsed treasure, like two per-
emptory traffic signs: one-way traffic, an arbitrary law that
Hispanos obey like a flock of sheep and only the traitor dares
to disregard!: as her index finger and her thumb investigate
the possibilities of liberation the near future holds in store, of
which there are already certain hints, and the sound effects
vary to match the spectral play of light: asteroids, planets,
constellations, dwarf stars, giant stars!: when the lace falls,
her breasts burst forth like an unexpected, joyous proclamation
of the arrival of spring: an impetuous hosanna, an exultant
hallelujah that the girl conceals with her slender hands as she
strides across the room, lithe and graceful, as though impelled
by the admiration that she arouses: her lips murmur prayerful
ejaculation, orisons rich in privileges and blessings, especially
if recited for an entire month and accompanied by the sacrament
of confession, a visit to a church, and prayers for the Pope:
a few moments later, she bends down, picks up a long leather
case, and removes from it the whip with which she daily casti-
gates herself: self-flagellation will now be performed, with ritual
exactitude: at each blow, her pious gasps grow louder, accompanied by the musical erection of an explosive, paroxysmal
Negro rhythm, the repeated muscular contractions apparently
bringing on orgasm: progressing from the vulgar and common
periphery toward the epicenter of dogma: slow, persistent,
dialectical rotary motions: a corkscrew or a propeller: pleading for masculine help with parched lips, provoking a sudden
flux of blood with her frenzied eyes: a sweet love wound, a
cruel dart transfixing the soul!: the crucifix is obviously not
enough: the vascular dilatation and the filiform secretion of
your serpent become intolerable: let the submissive and resigned
Hispano satisfy himself! manual manipulation isn't enough for
you!: when you grab the whip out of her hands and begin to
beat her yourself, a close-up of the satin triangle over her groin
will appear onscreen, and the mellifluous, persuasive voice of

the announcer will invite you and the other spectators in the
audience to take an unforgettable, instructive excursion down
into the depths, the folds, and the secret hiding places of the
Theological Bastion: a tour of the interior of the sanctum
sanctorum that before the tourist invasion, economic development, and the silver wedding anniversary of the Omnipresent,
you used to refer to as the Remote, Fantastic, Sacred Grotto
from Whose Bourne No Traveler Has Ever Returned

ladies and gentlemen
mesdames et messieurs
fair ladies and good gentlemen
the Cavern that you are about to visit is undoubtedly one of the
most typical and most fascinating historical curiosities of our
unique Peninsula
its metaphysical implications
its moral configuration
its rich, intense spirituality
make it a favorite rendezvous of Very Important Persons, and
amply justify the economic sacrifices you have made and the
inevitable inconveniences you have experienced in the course
of the long journey that has brought you here from the five
corners of this confused and turbulent modern world to which
our fate has destined us
originally conceived as a strategic military bulwark, it has been
able to withstand, thanks to its defenders' *sang-froid* and stub-
bornness, the onslaughts and the attacks of very powerful
enemies
entire armies have been dashed to pieces against its rocky
Toledan Alcázar, and more than one invincible armada has seen
its armor-plate shattered on the unyielding cliffs of its in-
domitable courage
today

thanks to our enormous adaptability to the present demands of tourists
with the proper dispensations and necessary papal bulls in hand
we are pleased to unveil the fabulous secret so carefully guarded
for so many centuries
a favorite excursion to Hercules' cave where the hero-god lived
a Moving Spectacle
Sublime
Unique
included in the Europe-Tours itinerary
recommended by the Diners Club and the Belgian Royal Automobile Club
with the special blessing of His Holiness the Pope
traveler's checks accepted here
we reserve the right to refuse admission
pers. sans ref. s'abst.
the tourists climb out of the air-conditioned, soundproofed, musicalized excursion bus and gather in a circle around the guide, in the huge parking lot recently constructed opposite the entrance to the Grotto
six bigwigs from the Bronx
ten furriers from Chicago
one gentleman farmer from Texas
one member of the D.A.R.
a delegation of speleologists
two avant-garde music critics
a married couple recently divorced
five war widows
the guide points to the vestibule of the vagina and describes the characteristic structure and function of each organ
the mons Veneris
the labia majora
the labia minora
the vaginal orifice

the clitoris
and the hymen
signs in a number of languages remind visitors of certain safety
precautions that must be observed
post-card and souvenir vendors pass among the group, handing
around necklaces, bracelets, fezzes, and pieces of pottery
loud-speakers broadcast religious music and commercials
and here you are, standing on the threshold of Mystery, at the
mouth of the infernal Cavern, in the middle of the dreary empty
space of what is reputedly the most formidable break in the
earth's crust in the world, a yawning crack leading to the
kingdom of Shadows, Dreams, and Night, an illustrious Aeneas
suddenly abandoned by the Sibyl
you will courageously break through the hymen and enter
the dark domain of Pluto, where you will seek in vain, amid
the fleshy proliferation of stalactites, the golden bough and the
black bulls destined to appease the wrath of the gods, the sterile
cow proverbially offered to Proserpina, and the lamb sacrificed to
the mother of the Eumenides
an Orpheus without a lyre, searching for Eurydice, Pollux
sacrificed for love of Castor, a new Theseus, an inspired Alcides,
you will worm through the oblique slit opened up in the pelvic
excavation, following the shadowy course of the Acheron and
skirting the vast, dead lagoon of the Styx, through the narrow,
winding neck of the uterus and the spongy vaginal sacs covered
with a strange, parasitic growth of blue-green algae, which
irresistibly remind you of the hallucinatory image of Discord
with her poisonous snake locks, and finally halting on being
confronted by an ancient elm tree, the age-old lair of fantastic
monsters and wild beasts, contemplating the fearsome countenance of Scylla, the fire-breathing Chimera, sedulously avoiding
a lethal encounter with Gorgons and Harpies, and taking a
leisurely stroll along the anterior and posterior surfaces of the
vagina and its two edges and tips, close now to the brackish

waters of the Cocytus, keeping a sharp eye out for Charon and
his fateful, eagerly awaited bark, surrounded by countless
wandering shades, among whose number you recognize the
silhouette of Palinurus, but you are still reluctant to put your
penny in the box and finally pass over to the deep shadows on
the opposite shore
you will cross the isthmus of the uterus and enter a vast, perverse cavity in the form of a pear with the broad base upward
and the slender top downward, in the center of which a gigantic
watchdog is barking furiously, thus frightening away the blood-
less shades of those who have attempted during their earthly
life to penetrate the secret of the Cave, shapeless embryos in
the workshop of veins and arteries, begotten by the foamy
exudate of human flesh in a drowsy transport of passion, who
roam all over these hideous, poisonous, nauseating surfaces,
hemmed in by walls of muscle tissue covered with disturbing,
sinuous submarine fauna, globular cells, star-shaped fruits,
horny spines, heads surrounded by tentacles with sucking disks,
articulated antennae moving about like whiplashes, and without
retreating a single step, you will throw a honeycomb in the
famished, greedy, triple mouth of Cerberus and take advantage
of his sudden drowsiness to steal past him into the Fallopian
tubes and their many meanders, all of them padded on the inside
with a soft, quivering epithelium, not deigning to notice the
nearby presence of Minos and his Silent Council, of star-crossed
Dido and Deiphobus, son of Priam, working your way through
the visceral conduit that becomes wider and wider, flaring out
like the bell of a trumpet, like a sort of flower or hairy ear, the
function of which is to suck in the ovum at the moment of
dehiscence and propel it toward the uterus by means of subtle
peristaltic contractions
inside the ovary now, a pinkish-white, almond-shaped structure,
which becomes congested with blood during menstruation and
turns gray at the menopause, the surface of which is smooth

during puberty and later becomes rough and wrinkled and
covered with scars, an organ made up of a fibrous central stroma
and a firm, white outer sheath: a shady oasis and a spacious
cradle welcoming every sort of fertile reptilian outpouring, be
it the product of deliberate vascular dilatation or a gratuitous
overflow
you continue on your way and reach
a redoubt protected by a triple wall, surrounded by the searing
flame of Phlegethone, with an impenetrable steel door behind
which Tisiphone, who sleeps neither by day nor by night, keeps
watch, wielding her whip and lacerating the flesh of desecrators,
of raging mad fornicators who once attempted to violate the
integrity of the obviously proudly defended ramparts and were
struck down by the divine wrath, thereupon falling into the
hands of Rhadamanthus the implacable and the Hydra with fifty
heads, losing your way amid the mephitic miasmas of a mossy,
damp expanse of vegetable deposits and immense rotting peat
bogs, a hideous, oozing, viscous world of canal, vesicles, glands,
nerves, arteries, secretions, membranes and sacs, the proteiform
realm of the flaccid and formless, of nasty creeping flora, of the
obscene bubbling of the inorganic
as Julian the avenger, possessed of the craftiness and ingenuity
of James Bond the invulnerable, you will post your advertisement at the entrance to the sanctuary just as the group of
tourists and the guide suddenly appear immediately behind you
and the Stygian lagoon becomes a romantic underground lake
where a dozen Charons in uniform play, with plangent arpeggios,
a sentimental violin tune aboard a raft cleverly disguised as a
shell-shaped Triton's float, and the D.A.R., the gentleman farmer
from Texas, the bigwigs from the Bronx, the war widows and
the furriers wipe tears from their eyes, A Marvelous Spectacle,
ladies and gentlemen, one of the Seven Wonders of the World,
and to the tune of Mendelssohn's "Wedding March," the last veil
is lifted, disclosing the vista of which you have already had

a tantalizing glimpse: white lilies and crimson roses, a verdant plain bathed in bright sunlight, on which the blessed are gamboling and frolicking, singing in chorus, and engaging in sports: paradise, in short, as promised to a chosen minority of the continent and chaste, and you discover, to your open-mouthed amazement, yes, there's no doubt of it, right there before your eyes, who would have ever believed it: the Cunt: yes, it's none other than the Cunt
you can't believe your eyes, right?
well, take a good look
it's the Cunt all right
the national emblem of the country of stupid cuntery
of all the cuntish cunters who've ever encunted the country of countless cuntifiers where everything is constantly cuntified and discuntified for the glorious encuntification of the most Sacred Cunt
the quintessential Cunt, symbol of your congenital, consecular, uncuntificated cunnery
of the cunnucular, cuntsubstantial, cunfuckatory, cuntipresent, cuntjunctory cuntgnition
of the Most-Cuntish Cunt
and you haughtily withdraw from The Presence and its luciferous dominions, and as the multicolored spotlight plays over you once again, you will savagely lash the blood-stained body of the damsel and torment her senses with baroque, hyperbolic cruelty
Tariq's hosts are awaiting your signal to fling themselves upon her and force open the portals of the ancient temple
you will whip her soundly, with swift unerring strokes, and will impassively witness the efficacious touch of their lips, open like a fresh wound, and the reptilian ecstasy of their pitilessly cruel asps
the futile struggle of the damsel who protests her innocence, pleads for mercy and forgiveness, before modestly yielding to her torturers and finally submitting, with bestial docility, to

their stubborn, imperious cobras
and in ringing, forcible tones, you will address them thus
hearken to my words
you Arabs with vulgar members, coarse rough skin, clumsy
hands, greedy mouths
prepare your poison-filled needle
virgins made fecund by long centuries of modesty and decency
are impatiently awaiting the horn-thrust
their tender thighs, their soft breasts are crying out to be
attacked, to be bitten
leap at the opportunity
violate the sanctuary and the grotto, the citadel and the cavern,
the bastion and the alcazar
penetrate the hollow mercilessly
the Cunt, the Cunt, the Cunt!
and you, Celestina, wise and diligent guardian of maidenheads,
my mother and teacher, help me spread the net to capture and
doom to death this prey that has too long escaped me
in my army you will find
        a hidden flame
        a tasty poison
        a sweet bitterness
        a most enjoyable pain
        a joyous torment
        a deliciously cruel wound
        a voluptuous death
for each and every Melibea that our Celestinesque, celestinal
country engenders, produces, consumes, and exports
as you utter these phrases
o wondrous miracle of the Word!
the example is repeated on a national scale
and each and every Hispano will immediately offer, in filial,
pimpish, cuckoldish emulation of this model, his mother, his
wife, his sister, or his cousin

Teodora and Rufina
Brigida, Teresa, and Anna
Pascuala, Isabel, and Juana
Paula, Antonia, and Catalina
to the African warriors who attack, flay, smash, and shatter
arms and legs, slit throats, tear out hearts, strew viscera all
about in sudden, wholesale, contagious slaughter
as simonists and desecrators make their miraculous appearance
little Arab genies with post cards and souvenirs who fight over
the bloody remains and offer them to the ecstatic tourists
entering
continuing to enter
venturing farther and farther inside
penetrating the vulva and the hymen, the vagina and the
uterus, the ovaries and the Fallopian tubes
the meandering subterranean galleries of an empty cave
the Cunt, the Cunt, the Cunt!

less than a hundred yards away, in the historic tower of the
castle, Don Álvaro continues to recite, with broad, sweeping,
inspired gestures, a vast poem, a noble, exemplary, patriotic
epic with countless verses: as he painfully makes his way
toward you, the joints of his chitinous carapace, encrusted
with calcareous salts, creak and strain, and his mask representing the perfect Christian gentleman seems to have grown even
larger: the dimensions of his facial features are noticeably
larger than the average and the stiffness of his armor plating
make his resemblance to a crustacean even more striking,
a man of firm principles and the unswerving faith of the simple
in heart, conscious of bearing on his shoulders the weight of
an age-old tradition, and bearing in his hands the torch of an
imperishable spiritual message: he will affably invite you to
palpate the dermato-skeletal structure of his members and you

will hear him deliver a grave discourse on this bare, sparse land of ancient, impeccable Christian lineage, a heritage transmitted down through the centuries by the most incorruptible, the most honorable ancestors: Castile, eternal and unbending, the cradle of martyrs, the smithy of heroes, the crucible of saints: the Meseta, habitually producing abundant harvests of courage, self-sacrifice, and prayers: tortured mountain crags, tragic wastelands: a homeland oozing pus and grandeur through the cracking crusts of its scars: and at each phrase his carapace becomes more rigid, and his features increase in size and grow more inflexible

(morphology?

a carapace composed of thick horny polygonal scales

spiny?

probably

chelonian or saurian?

a heart with two auricles and one ventricle, short lateral appendages, skin covered with scales, scutella, and plates)

and now the mask grows even larger and turns into an enormous, grotesque *mascarón* which utters talismanic names without losing one iota of its rigidity: Herrera del Duque, it says, Mota del Cuervo, Motilla del Palancar: it becomes bigger and bigger and bigger, takes on monstrous proportions, stretches and stretches, and then dries up, its immobility rivaling that of statues; genius and the appearance of genius, and vice versa: Manolete, Seneca, the Cid: as he obliges you to feel the texture of his members, which now reaches the upper limits of the Mohs scale of hardness: a dark gray, granitic topography: granite: an extremely hard rock consisting essentially of quartz, feldspar, and mica: possibly containing an admixture of other minerals: 70 per cent silica: and the imposing *mascarón* keeps increasing in size as it recites the entire list of Gothic kings and all of the dramatic works of Lope the Phoenix, reads fragments of *Blood and Sand*, enumerates the overseas territories possessed

by Spain, sings of Hispanic towns heroically resisting siege:
and the *mascarón* continues to increase in size, expands like a
balloon, hovers, descends, and becomes immobile: turned into
a pedestal of its own statue, or a statue of its own pedestal, a
pure essence, genius and the appearance of genius, a Figurehead
of sheer divine afflatus: when the diameter of the mask exceeds
the limits of the room and your Jamesbondish courage falters,
you will establish contact with the men of your harka and ask
for instructions
Number One calling
Number Two, I read you
carefully adjusting the earphones, you will speak through the
little metallic circle, carefully hidden behind the curtain
nobility: honor: mysticism: thirst for adventure: genius and
the appearance of genius: mask: over
houseflies: houseflies: bees: horseflies: fatal poison
is that all?
that's all
thanks: out
the sound waves fade out: the communication has lasted forty-
five seconds: no danger of interference at this hour on this
wave length
standing atop the portable library ladder, Don Álvaro, having
been elected a member of the Royal Academy, now rehearses his
acceptance speech, a discourse entitled "A Few Remarks on the
Concept of Honor in the Seventeenth-Century Spanish Theater":
his style is lofty, his diction perfect: an abundance of quota-
tions, gleaned from the many volumes lining the shelves, relieves
the intellectual aridity of his chosen theme, adorning it with
elegant, pleasing flowers of rhetoric: what marvelous harmony,
what eloquent periods, what striking images!: in each part of
the speech, and in each paragraph of each part, what felicitous
ellipses and transitions and turns of phrase!: what *brio*, what
passion, what fire!: Don Álvaro's eloquence reaches the heights

of the sublime: dazzling figures of speech, synecdoche, metonymy, metaphor, follow one upon the other in dizzying succession, like a breathtaking display of fireworks: hyperboles, syllepses, antitheses which his beautiful bass voice emphasizes as his fossil hands run down the rows of books on the shelves and take down a paperbound copy of a masterful drama of honor

> I shall be a father rather than a spouse
> hallowed justice meting out
> stern but equitable punishment
> for a shameless affront to honor

his immense *mascarón* expresses indescribable rapture: the incomparable magic of Spanish poetry, of your incomparably sublime prosody!: a treasure zealously guarded in the academies and temples of Classic Style, a majestic, perfect, immutable literary canon!: and Don Álvaro's countenance continues to grow bigger and bigger, to stretch and extend, to swell and swell: a living incarnation of the genius and the appearance of genius of the noblest flower of the race, continuing his recitation in the most beautiful rounded tones until suddenly he stops short, having discovered the crushed remains of a fly at the end of the moving dialogue: a fly? yes, that's correct, sir: a diptera possessing a single pair of membranous wings, a buccal sucking apparatus, a trumpet-shaped lower lip, two antennae, six legs: a common housefly, the abdominal contents of which have been spattered over the verses of the drama, creating a tiny, irregular, star-shaped stain: Don Álvaro's brow wrinkles and the dermato-skeletal joints of his carapace creak: this interference appears to have taken him by surprise, and after a few moments' hesitation, he selects another volume from the shelf and continues his spirited recitation

> He who takes his vengeance in full light of day
> Twice tarnishes his honor

Since he not only loses it
But allows the world to witness his loss
this time it's a bluebottle fly, a live one, with hairy legs, very
much alive, that immediately takes wing and buzzes off through
the open window overlooking the boulevard: another pause and
another pained expression: Don Álvaro's mask contorts,
grimaces, creaks, and decreases in size: cracks appear in his
carapace and a fair number of scales fall off of it: it is much
smaller now: its facial features diminish in volume and its
articulated appendages shrink in size: an optical illusion?:
no, a genuine metamorphosis: the fear he once aroused in you
suddenly disappears: and at the same time, as though obeying
a law of hydraulics, fear mounts within him, as through a
syphon: symptoms?: a cold sweat, tremors, anxiety, palpitations: with feigned nonchalance, he will now choose another
volume and with a painful effort open it at random
What's this? By Heaven!
. . . May God be my witness!
My house this day shall see
Punishment visited upon you
a tsetse fly, a bee, and a horsefly prevent him from continuing:
adopting the classic V-formation, they fly back and forth, performing daring acrobatic tricks as Don Álvaro's mask visibly
shrinks, his countenance losing its rigidity and each of his
facial features seemingly becoming independent: he makes a
pathetic effort to keep his limbs from trembling, clears his
throat emphatically, assumes martial postures: but it is no
use: the granitic crust crumbles, the violent process of erosion
continues at an even swifter rate: the stony mass begins to
collapse, to crack to pieces, to scale away: and his stubborn
resistance to this headlong process of demolition merely hastens
its pace: particles of fine dust keep trickling down, as in an
hourglass, and at the same time an amazing reduction in the

size of the cranium takes place, accompanied by terrifying facial contractions worthy of Frankenstein at his very best: the trio of insects fly about in close formation, hovering, looping, and spinning like a crack aerobatic team staging a spectacular show during a splendid military parade: serious doubts as to his most cherished values assail him and spread like gangrene: help, he cries, help!: illustrious historical figures, inexhaustible resources of the Spanish language, ethical emanations, metaphysical vistas, come to my rescue!: and in a mad fit of frenzy, he grabs another volume and declaims

No Spaniard ever hesitates for one moment
to visit death upon the offender of his honor
or postpone for an instant the moment of vengeance
the only result of which is to cause a dense swarm of insects to fly out of the moldy pages of the book and cover every volume drowsing on the shelves in the space of a few seconds: *romancero, auto sacramental, libro de caballería,* come to my rescue, I beg you!: Cid Campeador, Manolete, Meseta, help, help!: mysticism, tauromachy, stoicism!: Seneca, Seneca, Seneca!: submerged beneath the buzzing swarms of insects copulating and reproducing, reproducing and copulating: eggs that turn into larvae, larvae that turn into pupae, pupae that turn into insects: houseflies, bees, ants, horseflies, spiders going in and out of the books, devouring the paper, corrupting their style, contaminating their ideas: Don Álvaro's mask deflates, shrivels, becomes a mass of wrinkles, and his limbs suffer an irresistible attack of Saint Vitus Dance: he murmurs Guadarrama, Gredos, my Spain hurts me, but it is no use: his face continues to shrink and grow flabbier and flabbier, his eyes become watery, his voice sounds more and more feminine: he makes a pitiful attempt to adjust to the changing times, he essays a few youthful smiles, he hums a Rolling Stones hit: the insects continue to buzz about, to copulate, to multiply, to feed on the masterworks on the shelves: lofty ideas, famous apho-

risms, perfect verses are voraciously devoured and slowly dissolve in the recesses of their abdominal mass: the Sonnet, the Sonnet! Don Álvaro pleads: our national patrimony, an artistic treasure, an imperishable jewel!: but the flies suck the syllables of the fourteen-line poems dry, one after the other: they steadily gain ground, overrun the second quatrains, and head straight for the tercets, thus sealing the fate of these hapless verses: as the sawdust keeps leaking out of Don Álvaro's ripped belly and his mask shrinks to the size of the handle of a walking-cane: stoicism, he whines: prehistoric bulls, the caves of Altamira: and the fat, hairy, iridescent flies suck and suck, soar overhead, hover, dive: they are hanging from the ceiling in thick bunches now, the bookshelves are black with them, they are the lords and masters of the place: the perfect Christian gentleman's voice quavers like an adolescent boy soprano's, he wriggles and writhes, and the whites of his eyes show: the custodian of the library takes his pulse and predicts the fatal end that awaits him: the group of tourists, the guide, the beggars from the market place, the gagged woman, the apprentice weavers surround him and stand there motionless, awaiting the expression of his dying wishes: Don Álvaro's breathing is very labored: his pale tongue protrudes tensely from between his teeth as he desperately attempts to pronounce a word: CU, he stammers: CU-CU-CU: cure, culpable, culture, curious?: his voice fades with a dying fall as the buzzing of the flies grows louder: Cuba, Cumberland, Cúcuta, Curie, Cuitláhuac, Curaçao?: when the custodian of the library closes Don Álvaro's eyes and respectfully bares his head, a dense silence falls upon the room: there is no possible doubt: the perfect gentleman has died: and before turning the corpse over to the grief-stricken family you will draft the following pious epitaph

> your Christian breast was so full of lofty desires for eternity that there was no room left for fear, and clutching the hallowed ancient banner, beneath the castle and

the lion that crowns the impregnable fortress of Spain,
you shed your last precious drop of blood, a faithful
soldier of a brave legion to the very end

penitential psalms, hoarse-voiced *mea culpas*, dazzling cabal-
istic emblems!
the Hispanic procession emerges from the church of Santa María
la Mayor, preceded by the Guardia Civil on horseback in dress
uniform: seven thousand faithful worshipers of the Nocturnal
Adoration with their crosses, their tapers, their pennants, their
banners: six lodges of the Fraternal Order of Crusaders clad
in severe tunics: the municipal band playing religious music:
countless men of the cloth chanting Eucharistic hymns: extra-
diocesan, diocesan, and parish priests in brilliant array: the
deacons of the cathedral and collegiate churches cloaked in
gold-embroidered copes: the papal legate accompanied by Pro-
thonotaries Apostolic, national prelates, secret chamberlains,
and chamberers
the cortege descends the Calle de Bravo Murillo, continues down
the Calle Fuencarral, enters the Calle de la Montera, and at the
Puerta del Sol other brotherhoods join it to swell the ranks of
the solemn, cathartic Silent Procession
yes, sir, yes, the great capital with its skyscrapers and its
spacious boulevards, the great carefree, joyous city of *la dolce
vita*, the wide-open city in all the senses of the word, Madrid,
the birthplace of the gallant compliment and the schottishe, one
of the world's few remaining pleasure cities, Madrid Madrid
Madrid we are homesick for you here in Mexico, Madrid today,
I repeat, is preparing to do penance in the style of the Middle
Ages
chains and iron shackles clamped tight around ankles! naked,
freezing-cold, bleeding feet! thousands of wooden crosses, hair
shirts, scourges!

ten thousand kilos of iron, fair ladies and good gentlemen!: chains purchased at the Flea Market for the equivalent of $8.45 (U.S. currency) or rented for a dollar a night at local hardware stores because the last-minute demand for them was enormous and the normal supply was nowhere near enough!

shops along the Calle de la Paz and numerous cloistered convents have sold thousands upon thousands of hair shirts made by our little nuns, using nothing but a pair of pincers or pliers and rolls of barbed wire: the side to be worn next to the skin is studded with points as sharp as razors, and there are styles for every taste: to be worn around the arm, the thigh, or the waist, as the consumer chooses

these hooded penitents headed this way, reeling and staggering as in Bergman's unforgettable film, come, ladies and gentlemen, from all ranks of society: army officers and members of the nobility, bankers and industrial tycoons, famous celebrities and stars fraternize and rub elbows with the poorest and most humble plebes: their spirit of penitence makes them all equal in the eyes of Our Lord, and like the hermits and anchorites of old, they mortify their senses in order to make themselves worthy of one day entering the Kingdom of Heaven with souls purified of all sin

the cross you see in the foreground is fashioned of a telephone pole and weighs more than two hundred pounds: it is privately owned, and has been borne each year for some time now by its devout owner, a young man who possesses a considerable fortune: a true Spanish *caballero* whom you may have met just a few hours ago in our famous Chicote Bar or one of our typical cabarets, such as the Corral de la Morería: he has forsaken worldly pleasures for the moment, and following a noble, age-old tradition in our country, he has donned the costume of an anonymous penitent as he mortifies his flesh in the manner of his forebears

the cicerone has ended his spiel and the bigwigs from the Bronx,

the furriers from Chicago, the gentleman farmer from Texas, the delegation of speleologists, the avant-garde music critics, the recently divorced married couple, and the war widows are smiling in chorus, directed by the distinguished baton of Mrs. Potiphar: their squint-eyed gaze converges upon the penitent dressed in a sanbenito, with a peaked hood atop his head, a scapular round his neck, a noose around his throat, and a candle in his hand, bearing the telephone pole down the street with the typical Madrileño name of Vía de la Amargura, today renamed the Vía de Séneca el Grande: the sharp-eyed gaze of a lynx can be glimpsed through the narrow slits of his hood and there are signs of a faint smile through the dark breath hole: his light, agile step is not at all like the awkward, ducklike waddle of his neighbors: bathed in the golden splendor of Holy Week the floats pass by one by one, laden with flowers, and the floods of tears and great drops of blood streaming down the emaciated faces of the Christs and the Sorrowful Virgins bring the crowd's religious fervor to fever pitch and cause heart-rending *saetas* to ring out, filling the dark night with Arabic memories
the wary eyes of the hooded penitent bearing the telephone pole sweep across the lavish stage set, and as the procession rounds the corner and heads down the narrow winding Calleja del Moro, the fraternal orders and brotherhoods undergo an astonishing transformation: Dr. Jekyll suddenly becomes Mr. Hyde: painlessly, however, with no grimaces: smoothly, with no hitches: the bodies of austere Chevaliers of the Blessed Death begin to writhe to the sound of the flutes, their hips and shoulders miraculously loosen up and follow the beat of the bongos: possessed by the demon of tropical music, amid the swan floats, the oyster-shell floats, the statuesque black Venuses with feather headdresses and flouncing fan-shaped trains: throwing handfuls of confetti, lascivious, clinging coils of *serpentin*: miracles, magic, in American technicolor!: as the dazzling procession with its gleaming asteroids and little Japanese lanterns passes

by: the gentleman with the telephone pole has cast off his penitent's hood and a snow-white turban now crowns his grinning traitor's face: he is you, Julian, ennobled and surrounded with the bright halo of your age-old treasonous crime!: your bushy eyebrows joyously arched, framing your alert eyes, your full lips baring sharp white teeth made for love bites, for passionate, virile kisses: the implacable pupils of your eyes search for toothsome young victims and attentively follow the fleeting silhouette of a blond-haired Catholic damsel: mercilessly, mercilessly!: and with every stage trick at your command, the puppet master par excellence, you will veil the tortured crowd of penitents by lowering a radiant succession of curtains and gauze flies: the natives are drinking rum, the mulatto girls are gently blossoming in their carnival costumes: the kettle-drummers are pounding away as though proclaiming the Last Judgment: a lazy, languid island inhabited by gentle, lovable, tame blacks!: a luxurious décor of palm trees and ornamental plants!: and the procession of your fauna continues on and on amid passionate males and foolish virgins, down the streets of the festive pagan city, amid the tumultuous joy of carnival time

all the lights in the theater have been turned off: the reel has stopped turning

you alone, James Bond in the flesh, nonchalantly striding across the room toward the calypso orchestra, illuminated by gleaming spotlights

at the cocktail hour, when city traffic is usually heavier, a perfect specimen of the *capra hispanica* makes its appearance at the corner of Callao and Granvía, in front of the subway entrance: we then see it successively standing at the underwear counter at the Galerías Preciados, visiting different museums and churches, giving a talk on "Ortega and the Chase" at the

Ateneo, having a drink, of Spanish wine, with friends in the
Chicote, holding forth on economic oligarchy at the Pelayo and
on polymembrous verse at the Gijón: not to mention the inevitable visit to Parliament, where it sits in the gallery reserved
for distinguished visitors, as your eminent deputies who hold
office by the grace of a well-known party and the intercession of
divine providence endlessly debate the fifth amendment to the
preliminary draft of the proposed law on the installation of a
sewage system at Quintanar de la Orden, with tropes and meta-
phors that would qualify them for the most celebrated literary
jousts, for the most bitterly fought Battle of Flowers
despite the presence of numerous journalists and photographers
and the exposure kindly offered them by the most popular television interviewers and the network cameramen, their goings
and comings are greeted with utter indifference by the very
urbane, anonymous, mass-media-conditioned multitude: dressed
in Catalan wool, bound in Mallorcan suede, shod in elegant
Italian-troubadour style moccasins: resplendent in their brand-
new, impeccably tailored Sunday best, all of them capable of
being summed up under the common denominator of the
radically and startlingly new: new bourgeois, new aristocrats:
new shop clerks, new employees: new civil servants, new
priests: new directors, new lords and masters of the very new,
brightly promising situation: industrial development, a consumer society!: massages, saunas, reducing clinics!: rusty
automobile graveyards!: electro-domestic evenings in front of
the recently acquired television set!: in complete, solemn
possession of their new status: taming Seats, breaking in
Dodges, domesticating Volkswagens, forcing the instrument
panel of the latest model Citroën to obey the rectilinear Spanish
will: determined to ride the very crest of the wave, to be IN:
Carnaby Street, Pierre Cardin ties, Bonnie and Clyde berets and
fedoras: thinking like self-made men, to be sure, but with the
unmistakable accent of the Madrid street urchin

this situation definitely cannot continue: technical experts will improve the structures: our destiny is European and the encyclical shows us the way: let us
conduct a *mezza voce* dialogue to educate the people:
computer calculations will eliminate the apparent class
contradictions

as the *capra hispanica* sadly takes its leave of the downtown
commercial center and the residential sections and makes its
way toward the much larger working-class suburbs: obeying
the municipal regulations governing the flow of pedestrian
traffic along the sidewalks and crosswalks, the boarded passage-
ways around construction sites and the safety islands: in the
midst of the hard-working laboring class, maternally protected
beneath the sheltering wing of your very Spanish system of
vertical labor unions: a rational, far-sighted, harmonious,
flexible arrangement!: healing balm for age-old historic injustices, an effective defender of the worker against his own
class: so easily swayed, alas, by plebeian demagoguery, by the
siren song of extremist propaganda: drawing up, very sensibly
and impartially, the guidelines for the peaceful coexistence of
all Spaniards, taking advantage of your solid spiritual scaffolding and respecting your age-old traditions: the politics of a
philosopher and a system whose beneficial results are obvious:
low-cost housing, cars on easy credit terms!: Sunday excursions
to the Sierra!: European stardom for Di Stefano, undying fame
for El Cordobés!: wandering among the endless massive blocks
of cement, each exactly like the other, erected on the ruins of
yesterday's straw huts and tin shanties: on to the bare, deserted
stretch of beach bordering a petrified sea, as vast and indifferent
as the universe itself: the Meseta, a flat plain, rugged and
barren Castile!: an anchoritic landscape, the most austere of
colors: vast, stern, severe, dead-still: solemn oaks enveloped
in absolute silence, naked spikes of rock: a breath of eternity,
spiritual thirst, the arid passion of the Iberian soul!: having

escaped from the feverish cityscape, the *capra hispanica* breathes a sigh of relief: the clear mountain air fills its tortured lungs: an agrarian sense of repose, peace and quiet, far from the madding crowd! its restless spirit calmed, meek and gentle, it seeks out quiet wooded glens, humble, fragrant rock-roses: wending its way along forest paths and trails, it comes at last to the foot of the first steep range of mountains: and there, standing on a picturesque hillock, it feeds on the fresh, tender grass and drinks from a crystal-clear little stream: at the hermitage of Arenas de San Pedro, where the monks serve free messes of pottage to travelers, it takes a meal, along with its mentor and counterpart the Hispano: and then after a refreshing siesta, the two of them begin the difficult, arduous ascent: from rock to rock, from crag to crag: climbing ever higher, through familiar landscapes reminiscent of Santa Teresa, to the soaring peaks where silence and freedom eternally reign: romances in Gredos, between shepherd boys and ugly scullery-maids!: the melodious murmur of waterfalls, wild ravines, atavistic yearnings for immortality!

installed in the comfortable government-run Tourist Parador, the men of your harka patiently survey the scene through their binoculars, and in the wink of an eye the hunting party is organized: there is not a moment to lose: you are pressed for time: you must finish off this destructive fauna once and for all: the shortest path between two points is by way of the stars: once this sibylline aphorism has been drummed into their heads, your chargers will spread their heel wings and fly, lightly and swiftly, to the very peaks of the fateful sierra: Moors in turbans, with bushy black beards and radiant smiles!: your shadows flit across the bright polished green of the mountains, as weightless as your steeds and your scimitars, whose thin blades cleave the air and whose sharp tips point to the lofty heights where the *capra* increases and multiplies and the Hispano prospers: purviews, as Figaro would say, that are amazingly fertile: places where all you need do is tap your foot on the ground and the next moment the inseparable couple appears before your eyes, with its imperious poetic genius, its thirst for adventure, its transcendent spiritual message: the bovid and the hominid: the *capra* with the straight, hollow, nonramified horns, and the Hispano, a species possessed of a notable lack of good sense, an extremely lean, spare frame, a very dry skin, legs and arms each of which has five digitate terminuses, and a curious lingual appendage with which it expresses itself, sings, prays, and receives communion: a most peculiar symbiosis!: the pack of hounds, held on gleaming leashes, pursues you, and agile Bedouin huntsmen cleave the thin air with their rich panoply of lassos, snares, lures, and traps: expert trackers and sharp-eyed game-beaters follow your spoor, dispatching acrobatic teams on stealthy reconnaissance missions to discover your precise whereabouts: the model couple apparently scent the danger: hominid and *capra* explore the secret possibilities of the mountain foliage, the hidden passes that may be their salvation: it is immediately evident that a return to a troglodytic civilization is the most viable solution: Spanish prehistory, the source of your purest and brightest essences!: concealed by the thick growth, they approach the mouth of the cave and slip into it, trusting in the aid of the Lord: but since the Lord is terrified by the fierce cruelty of your harkas, He will cautiously refrain from intervening and instead hide His great shapeless head behind the cotton veil of a cloud: if this is not so, what other explanation is there for the sudden end of history?: the Hispano and the *capra* have furnished the cave comfortably, and in order to keep their spirits up and kill time, they raise and lower flags, organize marches and parades, recite the holy rosary and sing the Hymn of the Legion: isolation doubtless predisposes one to self-deception and false euphoria, for their strategic analyses in no way represent an objective and realistic estimate of the situation: the airborne African horde is now hovering

above the imaginary refuge and the first explorers are landing
with their impatient mastiffs: the search for the airstrip will
be immediately successful: the game-beaters occupy the neigh-
boring heights and any attempt to escape is doomed to failure:
a fiendishly clever trap, a net woven as if by magic, thanks to
the inspiring lesson in showmanship provided by your light-
footed flying steeds: the ends of the aerial host's turbans flutter
like flags and the thunderous neighing of the beasts mingles
with the prodigious outpouring of laughter from the men: the
coursers will gracefully alight near the Altamiresque grotto and
the feathered wings of that nice little god, Mercury, will beat
gently and then fold back around his slender legs: the denouement is close at hand now and the old medieval romances of the
Hispano and the turds of the *capra* are irrefutable proof of the
presence of victims in this spot: the horsemen have unsheathed
their curved scimitars and are crouching, silent and feline,
awaiting your orders: the great breadth and depth of the evil
make energetic, immediate therapy necessary: the couple must
die: their broken bodies will gleam like trophies at the end
of the pikes: their souls will ascend to the stars and their
corpses will push up daisies: a radical divorce!: and then
with your army's steeds saddled once again, you will gallop and
gallop, an aerial species, light as a feather, with your dense
horde of mounted acrobat-warriors at your side, along the crest-
line of Guadarrama and San Vicente, Fuenfría and Peña de
Francia, and if the obtuse Hispano and the stubborn *capra* cross
your path, you will throw yourself upon them and run them
through with your scimitar: the soul to the stars, yes indeed,
the soul will ascend to the stars and the body, nothing but
food for buzzards, will plummet to earth and push up daisies!:
and you will fly on and on with your powerful antidote:
gunsmoke-curing, preventive scorching: until you have forever
uprooted them from their rocks and crags, their Alpine raptures,
their lofty apotheoses: when this self-perpetuating, noxious

species becomes extinct and the new fauna imported from Australia takes over throughout the liberated countryside, you will gather your jubilant warriors together, and in Koranic language, order them to move on
a blind sun, thirst, fatigue!: with hundreds of his men, dust, sweat, and iron, Ulyan gallops across the terrible Castilian steppe toward the next resting place

you lack a language, Julian!
from platform and pulpit, from academic chairs and churches, from daises and speakers' stands, Hispanos proudly proclaim that language is their very own private property
it is ours, ours, ours, they say
it is we who created it
it belongs to us
we are its masters
scholars, holders of graduate degrees, oracles, wise men, experts, specialists wave the title deeds proving their rights of sovereignty, possession, usufruct
it's ours, ours, ours
under exclusive license
patented model
registered trade-mark
all rights reserved, worldwide
ours, ours, ours
the image of our soul
the mirror of our mind
ours, ours, ours
apostolic
transcendental
ecumenical
we transported it across the Atlantic, along with our morality and our laws, the ear of grain and the plow, religion, justice

to eighteen nations who today speak and think, pray, sing, write
as we do
daughter nations
hence their children
our grandchildren
are Castilians too
eternal essences
imperious poetic genius
an ascetic and militant conception of life
though we have lost our scepter, our empire, our sword
all our territories on which for centuries the sun never used
to set
we still have the Word left
we may lose Gredos
the Spanish earth
the *capra*
but never the Word
there may be fewer poplars
and more tourists
but the Word will remain constant
neither more nor less
and now the sublime chorus of their voices crosses the ocean
and swells like thunder, thousands and thousands of miles away
in the pulque-bars of Lagunilla in Mexico City
in the Calle de Corrientes in Buenos Aires
in the Jesús María district of Havana
and the Tlaxcalan
the Argentinian
the Yoruban
will be surprised and indignant to hear it and their glib tongues
will begin to wag

      hombre, what the fuck's gotten into those spics! the
      sonsabitches got it into their thick heads that their

gift of the gab's the living end. Ain't none of their
fuckin' business how I sling their damned lingo, and that
Lope-cat, or whatever his name is, don't cut no ice with
me, man. He probly a limp-dick bastard like all the
rest of 'em, couldn't get it up if you shoved a red-hot
chili up his ass, hombre! I'd like to see them fancy-
pants fairies try to make out with the pieces of tail
we got around here: it'd be a *noche triste*, that's for
sure! I know a couple of whores who'd turn 'em to tiger-
butter in no time. We may be little black sambos, but
we've got 'em comin' and goin' in the hot-lay department

hey, señor, you lookin' for fucky-fucky? virgin pussy,
señor? I got a sister, nice clean girl, good manners, very
cheap, hot stuff, special deal, okay, señor?
join forces with them, Julian
LA PROPRIÉTÉ C'EST LE VOL
ET
TÔT OU TARD
LA CLASSE POSSÉDANTE SERA DÉTRUITE
oh prophets of Baghdad, Córdoba, Damascus!: oh my beautiful,
noble language, the weapon of treason: a gleaming, sharp-
honed scimitar, an army of cruel, burnished blades!
rally round me, ye pure-blooded Bedouins: warriors who daily
confront death with a scornful smile, horsemen with coarse
lips, swelling jugular veins, rough-hewn features
gaze upon the tempting Straits with your piercing, rapacious
eyes: the succession of white waves furiously galloping toward
the enemy coast: foamy crests, like brood stallions neighing
furiously as they plunge into the sea: the burning sands of
Tarifa, the eagerly awaiting rock of Gibraltar!
your lexicon must be rescued: the age-old linguistic fortress

must be dismantled: the circulation of language must be paralyzed: its sap must be sucked dry: words must be removed one
by one until the crepuscular edifice, bled dry, collapses like
a house of cards

and galloping with them as they mount their furious attack, you
will lay waste to their fields of cotton and alfalfa and carob
beans

you will demolish arsenals and magazines, sink feluccas, pillage
alcoves

you will carry off sofas and divans, mattresses, muslins, and jars
you will kill albatrosses

you will deprive the astrologer of his azimuth, the alchemist of
his elixirs, the assassin of his scimitar

you will remove chess sets from casinos, and the asphalt from
highways

you will forbid salaams, masquerades, the hazarding of guesses

when the diner with a paunch as round as Sancho Panza's and a
gluttonous appetite sits down at the groaning board, with a
damask napkin tucked under his chin, and after saying the
customary blessing, is on the point of digging into the viands
set before him by headwaiters and costumed servants, you will
threaten him with your whalebone rod, backed by the authority
and the prestige of your imposing lexicographic diplomas

you are to eat, Señor Hispano, only according to the uses and
customs of the other islands I have inhabited: I am a grammarian, sir, and safeguard the purity of my native tongue with much
more zeal than my own health, poring over my books night and
day, studying the constitution of the Hispano so as to be able
to cure him should he happen to fall ill: and my principal
concern is watching over his meals and repasts, allowing him
to partake of only those dishes that seem to me to be of native
origin and forbidding him everything that is etymologically
foreign to him: and for this reason I order oranges, rice, and
apricots to be removed from the table

but in that case these roast partridges that have been set before me, which appear to be perfectly seasoned, will doubtless do me no harm

the esteemed Spanish gentleman is not to eat partridges as long as I live

and why is that?

why is that? because they have been seasoned with saffron

in that case, I pray the esteemed grammarian to take a look at all the dishes on the table, and tell me which of them will do me the most good or the least harm and allow me to eat my fill of it, for I swear on my life as a Hispano (and may the saints preserve me), I am dying of hunger: and whatever Your Lordship the grammarian may say, keeping me from eating will shorten my life rather than lengthen it

you are perfectly correct, Your Grace: and that is why I think it best that Your Grace refrain from eating those fricasseed rabbits on the table in front of you, for they are garnished with artichokes: and as for that roast of veal, Your Grace must refrain from partaking of it, for it is garnished with spinach

that steaming tureen farther down the table appears to me to be an olla-podrida, and such a dish is composed of so many diverse ingredients that I will undoubtedly find some small morsel within it that will be tasty and good for my health

absit!: banish any such thought from your head!: there is nothing in the world that is worse than an olla-podrida with tarragon and other such spices: and as for the desserts that may be offered you, there is not a single one that I can permit Your Grace to eat: custard is forbidden because it has caramel sauce: ice cream has sugar in it: and the fruit cup has been marinated in syrup: as for the delicious sherbet that Your Grace has just been served, to doubt is to offend: it is etymologically beyond the pale!

and leaving the Hispano full right and title to enjoy his hunger, you will gallop on through the flourishing, prosperous kingdom

of Peace, Development, and Order, and provoke financial disasters and frightful catastrophes on the stock market through the sudden elimination of all tariffs
you will leave shop owners to weigh and measure their merchandise without benefit of quintals or carats
you will remove algebra from the school curriculum and deprive accountants of the use of Arabic numerals
you will gallop on and on, enrolling alguazils, admirals, and alcaldes under your banner
you will requisition alcoholic beverages
you will close down the stables of *alezans*
you will spread infection and disease by doing away with the *alcantarillas*, the sewage system so laboriously built by the Moors
you will gallop and gallop, never resting, through the ravaged countryside, and when the ruin is total and the destruction complete, you will halt before the man of the Peninsula and point with your whalebone rod
oh, I forgot: remove the Guad-el-Kebir as well!

don't forget to do away with the *olés*
in the bullring, the navel of the Hispanic nation (continually absorbed in narcissistic self-contemplation), Seneca, the Nietzschean *torero* of virtue, the squat (but not squatting) stoic philosopher, is gravely and modestly passing on the rudiments of his exquisite salon philosophy: serene passes by a noble *caballero*, confronting, hand over his heart, the *bos primigenius*, a pure geometric theorem, resolving, in the perfectly rounded zero of your nothingness, the very Hispanic philosophical equation with gestures and postures that cause the dense crowd stuffed full of chick-peas to swoon with ecstasy: pontifical poses, regal, royalist passes to the right: advancing step by step, with studied nonchalance, toward the vast phenomenological perspective: with his unique native gift for intuitively grasping

spatial relations and forcing his audience to accept the incontrovertible mathematical and choreographic proof of the slippery,
slithery theorem: brilliant capework, astounding *manoletinas*,
verónicas, *zunzabiriquetas*, and *orteguinas*, clever, feather-light,
acrobatic syllogisms that have enormously enriched your cultural patrimony, century after century: ethero-musical elucubra-
tions emanating from your cinematic taurine steppes that bring
forth a chorus of *olés* from the depths of the cavernous glottis to
spur on the philosopher dancing in the naked center of the Great
Navel!: an enormous cavity, a terrifying slit in the suntanned
belly of the nation, just above the limp lettuce leaf and its bushy,
luxuriant, useless undergrowth: as Urus, brave but bedazzled,
attacks the dizzying, continuously moving casuistic target: the
axiomatic verticality of the expert, who slowly pivots on his
heels, illuminated by a blinding Leibnizian flash of intuition: by
the *philosophischen Schriften* of Gottfried Wilhelm Leibniz:
amid the thundering chorus of thousands of voices shouting at
fever pitch: wave after wave of *olés*, a *mare magnum* hailing
the perfect execution of the theorem, the cornerstone of your
Hispanic body of doctrine: the *olé*, Julian, the *olé*!: the
marvelous, age-old wa-l-lah! remove the vulgar rust that has
corroded its surface, restore its original luster! may the
messianic throats uttering it suddenly atrophy and fall silent:
without this mystico-visceral accompaniment the philosophical
dance of the *torero* will lose its majestic dignity, his movements
will become awkward, he will be suddenly panic-stricken: the
cape will fall from his hands, his suit of lights will dim, his
limbs will be seized with helpless tremors: trapped in the
obscene ring, he will make one empty gesture after another, like
a marionette awkwardly flopping and jerking about after the
puppet master has let go of the strings: the Arab Thur will
then launch his attack, with all the force of his long-contained
fury, and his horns will not be aimed at the sophistic cape: oh
what a fateful hour five o'clock in the afternoon is, five o'clock

on the dot, on every clock and watch, five o'clock in the afternoon shadow!: watch closely: the spectacle is magnificent: the
philosopher is standing there waiting, trembling from head to
foot, as though suddenly overcome with a dread attack of Saint
Vitus dance, and the horn passes straight through his body,
amid the silence decreed by law: why is no sound heard from
this great people trapped within the vague confines of this vast
arena?: not a single cry, not one lament: only your laughter,
Julian, the lord and master of the *wa-l-lah*, hovering above the
barren land, a ravaged navel without a voice, abandoned to the
erosion of the ages

part four

They're devouring me, they're devouring me in the very place where my sin was greatest

—ANONYMOUS: *Romance del rey Rodrigo*

He is trapped in Julian's grasp
his neck caught in a strangle-hold
Towering over him, Julian points at his throat
a cruel dagger, that chills his heart;
the more desperately he struggles
the tighter Julian's death-grip becomes

—JOSÉ DE ESPRONCEDA: *El Pelayo*

according to reports that would appear to be reliable, since they are supported by a vast accumulation of data based on your mythical and quintessentially Spanish theory of information (a theory which, as we know, is fed by wellsprings of profound, hallowed truths, as the foreigner is opportunely reminded by the vast mural commissioned by the young and dynamic herald, the eventual successor of your Seneca: a symbol of the first message ever recorded in the annals of history, famous throughout the world, as a well-known specialist would put it, for *la enorme quantità di informazione in una sola comunicazione*: since, *come è noto*, according to the aforementioned specialist, *la quantità di informazione dipende della probabilità: quanto meno probabile è l'apparizione de quelle unità di cui è composta una certa comunicazione, tanto maggiore è l'informazione in essa contenuta*: the blond, plump, auspicious messenger of the Lord transmitting to the blushing Virgin the improbable, and therefore very substantially informative, unit of communication having to do with the unexpected benefits of the visit of a dove which, because of its plumpness, whiteness, and brightness, gives rise to an excusable confusion in the mind of the pious contemplator of the mural, who is uncertain as to whether it is the Holy Ghost as invoked by the buxom Mahalia Jackson or an advertisement for Maggi chicken bouillon): in a certain small village deep in the woods there lives a little boy, the most beautiful child that the human mind can possibly imagine: the agencies have not announced how old he is, but they have reported that the youngster in question has a halo of red-gold hair that the very sun would envy: that his eyes are bright blue bits of sky that God has given him, his mouth as delicate as a strawberry, and his ears two pearly sea shells: Alvarito's mother naturally adores him: but his grandmother is even more passionately fond of him: she does not know what to do, how to caress this darling little angel, how to cosset him to show how much she idolizes him: Granny showers him with presents, and it is in fact she who knit him a little red riding hood, which looks so adorable on the curly-headed little blond boy that people take to calling him Little Red Riding Hood, and in fact eventually forget his real first name (there follows at this point a number of anatomico-moral descriptions of the aforementioned child: white skin, delicate hands, curly eyelashes, affectionate nature, pure and virtuous, *mutatis mutandis*, varying according to the particular communications code employed by the various information agencies and the gnosiological purpose for which each is intended):

oh Mama, what delicious little cakes: are they for me? (recipe: ¾ pound cooky crumbs, ½ cup powdered sugar, 6 egg yolks, 1 teaspoon cinnamon, 1 orange slice, 1 cup milk, sprinkling of hazelnuts)

no, my darling Little Red Riding Hood

you know how fond I am of them! (1½ cups milk, ½ cup powdered sugar, 4 eggs, ½ cup candied fruit, 2 tablespoons butter, 1 tablespoon rum, few drops vanilla)

they're for your granny: she's sent word that she's not feeling well

not feeling well? (alarmed): what's the matter with her?

I'm sure it's nothing serious: but I want you to go see her and take her these cakes and this little jar of butter

gosh darn! all right, I'll go right away

yes, please: put everything in this little basket and hurry to Granny's as fast as you can

Alvarito doesn't need to be coaxed: he climbs up on a chair, takes the basket down from the cupboard shelf, puts the little cakes and the butter in it, climbs carefully down off the chair, gives his beloved mama a kiss, and leaves his house

as he traverses the woods, he does a number of good deeds, performs several charitable acts that we should like to list in detail (in the frantically materialist-minded world we live in, the vectorial axis of the mass media as a general rule unfortunately skirts these ontological categories so fraught with luminous and transcendental meaning): he picks a caterpillar up off the road and places it along the edge, thus preventing its probable death beneath the shoe sole of some absent-minded passer-by: he props up the stem of a flower drooping in the summer heat: he puts out crumbs of bread for starving birds: he gently but firmly fustigates two scandalously immodest flies locked together *ex commodo* in fulminous, sonorous copulation: he assumes an elective office with the tacit approval of the inhabitants of the forest: one restless squirrel, one far-sighted rabbit, and an owl or two with a wise, introverted look about them: and he prays as well: brief ejaculations in Latin and prayers rich in indulgences, the approximate total of which, with expenses deducted, adds up to the astronomical figure of 31,273 years: my beloved Mother: Aqueduct of divine graces: Queen of heaven and earth: Advocate and refuge of sinners: Immaculate daughter of Joachim and Anna: as a consequence: fifteen souls in purgatory are relieved of their spiritual and corporeal punishments or have them reduced according to the most faithful and most obedient calculations of the I.B.M. machine: and there is even the possibility that a mentally retarded child or a Mongolian idiot may be rescued from limbo: a journey of a little over a kilometer put to good use, in short: time is money, as the English say: Alvarito continues on at a smart pace and finally arrives at one of the prefabricated chalets in the superdeluxe GUADDARAMA HOUSING DEVELOPMENT (do you enjoy breathing the pure, fresh air of the great forests? do you enjoy lingering on the banks of a quiet little stream trickling down to the vast plains below, listening to the hum of bumblebees? do you enjoy stretching out on soft grass, basking in the sun's warm caresses? do you enjoy drowsing beneath the green leaves of the trees, hearkening to the trill of the nightingale, the song of the lark? do you enjoy peacefully contemplating the crystalline depths of mountain lakes?

do you enjoy rocking your troubled spirit to sleep to the soothing rhythm of a babbling brook? do you enjoy scaling mountain
peaks and bursting into joyous song once you have reached the
summit? A SAFE INVESTMENT: CONVENIENT CREDIT PLAN:
15:35:07, according to the DAY-DATE ROLEX OYSTER: weight 3.7
ounces, 18-carat-gold band: automatic, antimagnetic, waterproof: knock, knock!
who's there?
it's Little Red Riding Hood, bringing you some little cakes and
a jar of butter from Mama
come in, child, come in: lift the latch and push the door open
functional interior suited to the axiological categories of the
landscape: an austere décor, indirect lighting, a living room
with a fireplace, a completely equipped kitchen, with formica
cabinet tops and breakfast table, a matching dining-room set,
parquet floors, wooden door and window frames, kerosene
furnace and central heating, a bathroom with a shower, a built-in
toilet deodorizer, a bidet with a central hot and cold mixing
tap: A REAL BARGAIN: A DREAM COME TRUE
how are you, Granny?
I've got a terrible cold
Ulbán (for there's not the slightest doubt: it's you!) disguises as
best he can the deep timbre of his voice (the raped, dis-
membered body of his granny is lying under the mattress)
quick, close the door, you're letting a cold draft in
what shall I do with the presents Mama gave me for you?
put them on the mantelpiece and come lie here beside me, please
yes, Granny
Alvarito, obedient as always, undresses and gets into the bed:
but the moment he slides in between the sheets he is amazed to
see how odd his granny looks this afternoon: an Arab with a
ruddy complexion, tiger's eyes, a handlebar mustache, razor-
sharp claws capable of tearing a pack of cards in two
oh, Granny, what big arms you have!

the better to hug you with, my dear
oh Granny, what big legs you have!
the better to run with, my little darling
oh, Granny, what big ears you have!
the better to hear you with, my little sweetheart
oh, Granny, what big eyes you have!
the better to see you with, my pet
oh, Granny, what a big snake you have!
the better to penetrate you with, you stupid little idiot!
and as you utter these words, you will bury the serpent in the
child's body and slit his throat with your gleaming Toledo blade
sound track: a scream from Alvarito, as when someone falls
into a well, never to wake up again

no
that's not the way
death is not enough
his destruction must be accompanied by the most refined tortures
famished dogs
bloodthirsty wolves
leeches
they will drink his young, fresh, pure blood
along with six other young lads and seven young virgins
he will be sacrificed
helpless and defenseless
to the monster shut up in the tortuous labyrinth of Crete by
King Minos
lion cubs
seemingly tame and gentle
will become metamorphosed at the very first bite
and will leap upon him
pitilessly
fiercely

sinking their teeth
burying their claws
in his pain-wracked body
as he stands chained to a rock in the Caucasus, an eagle hovers
overhead, tracing vast fateful circles in the sky
patiently waiting
and then suddenly
diving on him with dizzying swiftness
and devouring his liver
Alvarito-the-bird hops from branch to branch, but cannot resist
looking
cannot keep his eyes off the evil serpent
a secret force attracts him
hypnotizes him
overpowers him
the reptile's awesome, imperious gaze draws him closer
closer and closer and closer
as the serpent wraps him in its coils
slowly and voluptuously
and tenderly
very tenderly
(as one embraces a child)
strangles him
Alvarito-the-insect
all unsuspecting
flits gaily about
circling the lip of an insidious carnivorous plant
we have a premonition of what is about to happen
attracted by its gorgeous colors, the little innocent will alight
on one of the deadly hairy leaves
and that is precisely what happens
without our being able to prevent it
he is immediately trapped, like a fly on the sticky surface of
a strip of flypaper

the leaf
greedily enfolds him
immobilizes him with its sticky-sweet juices
sinks its hairs into his soft flesh
ladies and gentlemen
we beg you not to look at
this horrible sight
overly sensitive spectators may faint dead away
the plant has now encapsulated him
and is sucking out his thyroid and hormonal secretions
his bone marrow
his aortal artery
his ganglia
his mucous membranes
his brain
and when in a few days its leaves unroll again
close your eyes
or otherwise you will see
(and we earnestly advise against it)
a little heap of bones
with not one shred of meat left for the buzzards
stripped absolutely clean
at the bottom of a precipice
amid towering jagged peaks
a raging torrent flows
a bridge spans the abyss
a bridge that becomes narrower and narrower, until finally it
is no more than one thin plank
our young Álvaro crosses it
with flaming cheeks
and burning eyes
he is heedless of the yawning abyss
the dizzying chasm below
his eyes are riveted on

the seductive, provocative silhouette of a lascivious woman on
the other shore
Death is there
at his side
with a cold, ironic smile on her face
holding in her hands an hourglass, the sands of which have
almost run out
Álvaro reaches the wooden plank
and rides on farther and farther
in a moment
he will fall
he will be plunged
into the yawning chasm below
the gaping abyss that awaits him
he will die
we are certain he will die
a lingering, hideously painful death
if Bond does not come to his rescue
but Bond will not intervene
no one will intervene to save him
your irredeemable hatred of the past and the bastard child that
represents it
calls for a sacrificial death, and a splendid magic ritual to
accompany it
(the proper lighting effects, atmosphere, and setting and a
sober, discreet *mise-en-scène*)
probe your innermost heart
root out all pity
all sense of restraint
every tender feeling
every impulse to be kind and forgiving
(sex alone
and its naked violence)
you are Julian

you know the way
let no respect, no humanitarian considerations stand in your way

in a forgotten quarter of this city whose name you would like to forget (lovely, quiet streets, laid out by the generous compass of the land-surveyor, branded with the searing imprint of their transparent clear origins: iron fences topped with spikes, walls bristling with broken glass, romantic gardens, a faint scent of lime trees: a hushed, dreamlike universe: winding paths, reflecting pools, summerhouses, wicker chairs, pots of hydrangeas, croquet wickets, mah-jongg counters, silver teaspoons: morally uplifting reading, faded copies of *Signal*, old tennis courts overgrown with weeds: villas only recently occupied once again by their owners in the happy days of rationing and Falange handouts: a premonopolistic, bourgeois system, antedating the tourist invasion, the development plan, and the international apotheosis of the Ubiquitous One: a world that has disappeared today) you were a witness and a part of the story (not a love story, one of blood and crime), the violent, fascinating legend of Julian (whose long-ago treason is not a sad story, nor is it one unworthy of being celebrated in prose and verse: the most beautiful, the most splendid resources of your language will fail to do it justice): you and your robust companion, the serpent: an indispensable prolongation of yourself and your will: rebellious, viscous, ready to rise up, to leap upon the victim, and inject in it the deadly liquid that will slowly spread throughout its body and inevitably bring about its death: possessed of a thick, spherical hood and an imposing, giant trunk: if aroused by some stimulus, the serpent assumes a defensive stance, rising up vertically, a flat coil serving as a base, spreading its hood like a parasol and thrusting its head forward: this is what will no doubt happen this afternoon as the youngster is returning home from school, following his usual route, his book bag slung

over his shoulder: the youngster? what youngster?: you yourself a quarter of a century ago, a diligent, conscientious student,
who adores his mother and in turn is adored by her, who is
admired and cherished by his teachers and classmates: a thin,
frail youngster: huge eyes, pale white skin: not the slightest
trace of a beard profaning his softly rounded cheeks: not gay
and carefree, but on the contrary quite uneasy: plagued by
presentiments and desires, the graceful, coveted prey of demons
and incubi: crossing the street at the same hours every day,
always alone, lost in dark daydreams or absorbed in reading
some book: passing by the wooden watchman's shack where
you live: the fearsome guardian of the mysteriously interrupted
building project: the foundations of an immense villa destined
to flatter the vanity of some businessman who has made himself
a dizzyingly vast fortune in the black market: cranes, jackhammers, all sorts of machinery rusting under faded canvas
covers: bare, ugly scaffolding, iron skeletons: and there among
the buckets of tar and the sacks of cement, your shack: a
rudimentary stove, a shelf for your clothes, an old dented pail,
a kerosene lamp, an iron cot with rumpled covers: raindrops
patter monotonously on the corrugated-tin roof and as you
walk along your boots sink in the mud: an improvised walkway
consisting of a single plank leads to the water tank and the
toilet: there are footprints still visible in the soft clay soil,
and trapped in the mud is the high-heeled shoe of some
Cinderella who shared your bed for a few hours and then hastily
fled during your opaque, fitful sleep: disheveled, in tears,
filled with remorse, cursing herself for losing her head and
vowing never to do so again: this particular chapter is common
knowledge now, and the once quiet, peaceful atmosphere in this
neighborhood has given way to a vague, indefinable sense of
malaise: when they pass by your shack the respectable middle-
class people who live close by lower their voices and hasten
their step: all sorts of stories have been going the rounds about

you and the extraordinary dimensions of your snake: hurry up, child, don't loiter, mothers say to their daughters: but the young girls' eyes linger longer than they should on the wooden shack where you live, vainly attempting to penetrate the mystery that it conceals: it is said that these girls come to see him at night: how do they dare!: the very thought sends shivers up my back: bits of conversation that reach your ears in the early autumn twilight as fearful wraiths hurry down the street to the corner and a furtive Catholic hand makes the sign of the cross: may God preserve us from this man and his fierce attributes: don't look at him: they say his eyes can hypnotize you: and the street suddenly empties and even house pets flee you: wasn't a dead cat found hanging by the neck from one of the plane trees on the boulevard?: its rigid body swung back and forth in the wind for several days without any charitable soul bothering to take it down, and rumor has it that you are guilty of this misdeed, although there is no proof that it is your doing (you take endless precautions and yet you never seem to be careful enough): women and children desert this section of town, wandering off like a surly herd of sheep abandoned by their shepherd: the darkness intensifies the aura of danger and keeps you in a state of acute nervous tension: gardens surrounded by fences, mansions full of watchful eyes, damp vegetable odors, muted whispers of the wind among the myrtles: the gas lamps shed no more than a feeble glow, the lighted windows in the ivy-covered façades go dark one by one: the only glimmer of light is that shed by a flickering street lamp, as insomniac as the little vigil flame burning on an altar: and one night: or rather one evening, as so many times before, you will watch for the slender silhouette of the youngster coming home from school with his book bag slung over his shoulder to pass by, and suddenly find yourself face to face with him: thin and frail: huge eyes, pale white skin: not the slightest trace of a beard profaning his softly rounded cheeks: you yourself a quarter of

a century ago: doing homework for Natural Science class or
absorbed in trying to solve a difficult problem, walking along
unhurriedly to the edge of the construction site, then hastening
his step as if the rumor blackening your name had already
reached his ears: his heart begins to beat faster and the
blood drains from his cheeks: he will turn his head (fearfully
but also hopefully), having intuitively grasped, perhaps, the
irrefutable logic of your presence, of the strong, constricting
ties that will unite you later: bumping into the thin, horizontal
board fencing and suddenly fleeing (not his destiny, but this
brief instant) as fast as his legs can carry him: time gained,
time lost?: it all depends: both things, and neither: you will
never be able to say: a mere truce, perhaps, that later will
serve to enhance the tremendous importance of your encounter:
of the wordless pact that sooner or later will seal your mutual
fate: one day and another and yet another: vainly peering
through the cracks between the planks, lips brushing the wood,
inhaling deeply the heavy, disturbing odor of your lair: you and
your stout companion: the serpent: already erect and ready to
inject the deadly liquid secreted by its glands: poisonous fangs
situated in the anterior part of the jaw or erectile and retractable: an Oriental cobra or an Amazon rattlesnake: with scaly
rings, rising up in a defensive stance, thrusting its hood
forward: the child appears to be listening to the music, for he
is swaying back and forth, back and forth, following the invisible
movements of the magnetizer: your movements, Julian, there
inside the shack as you patiently await the moment to pierce
him and inject your poison: as will inevitably happen the
moment certainty takes possession of his tender heart and his
brief resistance suddenly collapses: irresistibly attracted by the
mystery concealed by the planks, already an unwitting captive
of the serpent and its expert charmer: from now on any pretext
will serve to justify his visits: the instant, dreamed of a
thousand times, when he arrives at your door and lightly grazes

it with his knuckles: a message he's been asked to deliver, the
wrong address, a drink of water, a lost balloon?: you will accept
no such excuses: there is no need to try to hide the truth: the
grave, mute look in his eyes says more than any possible words
he might utter: he will slowly walk down the deserted street,
and after making sure that no one is watching, he will slip
through the board fence surrounding the lonely site, traverse the
plank across the mire, and halt on the threshold of your shack:
Cinderella's shoe is clearly visible in the mud: the rain falls
monotonously: time seems suspended: will he escape once
again?: an interminable pause: then (reality? dream?) there
is a flurry of hurried knocks at the door: you open it, and there
he is: thin and frail: huge eyes, pale white skin: not the
slightest trace of a beard profaning his softly rounded cheeks:
you yourself a quarter of a century ago: an incredible encounter!: and you drag him into the bed with cool, deliberate
violence and show him your inseparable companion: the viper:
flat triangular head, forked tongue, hinged jaw that allows it
to swallow huge prey, divided lower maxillary, hollow fangs:
or perhaps a cobra: scaly coils, assuming a defensive stance,
hood thrust forward: toward the paralyzed, mute child, who
cannot take his eyes off you as the bellicose reptile rises up, and
on feeling him there so close beside you, your blood surges
toward him, wave upon wave, unable to contain itself: sweeping
him into your imprisoning arms: enormous, hairy, autonomous:
with a hoarse desire to squeeze his frail body and crush it: but
the hour to do so is not yet come, as both of your two protagonists
are well aware: the destructive process has not yet begun:
this is only the preamble to the story: and taming him with
flattery and soft caresses, you will initiate him into the cult
of the serpent: a deceptive love-discipline that makes it
more voracious and feeds its wrath: reechy rasputinous kisses
learned in church or in a bordello, from the mouth of a knowing
whore or the drivel of a tormented confessor: until finally

you slip the cobra in with a perfectly aimed, vigorous thrust, stifling the cry of terror with a sudden swift blow of your great paw: it's nothing, my pet, nothing: I am Bulian, your admirer and friend: the poor caretaker of an ill-advised, useless, abandoned building project: the social abyss that separates us has prevented me from confessing my passionate love for you, but the love you have so generously shown me may yet redeem me: hearken to my words: have faith in me: a wicked fairy, in an access of menopausal fury, reduced me to this sad state and shut me up in a dark, cruel tomb with no other company save that of a starving snake: only the radiant beauty of a graceful youth can appease her wrath: if you were willing to suffer in my place, I should be eternally grateful: do not allow my savage countenance to frighten you, I pray you: my tenderness lies entirely below the surface: and the love you inspire in me is boundless: I should like to slash my breast open with a knife, slip you into the very depths of my heart, and then seal my breast again: a false declaration, by a swindler or a poet, from another place, another time, that you will murmur to him: or another version: without a mask or a smile or poison: inserting the viper with one sudden, naked thrust: I don't care whether you like it or not, you're going to take every last inch of it: and he (it's better this way) screams and screams: and you keep penetrating deeper and deeper: go ahead, bawl your head off if you like, nobody can hear you (the sober-faced neighborhood ostriches are prudently hiding in their well-protected redoubts): and he keeps screaming (it's better this way) and you keep flailing away: it's no use struggling, you're going to get it anyway: you finally decide you definitely prefer the second version: it's livelier, faster-paced, and also more direct: the child tormented by the asp and the asp aroused by the child: and in the background the soft flute melody, skillfully executed by you, the charmer: as the child sobs and trembles and the pacified serpent returns to its lair: I'll be waiting for you tomorrow, my pet: we'll begin all over again tomorrow: and the child breaks the spell: overcome with remorse, he solemnly swears that it won't happen again, invoking God and the Blessed Virgin and the Saints, without daring to look his pure, immaculate, forgiving mother in the face, struggling to work himself loose from the web he is caught in, the sticky ribbon he is stuck fast on, kneeling before the altar and tearfully reciting the act of contrition: but it is no use and both of you know it: when the hour has come, on his way home from school, his footsteps will irresistibly lead him to the deserted street where the sly caretaker is waiting: the sky is dark and overcast, the wind is stripping the branches from the trees and the neighbors have timidly taken refuge inside their gloomy mansions: damp, moss-covered villas with canopied entrances, statues, lightning rods, weather vanes, little cupolas: the usual wistarias, mimosas, geraniums, rose bushes, morning-glories: a desolate, declining world which you have traversed and which he is traversing and will continue to traverse for many afternoons: this afternoon in particular: a selfish world closed in upon itself, knowing nothing of work or of life: with no memories of a revolution not far removed in time and a war not far distant in space: the miserable society of the forever accursed '40's: and failing to live up to his good resolutions, he (you) will again slip through the board fence, cross the wooden plank, halt on the threshold of your shack: Cinderella's shoe is clearly visible in the mud: the rain falls monotonously: time seems suspended: will he escape today?: an interminable pause: and then (reality? dream?) a flurry of hurried knocks on the door again: you open it: and there he is: docile as a lamb, knowing what is in store for him, ready to submit to the authority of the serpent and the magnetism of his charmer: and piping a tune on the invisible flute of the son of Hermes (no cloven hoofs, and no horns: robust limbs, shaggy, coarse hair) you will lead the

snake (your stout companion) to the secret (nonvirgin) countryside and slowly and carefully explore the opening (a slit, a
half moon) that cleaves (divides) the coveted parallel dunes,
suddenly crowning them with a brutal trunk, lopped off an
Arabic palm tree: a drug-induced hallucination, a real image?:
a desert serpent, rather, supple and flexible, searching, exploring, crawling, caressing, nourishing: rising up in a defensive
stance, intractably stubborn and rebellious: and this time the
child will not cry out: he will mutely yield to your advances:
the enslaving yoke of your arms and the leisurely feast of the
serpent: following which, you will ask him for money: Urbano
is poor and you are powerful: couldn't you help him out a
bit?: the Good Lord will repay you: a hundred pesetas, five
hundred, a thousand: your mama gives you all the money you
ask her for: you've got a nice fat savings account, haven't you,
you rascal?: don't tell me you'd refuse me a few measly
pennies: to help out my family back in the village where I was
born: good people, not riffraff from heaven only knows where:
born right here: nice, quiet folk: one of them a handyman,
another earning a living as best he can, another working for the
city: no trouble to anyone: and when he turns up the next day
with every penny he's gotten his hands on, you will ask for more:
my brother's getting married, my father's sick, my mother's been
hurt in an accident: they're in desperate need of money: a
thousand, two thousand?: no, lots more than that: you're rich,
your mama never refuses you anything: five thousand, ten
thousand: ask your mama: fifteen thousand, twenty thousand:
for poor Julian: and he brings you money every day, and every
day you ask for more, and meanwhile the serpent, obeying the
snake-charmer's music, rises up in front of him and slowly
spreads its round hood: ready to spit, to inject the poison that
progressively paralyzes his will and makes him the prisoner of
yours: resignedly submitting to your rigorous treatment of him,
to the cruel, violent embraces with which you generously reward

his awed respect of you: and once he has exhausted his list of pretexts for wangling money out of his mama (books, his stamp collection, presents, hiking trips, minerals, insects), he will turn up empty-handed at your shack one afternoon, and you will beat him: SPARE THE ROD AND SPOIL THE CHILD: you will take it down from the wall and force him to strip naked, kneel at the serpent's feet, and beg its forgiveness: and the snake will energetically pump out its abundant, fluid, yellow disdain: whereupon you will raise the scourge and lash his back three times with it: deep, narrow, parallel marks cut into the flesh, the symbol of the new, accepted situation: the tie between you a most unusual one: cruel and lucid: all the closer for being so long postponed: and with feigned pity, you will draw him to your bosom and gently dry his tears: don't pay any attention, dear boy, don't be angry: you must pardon poor Julian: love has blinded him: that's what passion does to a person, you know: he needs money again: just a few thousand to tide him over: you're rich, you're rolling in money, and yet you won't help him out: listen, you little prick, is that any way to act?: sly, treacherous words that will germinate in his mind and suddenly burst into blossom like outsize Japanese flowers, causing him to lose his appetite, suffer from insomnia, and begin stealing: that very night he will slip into his mother's bedroom and swipe several thousand-peseta bills: you recognize the place perfectly (as the worm recognizes the heart of the fruit), even though you have not visited it for some time (the punitive fangs meting out perfect justice will soon demolish it): wallpaper with rose-buds and trefoils, a standing wardrobe with a mirror, a Gothic *prie-dieu*, a canopied bed: the parquet floor creaks, the purse is in the top drawer of the dressing table: inside it, lying next to a dried bouquet of faded roses, the photograph of her dead spouse, and another one of you, a gangly youngster stand-ing ramrod-straight in your First-Communion suit: from the window the deserted street can be seen, and the rain dripping

down on the dreary, gloomy garden: once, twice, three times:
without Mama's noticing and without satisfying the charmer's
insatiable greed: a ravening beast now, demanding more and
more and more: for the moment stealing is easy: Doña Isabel
la Católica suspects nothing: but what if she should catch him
in the act?: she who would rather see him dead than in a state
of sin, what would she say?: the child spies the premonitory
stigmata and covers his body in horror: clearly visible already,
strikingly evident: it is only his mother who does not see them:
a blindness doubtless occasioned by love, which he must take
advantage of, is at present taking advantage of, and will continue to take advantage of: slyly and craftily, pretending to
study and pray, secretly divided in two: an outer shell and an
inner pulp: the child who dutifully attends school and church,
and the one who seeks out the serpent and worships it in the
construction site: a spurious angel and a genuine demon: and
the world likewise divided in two: home and school, piety and
material comforts, the Lord's Table and the groaning family
board on one hand: on the other hand, a shack and mud, the
whip and the cot, the slow writhing of the snake, the piercing
wail of the flute: he goes down the deserted street every day,
and after making sure that no one is watching, slips through the
board fence, crosses the plank, halts on the threshold of the
shack: thin and frail: huge eyes, pale white skin: but today the
whip leaves shameful marks on his back and the poison that the
serpent injects in him is beginning to undermine his health:
courage, nobility of spirit, patriotism, filial piety, pride,
chivalry, heroism give way to indolence and dissipation: a
young tree, just beginning to blossom, whose leaves wither,
whose branches rot: no more buds, foliage, flowers, its trunk
has suffered a mortal blow, its vital sap is trickling out
drop by drop: a deep slash through which its energy, its
strength, its vigor, its spiritual vitality will slowly drain away:
abjectly advancing toward the serpent and vainly attempting

to tame it: a baroque cobra, triumphantly rising up to its full length, enormous and voracious, with its brazen, not at all monastic hood thrust forward: a ringed boa creeping about, exploring, writhing, coiling, embracing, strangling, suffocating: an Oriental asp or an Amazon rattlesnake: the more often the child submits to it the greater its spongelike greed: more, more, more!: a barrel with holes pierced in it that never fills up no matter how much water is poured into it: and the petty thefts and the guilt-ridden visits to the shack continue: the fluid yellow disdain of the serpent and the writhing dance of the whip: until the day that the adored mother finally discovers the child's thefts, and in a fit of terror, he comes to see you: you will force him to take yet another step along the downward path and the timbre of your voice is such that your command must be obeyed without question: the faithful old servant, the governess who has served him (and served you) with such selfless devotion for so many years must be accused of stealing: having been summoned by the mother, the police carefully search the house and discover, beneath the governess's mattress, the jewels and the family mementos that you have previously hidden there: sobering vision of the unfortunate woman, who denies everything, whines, begs, sobs, and finally is dragged off into the hermetically sealed police van hauling her straight to jail: his fate is now written in the stars, as he is well aware: the iron rule of the serpent and the collapse of his own will: total capitulation, unconditional surrender whenever requested: fluid disdain, the dance of the whip, cryptic reptilian intromission: the whip marks on his back grow more numerous, and the thick trickles of black blood: the subtle poison that you inject infects him and his wounds ooze pus: only the childish face without the slightest trace of a beard remains deceptively unchanged now: the pious mother still suspects nothing and the ritual continues: neglected studies, Judas-kisses, sacrilegious communions that he receives despite himself, and will continue to receive: oh insinuating magic of the snake and its expert charmer!: and yet, and yet: the moment the Pandora's box is opened, sickness, misery, anguish overcome him: a raging fire will turn the child's heart, still pure and generous, into a chunk of hardened lava: his body will become covered with pustules, he will feel wracking pains in his very bones, he will suffer constant headaches that allow him not a moment's respite: little by little symptoms of the disease will appear on his skin, on his eyelids, in his intestines: he will be tormented by insomnia despite his desperate craving for sleep: you imperceptibly tighten the screws, and the afternoon that he tries to get away from you and takes a roundabout way home in order not to pass by the construction site, you will lie in wait for him at a certain street corner and drag him to the shack by brute force: the bloody whip is waiting there, but you will not use it: the punishment will be more severe this time: you will rip off his clothes and examine, with loathing and disgust, the foul scars: you son-of-a-bitch, you mother-fucker, you bastard: who do you take me for?: since when does a filthy pervert like you dare defy Julian?: don't you know I'm the one who gives the orders around here?: this time you're going to pay dearly for what you've done: with the child's eyes staring into yours, you savor the fascination in his dilated pupils, your huge hands clamped around his throat, slowly squeezing tighter and tighter and tighter: some day I'm going to kill you, you hear?: and when you let go, you will cuff him in the face several times, shouting like a madman: as he rubs his swollen cheeks and pitifully wipes away the blood: if your mother asks you any questions, tell her you fell down: sweep the floor now and then clear out of here: oh, don't forget the family jewels: you are to bring them to me tomorrow, without fail: the child does as he is told, and drags himself painfully back to the bosom of his family: his toad's face is covered with bloody lumps and bruises

that inspire pity and revulsion: but the child's innocent, unsuspecting mother, absorbed in her devotions as always, accepts
his story of the fall without question: a momentary truce, but
a truce nonetheless: and the disease rages unchecked, tightening its tyrannical hold on him: as all doctors know, and even
the most Voltairean and impious of them readily confess: in
the most acute phase, the palate becomes pitted with sores:
very often the nasal cartilage rots away and the patient's face
is permanently disfigured: he looks like a ghost: his joints
become very brittle: general paralysis sets in: the end is inevitable: you will outdistance it (your rigor is extreme, and
the last bitter drop in the cup will not be spared him) and
take the most severe measures: the child returns immediately
with the jewels and you throw them in the mud: from now on,
nothing he does can possibly satisfy you: he is now so hideous-
looking that he arouses not one ounce of pity: although he
coaxes and wheedles and tries to entice the snake, to win favors
once generously granted him but now dwindled to next to
nothing, the serpent will turn its back on him: obediently
following the silent melody of the invisible flute, it will return
to its hispid retreat, but not without first pumping out (supreme
contempt) its yellow, fluid disdain: and one afternoon (bitter-
cold, a lowering sky, gusting winds) you will receive him with
a warm, cheery smile and order him to bring his mother: his
mother?: yes, your mama, why not?: Ulyan lives by himself
and he sorely misses having a woman around: your mama is
still young and pretty: I've seen her a number of times, coming
home from church with her missal in her hand: just look at
this shack: it's filthy dirty and dreary and lonely: it needs a
woman's presence: I like the looks of your darling mama and
I'm sure we'd get along very well together: does that surprise
you?: come on, don't hand me that!: I'm sure the thought's
often crossed your mind: your mother and the snake, the snake
and your mother: she's curious, too, she's dying to get to know

it: religion, morality, you say?: all nonsense!: women are all alike: the serpent (my stout companion) commands: and all of them (rich or poor, young or old) obey: none of them (not one, do you hear?) ever disputes or resists its power: your beloved mama is just like all the rest of them: do you doubt it?: bring her here tomorrow and you'll see: I'll sit her down here beside me, as I did with you, and initiate her into the ritual ceremonies of the cult: surrender, liquid disdain, whippings: and you'll be right here watching it all: your darling mama and the serpent, the serpent and your darling mama: your proposal arouses in him a chill of pleasure (as you knew it would) which betrays itself by infallible signs, whereupon you will lean down and grab him roughly by the arm: come here, you little whoring son-of-a-bitch, and tell me the truth: would you like to see that?: admit it: you'd like to, wouldn't you? and then suddenly screaming: well, you'll see it, you little fairy, you'll see it: with your own eyes: I swear on the head of my mother that you'll see it, or my name isn't Julian: it's the end of the tunnel, the cup is empty: and you will impassively stand there watching the spasms and listening to the last gasps of his dying will, the subtle yet not at all unexpected prelude to an exquisitely painful death: if you don't bring her, I'll go see her myself and tell her all the things you've done: your lies, the money, the jewels, the false witness against the governess: she would far rather see you dead!: the thought of the sins you've committed will drive her out of her mind: and having trapped him in the dilemma (an omnivorous flower) you will decree: either you bring her here with you (and that is what I advise you to do, my boy) or you kill yourself: tie a rope to the ceiling and hang yourself: get it over with once and for all: that's the way filthy perverts always end up: oh, and above all, don't expect any help from me: you're to do it all by yourself, by your own unworthy hand: but first you're to write a note explaining why: I'm in a foreign country and I don't want any trouble with the police: it's the end: the second hand sweeps implacably round the face of the watch: the child would like to repent of his crimes, but he no longer has the strength to: his feelings and his faculties have been dulled, he has lost his faith: eternal punishment leaves him totally indifferent, and like you he awaits the guillotine: the curtain falling as swiftly as a deadly blade: his hand with the deformed fingers will pen the cynical and painful farewell that coxcombic night birds will later recite *ex cathedra* to serve as an example and a lesson to future generations of quintessentially little Hispano bastards: like a sleepwalker, he will seize the rope you hold out to him and attach it to the ceiling: your piercing gaze follows his every robotlike movement, and your stout companion, the snake, emerges from its hairy retreat and also watches him, rising up the full length of its body, its hood thrust forward: weaving back and forth to the haunting, piercing, hypnotic melody that you are playing: as the child, standing on a chair, carefully knots the disproportionately long, voracious length of rope around his neck: and lets himself fall: pent-up fervor that explodes like a splendid fireworks display: swaying back and forth: and as the entire life of a dying man flashes past his eyes in the space of a few seconds, so the child's original innocence fleetingly reappears: thin and frail, huge eyes, pale white skin: not the slightest trace of a beard profaning his softly rounded cheeks: and like the falcon diving on its prey, you will hasten the miracle: pressing him to your bosom: a troglodytic reptile, a hircine flagellator: in a fulgurating symbiosis: impugning death threateningly hovering overhead: not a monster, or a two-faced creature, or a Janus: you yourself at last, become one and indivisible, in the very depths of your tortured animality

the death and profanation of the child sow panic among the people, and the Hispanos humbly fall to their knees, hysterically attempting to exorcise the danger: from his pulpit in the House of Fear, an oracle attributes the recent disasters to profligacy and the decline in moral standards: his face is pale and ascetic: illuminated by a theatrical spotlight which accentuates the almost caricatural simplicity of his features, outlined in the crudest of brush strokes, like a mask: amid the reverent silence of the faithful, he lauds virtue, fustigates vices, predicts Julian's defeat: hidden within the confessional, you patiently listen to this dull, monotonous harangue: a procession of female penitents kneels on the other side of the grille, and in a soft, persuasive voice you urge them to commit lustful and criminal acts: the men of your harka have removed their turbans and hidden their weapons beneath tattered rented cassocks: their stout serpents bulge indiscreetly underneath their long robes and remain fervidly tense and erect in the presence of these women who, with arms outstretched, as though pinned on a cross, are desperately attempting to appease the divine wrath: some of them deposit alms in the poor boxes: others light candles and votive lamps before the images of saints: grief-stricken murmurs mount heavenward, mingling with the odor of incense: when the flunky winds up his sermon and offers the faithful communion, all the women kneel and stick out their viscous tongues to receive the host and greedily swallow it in one gulp, with a swift, practiced, retractile movement: fine grains of hashish, which you have slyly mixed in with the communion wafers during a moment of inattention on the part of the acolyte, provoke a sudden attack of sexual fever: the crowd of pious female bigots rend their garments, roll about on the floor, spit, drool, and begin to masturbate: raising their skirts, they attempt to couple with each other, paying no attention to the distraught protests of the augur: the moment has come for your harkis to spring into action: their ridiculous disguises fall to the floor, immaculate white silk turbans cover their black turbans of kinky hair: they pitilessly portion out the sacred

COUNT JULIAN : 197

booty among themselves, they charge and bury their sharp, poison-filled needles in the tender flesh: one orgiastic scene follows another, accompanied by cries of terror and ecstasy from the damsels penetrated by the Arabs' serpents: the blood flows copiously, and still the fury of the Moors is not appeased: death imposes its implacable logic: you witness this violent, cruel spectacle from the vast transept of the temple: standing close by the Doll's shrine: a wooden mannequin with moving joints, clad in a blue-and-gold mantle, its heart pierced with pins like a seamstress's pincushion: cradling in its arms the Child, with natural reddish-blond hair combed in Shirley Temple corkscrew curls, clutching in its hand a toy sword: the face of the Doll is both plump-cheeked and emaciated: its cheeks are streaked with thick red plaster rivulets, like trickles of blood: in its opaque eyes with crimson-tinted eyelids, you discern what seems to be a glowering, restless, discontented gaze: by climbing on the top of the mutilated body of the magus, you reach the foot of the statue and slowly begin to strip it of its jewels and adorn-ments: in its opaque eyes, with the eyelids painted crimson, you catch a grim look, a look of anxiety and displeasure: your glance lingers on the statue's diamond earrings: be careful, the Doll says, they're fixed permanently in my earlobes: they pierced them when I was a Child: it's a custom in this country: you yank them out with one jerk: the Doll blinks slightly, but endures the pain with dignity: the hand holding the Son appears to close into a fist, and you suddenly note the presence of two emerald rings, one on the index finger and one on the third finger: you try to remove them, but cannot: the fingers are too plump: perhaps with a little soap or vaseline, She suggests: never mind, you reply: it's easier with scissors: the severed fingers will become part of your rich booty, and the Doll can scarcely hold back her tears: you wicked rascal, she says: suddenly the roof of the House of Fear with its supporting members covered with gilded volutes and floral decorations collapses: columns and capitals, altarpieces and grilles, the heads of winged angels, contorted faces of little carved demons: the splendid, hallucinatory stage setting and all its scary, grandiose props come tumbling down: plaster arms and legs, crutches, locks of hair, furry pelts, ex-votos fall on the human clusters fornicating and gasping for breath amid blood, sweat, and sperm: the Doll's eyes seem to grow larger and larger as vertigo overcomes her, as though the very earth beneath her feet were giving way: without becoming any the less rigid, she tries desperately to maintain her balance: she turns round and round, staggers forward a few paces, reels back, and finally collapses: the Boy Doll shows increasing signs of irritation, and suddenly maliciously pricks her sorrowing, grieving heart with the tip of his foil: the simultaneous fall of the two dolls and their screams put an end to this fabulous, crazy Happening

to the market, to the market!: the absolute kingdom of the improbable, stripped of all its glittering trappings from the prop department of Metro or Paramount: a prolongation of the typically Tangerine Calle de la Playa, in the working-class suburbs into which the prudent middle strata of society oscillating between the solid and the gaseous timidly venture when the sun reaches the zenith: there is nothing happening in this district now: it is drowsing like an empty fairgrounds or a deserted traveling carnival: you will be all by yourself once again, unless you go down one of the dark narrow side streets, pushing and shoving your way through a court of miracles: following along behind the club-footed beggar king who resembles Nijinsky, guided by the blinking semaphore of his one bright-blue glass eye: a Cyclopean channel buoy bobbing up and down on the waves, sending out its helpful signals and leading you to one of the little alleyways crowded with hominids who

defy the arbitrary, bourgeois laws of verisimilitude: cripples,
hunchbacks, the lame and the halt and the blind: creatures
missing one or several limbs, having been deprived of them with
that disturbing frequency with which poor people in underdeveloped countries lose various organs and extremities, like
crabs: an urban chaos of shouts, voices, the honking of horns:
an old man on a white (Dioscuran?) horse, a donkey staggering
beneath the weight of its rider, an angrily sputtering moving
van giving forth with the opening bars of the march from *The
Bridge over the River Kwai*, a humpbacked dwarf toting an immense standing wardrobe with a mirror, a cyclist with the
talents of a high-wire acrobat balancing a tray with an enormous pyramid of pastries atop it on his head: peddlers of socks,
ties, plastic sandals nimbly circulating among the crowd with
their collapsible display stands, and a fat lady, with the haughty
air of a prima donna, elbowing her way through the dense mass
of humanity like an icebreaker: the vehicle is jam-packed, and
bunches of people are hanging out the side door and even the
windows: impossible to escape: crammed in body against body,
fused into a single tentacular, vociferous mass: hey, don't
push!: stop shoving, you stupid idiots!: you're the one who's
a stupid idiot, you son-of-a-bitch!: the woman next to you
lovingly dandles an angry hen perched on her lap on top of a
basket of eggs, a child is crying, and the radio, turned all the
way up, is blaring out Chopin's *Les Sylphides*: you masher,
stop trying to feel me up!: don't crowd me like that, lady!:
you stupid cunt, take your hands off me!: the cyclist continues
to perform acrobatic tricks and the pyramid of pastries remains
intact: the *prima donna assoluta* opens a protective parasol, paying no attention to the angry screams and shouts of protest:
the hen cackles, the baby wails, the radio blares out Xopen's
Les Syphilides: you are caught between the devil and the deep
blue sea, helplessly trapped between the prima donna, the

peasant woman with the basket of eggs, and the acrobatic cyclist: the sweat rolls down your back as though you were in a Turkish bath: a strange creature is dragging itself painfully along the floor at your feet, begging for your attention, as mute as a reproach: its presence goes beyond the limits of a drug-induced hallucination, its frail corporeal reality is undeniable: a sinuous leg is endeavoring to coil itself around its head and the creature's front hoofs are shod in odd-looking footwear adapted to its peculiar creeping method of locomotion: a spider, a tarantula, a centipede? tracheal respiration, flexible antennae, a poisonous stinger?: the air is doubtless very thin down there in those dark inferior regions and the unclassifiable creature is panting and trying to hoist itself up to grab the bottom of your jacket: the child is wailing, the *primissima* is flowering beneath her parasol, the aerial cyclist is doing a balancing act with the miraculous tray piled full of pastries: the mendicant insect is avidly seeking the warmth of your lap, its pincers are freeing the captive buttons one by one, its mouth is working its way into the hircine lair, and its piteous, anxious voice reaches your ears: gooddaysir, mamapoorthingthesameasalwaysoverseventy-herhealthworries: the hen and its cackling, the child and its wailing, Xopen and his syphilis!: your hands have clamped themselves around the creature's neck and the sound track drowns out its sharp scream: a balloon deflating, sawdust leaking out, a crushed abdomen spattering its liquid abdominal contents: the prima donna executes trills in the countertenor register, the cyclist pedals along the tightrope, the maternal peasant woman dandles the hen and the basketful of eggs, still intact, on her lap: noises, noises, music, voices, interferences!: the nocturnal passenger bus continues its phantom journey and will deposit you at the intersection of the lonely street slanting steeply upward and the deadly still, deserted Calle de Portugal amid the piles of garbage in the market (old papers, bones, fruit rinds) and the emanations and odors they give off (secretion, putrefaction, carrion) the smooth, bare, shiny dead body is immediately visible: a pink celluloid boy doll, hideously disfigured by the vengeful fury of its murderer: arms and legs lopped off, empty eye sockets, heart pierced with a long, sharp gold pin that instead of a head has a curious plume of metallic feathers: the water in the gutter sweeps it away along with the stinking garbage and rubbish of the Zoco Grande: past the stairway where at dawn blank-faced Riff peasant women will squat, patiently displaying their pitifully meager wares: tiny bunches of fresh mint, prickly pears, pathetically small bunches of dates that no one is buying and no one will buy: face up, with an orange peel atop its chest, the celluloid doll floats down to the corner of the Calle de Portugal, and there at the intersection it turns round and round, sinks, bobs to the surface once more, turns round and round again, trapped in the little whirlpool caused by the confluence of two currents flowing in opposite directions: when it finally emerges from the miniature maelstrom, the waste water deposits it in the center of the street: a skinny, famished dog sniffs it for some time and then fearfully turns tail and runs away: the doll is now lying in a crude cradle, and a Moorish necromancer and little sorcerer's apprentices from the mosque of the Aisauas come to pay it homage: little green wax candles, skins shed by serpents, the bristly hairs of a he-goat are piled up on the straw around it as a sign of obedience and submission to its will: then the worshipers line up in Indian file, and with the doll on a stretcher, begin parading smartly down the street: along the Calle de la Playa in the direction of the boulevard: at their head the European youngster with a Texas sombrero on his head and two silver-plated revolvers stuck in his belt: the city remains silent and tense, as though on alert, and the flute of the knife-grinder can be heard in the distance, a melody so faint as to be unreal: full of sly hints, invitations, promises: bare and spare, tenuous, subtle: persuasive: as the cortege files past the rough-hewn, angular stone houses, escorted by graceful shadows, svelte presences: Mohammedan devotions that the night conceals, that the fleecy clouds blur: burnooses, veils, gauze headdresses standing out against a background of little carved animals and decorative plasterwork, forests of columns, stylized leaves: and now the doll comes to life once more, suddenly recovers its sight, all its lost members, and the use of them: clad in an immaculate djellaba, a snow-white turban atop its head, it invokes the name of Allah in faultless Arabic, and manifests its ardent desire to become a convert to Islam: the procession has now reached the Avenida de España and is marching down the median strip beneath the palm trees, whose luxuriant fronds fan out like the spray of a fountain, still guided by the bucolic modulations of the flute melody: at its soft summons, men and women abandon their humble, monotonous tasks and silently join the procession: the melody will gradually charm beggars and soldiers, peasants, tourists: the children will direct the mimetic human stream by gesturing, and rejoice at the sight of the instruments that the expert conjuror will generously distribute to them: clarinets and saxophones, violins and oboes, tambourines and timbrels, rebecs: as it passes by, the impromptu orchestra will receive the silent approbation of the specters prowling up and down the boulevard: with their instruments muted the orchestra will weave in, almost imperceptibly, the descending theme of the adagio, as though to lull the listeners, to put them to sleep: when they reach the Hotel El Djénina, the musicians will fall silent, one after the other, and as in Haydn's *Farewell Symphony*, written for Prince Esterhazy, they will blow out the green candles one by one, put away their scores, lay their instruments back in their cases, before stealing away from the phantasmagorical, nocturnal procession: on three occasions, three times during the steep climb up Grotius, the major theme will be heard again, played each time by fewer and fewer instruments, until finally the movement, and with it the entire symphony, fades away into a hauntingly sad flute solo: thus softly sighs the lyre that in gentle concert wounded the wind's pride, the gentle rustle of the breeze: the last child-musicians will bid you farewell with graceful curtsies and throw you kisses, as in a courtly minuet: they will leap over the wall of the nearby vacant lot and bury the corpse of the mangy cat in the wild fronds: as yesterday, as today, as every day: you will push the door of the building open, press the buzzer, immure yourself within your apartment: the kitchen window is still wide open and clouds of insects are swarming over the chicken giblets and the little mounds of powdered sugar: it is time for the torrent of Pompeian lava, for the dipteral and hymenopteral hecatomb: once the ritual is completed, you will turn out the light, having first made certain, as a scrupulously careful huntsman, that escape is materially impossible, that the trap is absolutely perfect: you will urinate, brush your teeth, go into your bedroom: the same immovable décor as always awaits you: two chairs, the wardrobe built into the wall, the night table, the gas stove: a map of Morocco, scale 1 : 1,000,000, printed by Hallweg, Bern, Switzerland: a colored print showing different varieties of leaves: ensheathed (wheat), cordate (buckwheat), dentate (nettle), digitate (chestnut), verticillate (madder): the lamp on the night stand, the ashtray full of cigarette butts, the schoolchild's red composition book with the multiplication table printed on the back cover, the little folder of cigarette paper, the kind that Tariq uses to roll joints: nothing more?: oh, yes, the light fixture on the ceiling, with four arms and glass teardrops: two of the bulbs have burned out, as a matter of fact, must remember to hunt up new ones: you will open the book of the Poet and read a few verses as you undress: then you will draw the cord of the venetian blind without so much as glancing at the enemy coast, at the scar dripping poison on the other shore of the sea: sleep weighs heavily on your eyelids and you close your eyes: as you know, all too well: tomorrow will be another day, the invasion will begin all over again

notice

This work was written with the posthumous or unwitting collaboration of:

Alfonso X el Sabio
Alonso, Dámaso
Arrarás, Joaquín
Azorín
Berceo, Gonzalo de
Buñuel, Luis
Calderón de la Barca, Pedro
Caro, Rodrigo
Castro, Américo
Castro, Guillén de
Cervantes, Miguel de
Corral, Pedro de
Darío, Rubén
Espinel, Vicente
Espronceda, José de
Ganivet, Ángel
García Lorca, Federico
García Morente, Manuel
Góngora, Luis de
Ibn Hazam
Jiménez, Juan Ramón
Larra, Mariano José de
León, Fray Luis de

López Alarcón, Enrique
López García, Bernardo
Machado, Antonio
Machado, Manuel
Menéndez Pelayo, Marcelino
Menéndez Pidal, Ramón
Mora, José Joaquín de
Mutannabí
Ortega y Gasset, José
Otero, Blas de
Pérez de Ayala, Ramón
Pérez de Guzmán, Fernán
Pérez del Pulgar, Hernán
Primo de Rivera, José Antonio
Quevedo, Francisco de
Rojas, Fernando de
Sánchez Albornoz, Claudio
Teresa de Ávila
Tirso de Molina
Unamuno, Miguel de
Vega, Lope de
Vélez de Guevara, Luis

as well as that of Monsignor Tihámer Toth, Perrault, Virgil, Lermontov, Ian Fleming, Umberto Eco, and Agustín Lara—and in addition, materials taken from various periodicals, textbooks, and popular medical encyclopedias.

Juan Goytisolo
MARKS OF IDENTITY

'For me *Marks of Identity* was my first novel. It was forbidden publication in Spain. For twelve years after that everything I wrote was forbidden in Spain. So I realized that my decision to attack the Spanish language through its culture was correct. But what was most important for me was that I no longer exercised censorship on myself, I was a free writer. This search for and conquest of freedom was the most important thing to me.'

Juan Goytisolo, in an interview with CITY LIMITS

'Juan Goytisolo is by some distance the most important living novelist from Spain . . . and *Marks of Identity* is undoubtedly his most important novel, some would say the most significant work by a Spanish writer since 1939, a truly historic milestone.'

THE GUARDIAN

'A masterpiece which should whet the appetites of British readers for the rest of the trilogy.'

TIMES LITERARY SUPPLEMENT

352 pages £8.95 (paper)

Juan Goytisolo
LANDSCAPES AFTER THE BATTLE

'Juan Goytisolo is one of the most rigorous and original contemporary writers. His books are a strange mixture of pitiless autobiography, the debunking of mythologies and conformist fetishes, passionate exploration of the periphery of the West – in particular of the Arab world which he knows intimately – and audacious linguistic experiment. All these qualities feature in *Landscapes After the Battle*, an unsettling, apocalyptic work, splendidly translated by Helen Lane.'   MARIO VARGAS LLOSA

'*Landscapes After the Battle* . . . a cratered terrain littered with obscenities and linguistic violence, an assault on "good taste" and the reader's notions of what a novel should be.'   THE OBSERVER

'Fierce, highly unpleasant and very funny.'
THE GUARDIAN

'A short, exhilarating tour of the emergence of pop culture, sexual liberation and ethnic militancy.'
NEW STATESMAN

'Helen Lane's rendering reads beautifully, capturing the whimsicality and rhythms of the Spanish without sacrificing accuracy, but rightly branching out where literal translation simply does not work.'
TIMES LITERARY SUPPLEMENT

176 pages £7.95 (paper)

Also published by Serpent's Tail

Daniel Moyano
THE DEVIL'S TRILL

'The first English publication, in superb translation, of one of Argentina's finest writers (in exile). Moyano, like his hero Triclinio, finds harmonies in discord and, playing ironic acompaniment to the Devil's tunes, brings music out of madness.... With fine wit and artistry, Moyano has written a political parable that movingly sings the triumph of the human spirit.'

SUNDAY TIMES

'Daniel Moyano is a superb writer.... The absence of an English translation of his writing is one of those literary lapses one reads about as happening to other places and other ages.'

ANDREW GRAHAM-YOOLL

'An eloquent defence of artistic integrity and freedom ... the book is a real triumph.'

JOHN KING

'Daniel Moyano's deep realism blends both modern and classical prose, progressive thought and a profound faith in the ability of human beings to suvive.'

RAFAEL CONTE

128 pages £6.50 (paper)

Also published by Serpent's Tail

Raul Nuñez
THE LONELY HEARTS CLUB

'Magnificent.'   BLITZ

'The singles scene of Barcelona's lonely low life.
Sweet and seedy.'   ELLE

'A celebration of the wit and squalor of Barcelona's
mean streets.'   CITY LIMITS

'This tough and funny story of low life in Barcelona
manages to convey the immense charm of that city
without once mentioning Gaudi. . . . A story of
striking freshness, all the fresher for being so casually
conveyed.'   THE INDEPENDENT

'A sardonic view of human relations . . .'
                                                 THE GUARDIAN

'Threatens to do for Barcelona what *No Mean City*
once did for Glasgow.'   GLASGOW HERALD

'A funny low life novel of Barcelona.'   THE TIMES

160 pages £6.95 (paper)

.Manuel Vazquez Montalban
MURDER IN THE CENTRAL COMMITTEE
and
SOUTHERN SEAS

'More Montalban please!' CITY LIMITS

'There are three other Montalban novels. I cannot wait for them to be published here.'
NEW STATESMAN

'At last a thriller worthy of the name: a taut, intelligent tour de force set in the shadowy minefield of post-Franco politics.' JULIE BURCHILL

'A must for all connoisseurs of political infighting... the factional quarrels of the left make an all too plausible setting for murder.' ELIZABETH WILSON

'Excellent stuff.' TIME OUT

'Montalban's style is grounded in sensory detail, and he writes with authority and compassion – a Le Carré-like sorrow . . .' PUBLISHERS WEEKLY

'Shows to the full the excellencies of plotting and character which have won him literary prizes in France and Spain. His insights into the murky undercurrents of life in post-Franco Spain are quite fascinating.' BRITISH BULLETIN OF PUBLICATIONS

Both titles: 224 pages £5.95 (paper)

Books are to